Confessions of a Jane Austen Addict

Center Point
Large Print

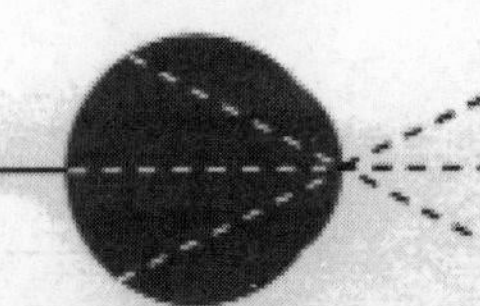

This Large Print Book carries the
Seal of Approval of N.A.V.H.

Confessions of a Jane Austen Addict

LAURIE VIERA RIGLER

CENTER POINT PUBLISHING
THORNDIKE, MAINE

This Center Point Large Print edition
is published in the year 2009 by arrangement with
Dutton, a member of Penguin Group (USA) Inc.

The text of this Large Print edition is unabridged.
In other aspects, this book may vary
from the original edition.
Printed in the United States of America.
Set in 16-point Times New Roman type.

ISBN: 978-1-60285-625-7

Library of Congress Cataloging-in-Publication Data

Rigler, Laurie Viera.
Confessions of a Jane Austen addict / Laurie Viera Rigler.
p. cm.
ISBN 978-1-60285-625-7 (lib. bdg. : alk. paper)
1. Single women--Fiction. 2. Time travel--Fiction.
3. Man-woman relationships--Fiction.
4. England--Social life and customs--19th century--Fiction.
5. Austen, Jane, 1775-1817--Influence--Fiction. 6. Large type books. I. Title.
PS3618.I427C66 2009
813'.6--dc22
2009027802

I dedicate this book to Austen addicts past, present, and future; and most of all, to Jane Austen, whose bit of ivory is an endless source of wisdom and joy for this humble admirer. If there is any justice in the world, Miss Austen, then there is a parallel reality in which that lovely young man from the seaside didn't die young, you lived to write at least six more novels, and the two of you grew happily old together, preferably without children.

Till this moment, I never knew myself.

—JANE AUSTEN,

PRIDE AND PREJUDICE

One

Why is it so dark in here? And that smell, like dried lavender mixed with ammonia.

A door thrown open, curtains thrust aside noisily. I squint in the harsh light. A stout woman with black hair in a messy upsweep unlatches a window while a scowling older man hisses orders. The woman ducks her head and shrinks into her shoulders, as if to hide from the man's voice.

Who are these people? And what's with those outfits?

The woman's dress is long and drab with a large white apron, down to the floor. The man's suit and vest look like cast-offs from the Merchant-Ivory costume department. Even his glasses are vintage.

But that's the least of it. This is clearly not my room.

My nose wrinkles at the ripe smell of unwashed body, and I realize that the man and the woman are standing at the foot of my bed staring at me. Am I the source of that smell? Is that why they're looking at me?

Apparently, I am having a dream, and a highly olfactory one at that. Strange, though. I can't recall ever having been aware of dreaming during the dream itself. Lucid dreaming, that's what Frank called it. Claimed he used to have them all the time when he was seeing some Jungian therapist.

Why are they looking at me like that?

"Miss Mansfield? Are you awake?"

It's the man who's speaking to me, moving toward the bed as he does. I can now connect the stench with its source. His face has the bulging-eyed look of a trout surprised to find itself attached to a hook. I stifle a giggle.

"Miss Mansfield," he says again. "Can you hear me?"

Miss Mansfield. That's a good one. Especially the British accent. That's what I get for being such a Jane Austen addict. No wonder some bipedal trout in a dream is calling me something that could be right out of an Austen novel—though last night I fell asleep reading *Pride and Prejudice*, not *Mansfield Park.*

"Miss Mansfield?"

Should I answer? No need to be polite. After all, it's my dream, isn't it? He's just some cryptic symbol. Of what, however, I have no idea. He does look really worried, though, poor guy. Perhaps he's a symbol of some subconscious desire I have to be more tolerant of people with poor personal hygiene.

"Miss Mansfield. Can you hear me?"

"Why are you calling me that?" I finally say.

He gasps, his bulging eyes magnified by his glasses. Perhaps I should have played along. After all, he can't be expected to know he's just a construction of my subconscious mind. Should I be the one to break the news?

He backs up from the bed, pulling a handkerchief from his jacket and wiping his sweaty upper lip.

"Barnes," he says to the one with the apron, "tell your mistress that Miss Mansfield has opened her eyes. Inform her that I will be with her shortly."

"Very good, sir," says the woman, with an unmistakable note of relief in her voice, and closes the door.

I lie under the covers and observe while the man, who is evidently a doctor, feels my pulse, touches my cheek and forehead, and frowns. Then he opens a brown leather satchel and takes out a china bowl that's kind of like a soup bowl except that it looks like someone took a big bite out of its edge. Next he opens a little leather case with some sharp instruments in it, then gives me a sort of half grin with his blubbery fish lips.

"I shall be back in just a few minutes, Miss Mansfield. A little bleeding will be just the thing."

I remember that Frank once said lucid dreams have a decided advantage over regular dreams. If a lucid dream becomes unpleasant, all you have to do is say what you want out loud or take some kind of definitive action and proclaim your control over how the dream goes. And, like magic, a menacing rat will change into a cuddly puppy or a smelly doctor with a lancet will change into a . . . let's see, how about a vase of roses?

"Enough!" I shout at the doctor. "I pronounce you to be a vase of roses!"

Strange. This is not my voice. And this working class girl from Los Angeles by way of Long Island definitely does not have a fancy British accent.

"Lord bless me!" says the doctor, backing away with fright-widened eyes. And then he's out the door.

It figures Frank would brag about being able to change a nightmare into a nice dream when he really had no idea what he was talking about. What options do I have now? I could certainly will myself awake, can't I? Focus, focus. Come on, wake up!

I squeeze my eyes shut. Wake up!

I open my eyes. I'm still here.

All right then, no need to panic. I'll probably wake up before he comes back to cut me. And it's not like he'd actually be cutting me anyway.

I get out of bed, stand up. I'm a little wobbly. Weak, in fact. My logic knows this is a dream, but it's a damned realistic one. I have to take some action. Action is power, power is control, and I need control in case the doctor comes back in to finish his task.

I feel the little hairs rising on the back of my neck. Someone is in the room with me. A dark-haired woman in a long white dress. I can see her reflection in the mirror that stands in the corner of the room. I can feel the adrenaline rush as I whip around.

There's no one behind me.

There she is again, in the mirror. I move closer to her reflection, not daring to turn around. My forehead throbs, and I press it with my hand. The woman in the mirror does the same. I drop my hand to my side, and she mimics my motions.

I turn around and see no one behind me, then turn back again to face the mirror. The woman's image continues to stare back at me.

The flesh rises on my arms. Calm down now; this isn't real.

I look at the strange reflection staring back at me. I feel the unfamiliar weight of skin and bones resting on me, yet not any part of me. It is a costume, a mask. Yet the more I gaze at that reflection, the more the skin seems to merge with myself inside of it. It's closing in on me, becoming me, but it's not me. Is this how lucid dreams are supposed to feel? How am I supposed to know? I've never had one before.

I suppose the unfamiliar is always unsettling at first. And I'm not about to let a dream freak me out. Especially when the reflection staring back at me from the mirror is so much more attractive than I am in waking life. The hair is long and dark, almost black and slightly wavy. The pale, unadorned face is much prettier than I've ever been without any makeup. The body isn't bad either. Tall, slender figure with nice curves, at least from what I can tell through the white, high-necked granny nightgown. I cup my hands around the breasts, which are certainly smaller than mine but seem to go with the rest of the body. That body is so unlike my own petite frame, with breasts far too large to be proportional, short legs, and a tendency to look enormous with only five extra pounds on me. Breasts as big as mine only look great on tall, slim women, who often must resort to surgery to achieve that effect, since tall, slim women usually come equipped with smaller accessories.

Gazing at the mirror begins to make my head throb. It's safer to look at the room, which is unlike anything I've ever woken up in. A four-poster bed with a canopy, the kind I've always dreamed of having. But I *am* dreaming, I remind myself. Thick, burgundy velvet curtains, a view from the window to lawns, trees, flower beds, and an herb garden. A pink marble fireplace. An intricately carved chest of drawers. An armoire with inlaid designs in the wood. An ornately framed mirror in addition to the one on the dressing table and the other one on a stand. Wherever I look I see the black-haired woman. As in the home of Sir Walter Eliot, Jane Austen's very own metrosexual, there's no getting away from myself in this room. Or at least there's no getting away from that alien reflection. Fortunately, she's not hard to look at. No puffy hangover bags under the eyes, no red blotches on the skin from sleeping with my cheek on my hand, no lank blond hair plastered to one side of my face.

I sit down at the dressing table and pick up a silver brush, open an inlaid wooden box, and finger the sparkling rings, pins, and pearl necklaces inside. More wish fulfillment. I can't begin to count the times I've agonized over my checkbook and wished I didn't have to decide which was more important, paying the electric bill on time or buying groceries, although sometimes I did neither and had my highlights done instead. It's unlikely that a person with a bedroom like this and a well-stocked jewelry box ever has to prioritize such things. Of course, I also appear to be in a pre-electricity dream era, which would remove one factor from the equation.

Anyway, who could blame my subconscious for concocting such an escapist fantasy to a Jane Austen–like world, knife-happy doctor notwithstanding. After all, the last couple of months haven't exactly been a picnic.

Don't want to think about that now. Just want to lie back down in this comfy bed.

Two

A knock at the door. Before I can say anything, it opens, and in walks the doctor. He looks at me warily, then right behind him comes a petite, curvaceous woman, maybe fifty years old, in a long, empire-waistline dress. Golden blond curls and tendrils frame her face and neck, but most of her hair is covered by one of those pouffy, lacy shower caps masquerading as hats. She'd probably look younger if she didn't wear it, and I have half a mind to tell her so.

The woman glides over to me, places a cool hand on my forehead, and, as if as an afterthought, gives me a quick kiss on the cheek. "Well, Jane, I am pleased to see you back among the living."

What's this about?

Her ice-blue eyes examine me. "Have you nothing to say to me, child?"

I most certainly don't. She looks over at the doctor, who frowns in reply.

"It is best you leave us now, Mrs. Mansfield," he says. "Barnes will attend me." He glances meaningfully at the bowl and lancet.

The one called Mrs. Mansfield arches an eyebrow and shrugs. "Well, I suppose you must." She strides over to the door and hisses in a stage whisper for Barnes, who scuttles in.

Doc bows at Mrs. Mansfield, then smiles at me.

His teeth are yellow-and-brown spatulate things.

No way is this creature going to stick anything into my arm. I've always been squeamish, but this is too much. Last time I had my blood drawn was at the gynecologist's, and I had to lie down in an empty examination room for twenty minutes because I almost fainted, and assistants were running around getting me cups of orange juice and cookies to give me a sugar jolt. Somehow knowing this is a dream doesn't make the prospect of a bleeding seem any less frightening. Besides, by the look of things this is the early part of the nineteenth century, and though I'm no historian, I know that in Jane Austen's day, antisepsis was still decades away from becoming standard practice. Even though it's a dream and might have its own Wonderland sort of logic, I'm not about to take any chances. Who knows where that lancet has been before?

"Wait!" I shout as loudly as I can in that strange British voice.

Doc, Barnes, and the petite woman all look at me at once.

"Listen, you guys," I say. "I'm having a dream, and none of this is real. So why don't you just put those instruments of torture away right now, because you're wasting your time. Any minute I'm going to wake up, and you'll all go back to . . . I don't know, wherever it is you go."

Mrs. Mansfield's eyes are steel. "Jane. You will

refrain from speaking such nonsense. And to your mother of all people."

"Mother? You're not my mother."

The doctor steps in. "My dear lady," he says to Mrs. Mansfield. "She is certainly not in her right mind. Do be good enough to leave us so that I might bring her to her senses. I have seen such cases of brain fever before, and I flatter myself to say that I have been successful in bringing about a complete cure."

"Forget it, pal," I say. "You're not coming within ten feet of me, even if this is a dream. And I'm sorry, ma'am, but you don't exist. I don't even exist, at least not here. My name is Courtney Stone, and I live in L.A. You know, California? In the twenty-first century? I have my own mother and my own life. Not much of a life, but it's the only one I've got. I'm sorry if you think you're real, but there's nothing I can do about that. Now why don't you all just please leave me alone until I wake up."

Mrs. Mansfield's icy blues are like lasers.

"Don't waste your time, sweetheart," I say to her. "I suppose that might be an intimidating look—if you were real, that is."

The doctor whispers to Mrs. Mansfield, motions to Barnes, and the three of them scurry out of the room. Yes!

I lie here in bed, suddenly too weak and heavy to do anything but enjoy the respite. I must have dozed off (if one could actually doze while dreaming), because the next thing I know, I'm waking to the sound of Mrs. Mansfield coming back into the room. She closes the door behind her, sits on the edge of the bed, leans over me, and grasps my shoulders, hard. I'm so thrown by the steeliness of her voice and the viselike grip of her fingers that I can't even protest.

Her eyes narrow to slits. "Now you listen to me, Jane. Mr. Jones believes that the only hope for your recovery awaits you in an asylum, but I can assure you that no daughter of mine will ever enter a house for madmen. It would be a disgrace to the Mansfield name that I will not abide. And should you ever leave such a place, your fate as a spinster would be guaranteed. Not that the danger of that is slight at the age of thirty, even without the epithet of madwoman. You would be shunned by society, and all your family would share in your disgrace."

She lets go of my shoulders and pauses to see my reaction.

"You know, you really should rethink the hat. You're not a bad-looking woman."

"This is no joke," she says, springing off the bed and standing over me, index finger pointing in my face. "If you persist in this shameful conduct, I will allow Mr. Jones to take you forthwith, and I shall let it be known that you have died as a result of your riding accident. Your father would resist such a course of action, but I daresay he would come to a right way of thinking, especially when he realizes the disgrace to be visited upon your sister and brother. And indeed, you will be every bit as dead to me if you enter an asylum as you would be lying in your grave. In fact, from what Mr. Jones has just told me, I am persuaded you will wish yourself in the ground should you choose such accommodations over a more reasonable course of action."

I attempt a laugh while visions of some squalid, nineteenth-century version of *One Flew Over the Cuckoo's Nest* dance through my head.

"You're not serious," I say.

She raises an eyebrow. "I would not take such a gamble if I were you. I do not believe you are insane, and I am about to prove I am right. No sane person would ever give up your comfortable situation for such an alternative. And if—heaven forbid—I am wrong, then this removal will be best for all concerned."

My fears must be visible on my face, for Mrs. Mansfield's seems to relax in a sort of triumph.

"All right," I say. "You win."

"Good." She begins to pace the room. "Of course, I will have to give that dreadful Mr. Jones a little something—more than a little something, no doubt—to ensure his silence. I'll not have him gossiping to all the neighborhood. As for Barnes, she is trustworthy, to be sure; however, it cannot hurt to make her trust a more profitable enterprise."

As if recollecting my presence, she turns to me

and says, "As for you, Jane, I insist you say nothing of this to your father. He is very fond of you, though I have no idea why, and this matter would upset him terribly. From now on, you will conduct yourself as you should, and there will be no more talk of not being the person who you so clearly are."

"I'll try," I say. "Though I can't promise I can pretend to be someone I'm not for very long. However, I have a feeling this will all end very soon."

Mrs. Mansfield raises an eyebrow. "Whatever do you mean by that?"

"You told me not to talk of it, so let's just leave it at that, okay?"

" 'O-Kay'? And what sort of word is that, pray tell?"

"Never mind," I say. "Forget about it."

"With pleasure."

Interesting. Though the psyche of a twenty-first-century woman has created this dream, it is somehow a hermetically sealed world, isolated from modern references.

Throughout all this talk of asylums and riding accidents, my head has begun to throb again. I press my hand to my forehead.

Mrs. Mansfield eyes me. "I suppose that blow to your head could account for your odd behavior. It was a nasty fall, to be sure. However, you are not the only one who suffered. For almost three whole days, while you slept the sleep of the innocent, I was in a constant state of suspense. Would you awake, or would you die? Should I order our mourning clothes, or should I wait another day?"

"Not to mention all the funeral arrangements."

"You have not the smallest notion of what that can do to a person." Mrs. Mansfield stifles a yawn. "Dear me, I am exhausted." She looks at me, and her eyes narrow. "I shall summon Mr. Jones, and you shall make certain there is no doubt in his mind as to the soundness of your mental state. Have I made myself understood?"

"Uh-huh."

"You will speak like a well-bred young lady, or you will be sorry you were born."

She locks my eyes with her own, and I am the first to look down. "Do you understand me?"

"Yes—ma'am." I can't believe I'm allowing her to intimidate me.

"Excellent." Mrs. Mansfield bestows a glacial smile upon me and leaves the room, and I lie there trying to make sense of the situation, and trying to talk myself out of a growing queasiness in the pit of my stomach. After all, why get all bent out of shape over a dream? So what if it seems that I'm stuck in it for the time being; it's bound to end eventually. Might as well take advantage of my lucidity and deconstruct it while still in it.

Not that it would take a rocket scientist to do so. Aside from my addiction to all things Austen providing the setting, the mother figure's narcissism is clearly a caricature of my own mother's self-centeredness. Like Mrs. Mansfield, Mom is mostly interested in my life inasmuch as it affects her own.

On the other hand, Mrs. M doesn't appear to have my mother's self-medication issues. Though I'm sure there's a sherry bottle around somewhere. Mrs. M certainly doesn't appear to have been swilling, but then again, Mom never actually looks hammered either.

Still, Mom doesn't have Mrs. M's killer instincts. Fact is, despite her selfishness, or maybe even because of it, I can always ask Mom for help in a pinch. She seems to get on some kind of high fueled by maternal hormones and self-importance whenever I'm in extremis. Suddenly, she develops an in-depth interest in my life, feeding off the drama like a soap opera junkie anxious for the next installment. My breakups, heartbreaks, and financial crises give her something to talk about with her friends, especially her role as glorified rescuer of the distressed. Inevitably, whenever I emerge from a crisis and get my life back to normal, dear Mom lapses back into her routine lack of interest.

Suddenly, I am struck by a realization. The doctor called me "Miss Mansfield"; the mother figure called me "Jane." Jane Mansfield! Too bad this Jane Mansfield's breast size doesn't live up to the name. And too bad I am doomed to be an anachronism, because I'm sure no one in this period-piece dream would get the joke.

The appearance in my doorway of Mrs. Mansfield and the doctor puts an end to those musings. Perhaps my amusement still shows on my face, because Mrs. Mansfield looks at me warningly.

"I was just telling Mr. Jones how well you are feeling now, Jane. Why do you not put his mind at ease?"

I open my mouth and say, in perfectly nineteenth-century lady-like language, "I assure you I am perfectly well now, Mr. Jones. I was momentarily confused when I awoke, but I am quite recovered." I almost giggle at the sound of my voice. It's like being in the seventh grade play. Or even better, in a Jane Austen novel.

And to Mrs. Mansfield I add, "Forgive me for worrying you . . . Mama."

"Mama" pats me on the cheek, then turns to the doctor again, looking at him smugly.

He frowns a bit, no doubt disappointed at having his fun spoiled. But he clears his throat and then favors us both with a broad smile. "This is all very promising, I daresay, Mrs. Mansfield. Nevertheless, unless I can satisfy myself with medical proof of Miss Mansfield's health, I would be remiss in advising you to keep her here. After all, what if she should become violent? In such cases as these, you know, it is not uncommon."

Mrs. Mansfield's confident look vanishes.

"Be not alarmed, madam," says the doctor. "If you leave Miss Mansfield to my care for but half an hour, I shall bleed out of her any vicious humors that might bring forth such an inclination. Then we might all rest easy."

Dear God. I have to talk them out of this. As Mr. Jones reaches for his bag, I silently hiss my vehement refusal at Mrs. Mansfield. She chooses to ignore me.

"Very well," she says to my would-be torturer. "I shall send Barnes to you directly."

"Jane," she says to me, "you shall cooperate fully with Mr. Jones."

This isn't happening. I have to do something, say something. "Wait a moment, Mother," I say, again marveling at the alien voice coming out of my mouth. "I am perfectly well and there is no need to put Mr. Jones to any more trouble. Besides, I am already in a weakened state; if I should lose blood I am likely to feel much worse rather than much better."

Mr. Jones smiles at me as one would to a child who has just said that the sun must be hot indeed to survive its nightly descent into the ocean.

"I can assure you, Miss Mansfield," he says with barely restrained triumph, "that draining the offensive humors in the blood will do quite the opposite of weakening you." And, turning to Mrs. Mansfield, he makes a polite bow. She nods and approaches the bed, leaning over as if to give me a kiss.

"You will do as he says," she hisses into my ear. "His silence depends on his being satisfied that it was he who enacted the cure."

When she attempts to straighten herself up again, I clutch at her dress, but she extricates herself with those surprisingly strong fingers, and with one quick dagger look at me, leaves the room.

Barnes, who has evidently been waiting outside, steps in. Jones moves toward me, surgical knife and bowl in hand. I scream, and he motions to Barnes to hold me still. I must be really weak, because she doesn't have much trouble restraining me. I watch in horror as he lowers the knife. Oh God, please let me wake up from this nightmare. The knife touches my arm and . . . that is all I remember.

Three

When I open my eyes, it's dark in the room. Mrs. Mansfield is standing over my bed, a candle in her hand.

"Poor dear. You have been sleeping for hours. Will you have some dinner now?"

I shake my head, wanting more than anything to throttle her.

"Now, Jane. You haven't eaten in almost four days."

"Like you care. That vampire nearly drained me dry. I'm so weak I can hardly move." I show her my arm with the offending cut, glaring at her accusingly.

She shrugs. "All the more reason for you to eat something. Cook made your favorite." She bustles around the room, lighting candles with the one in her hand.

"Whatever."

She touches my arm lightly. "I shall have a tray sent up." And turns to go.

She pauses in the doorway. "You are wrong, you know. I do care. Someday you will understand that I did what I had to do. For you."

I turn my head, and I hear her leave the room.

Who is this woman? Does she really think she cares about me or, more accurately, Jane? I fume for a while, becoming aware of the emptiness in my stomach. I'm so hungry that I'm on the verge of having a stomachache. Where is that alleged tray? It's bizarre that I can have this intense and visceral feeling of bodily hunger in the midst of a dream.

And that isn't the only bodily feeling I'm having. I have an absolutely pressing need to take a pee, too. And have no idea where the bathroom is. Or *if* the bathroom even exists.

Just as I'm forming a desperate plan of dragging myself out of bed to urinate into the washbasin, Barnes arrives laden with a huge tray of delicious smelling food. She looks at me anxiously, as if afraid to approach.

"Please," I say to her. "Could you help me?"

She rushes to my side, depositing the tray with a clatter on the dressing table.

"What is it, miss? Please don't be ill again."

"It's not that. I need to go to the bathroom."

Her face goes blank momentarily, and then she frowns. "You'll be wanting a bath now, miss?"

"I want the toilet, privy. Whatever you call it. I have to, you know—pee!"

"Oh, of course." She reaches under the bed and produces a china pot painted all over with little flowers, and thrusts it in my direction.

"You expect me to pee in that?" The thought is revolting, but if I don't relieve myself soon, the alternative will be much worse.

I reach for the pot. "Here, let me. I can handle

this myself." But when she releases the pot into my grasp I almost drop it, I'm so weak. Shocked at the state of my physical condition and too desperate to think any more of modesty, I surrender to Barnes's helpful hands. Quickly covering the pot with a cloth, Barnes rushes out of the room, promising to return posthaste to see to my dinner.

I sink back on the bed, sweet relief flooding through me, and the aroma of some kind of roasted meat from the tray making my mouth water. I hope Barnes intends to wash her hands before she reappears.

Barnes is back in a flash, but I can't tell if she's attended to personal hygiene, and it's too awkward to ask outright. Anyway, I'm too famished to care much and gratefully surrender to her feeding me roast beef and potatoes. Yummy. It's not long before I can't eat another bite, though I really haven't consumed much of what was on the tray.

As Barnes bustles about covering dishes, she looks at me shyly and says, "You're not in anger at me for helping Mr. Jones, are you, miss? I was only doing my job, and me and you was always such good friends. Surely you know I want what's best for you."

Her face flushes red as she lowers her eyes and busies herself again with the tray.

"No, of course I'm not angry," I say.

"My brother has been beside himself these past few days, worrying and fretting."

She's looking at me, almost expectantly.

"Your brother?"

"He's beside himself with joy at your recovery, as we all are, miss. But he seems more distracted than ever. And the worse he gets, the more trouble Mr. Dowling gives him. First there was the two crystal glasses he knocked over and broke the other day, and then today he was late for breakfast on account of Cook letting him have a bit too much brandy last night. Why, Mr. Dowling is this close to dismissing him. Which might not be the worst thing."

She has been twisting a handkerchief in her hands, but now looks up at me, as if wanting a response. "Perhaps you are of the same mind, miss?"

"I . . . I'm sure you know what's best for your brother. Sometimes even a lateral move can lead to more rewarding opportunities." Suddenly I am channeling a human resources drone.

Barnes has a sort of glazed look in her eyes. "Right, miss. Anyway, I says to him, what good can come of this if you stay? But he won't hear none of it. Will you think of none but yourself, I says? You'll have nothing to live on, and neither will I. Because sure as I'm standing here, I'd lose my place as well. And there would be nothing to send my mother, and . . ."

Barnes's voice cracks, and she starts to cry. "Dismiss me if you must for speaking so freely, miss, but please do not throw everything away. You'll be cut off without a penny, and I can't bear to think of you starving in the streets . . ."

Now she loses it. She keeps trying to control herself, apologizing incoherently, blowing her nose into a handkerchief, eyes streaming, and all I can do is keep telling her that it's okay for her to cry. But I have no idea what she's talking about.

Unless—could it be that the fretting, about-to-be-fired brother has something to do with my starving in the streets? Is Barnes implying I've been doing the nasty with a member of the serving classes? Perhaps ordering him to service me?

Barnes looks like she's just been slapped, and I realize I've got a smirk on my face. Poor Barnes. How could I be so insensitive? Just because I know this isn't real doesn't mean that she knows it, too. If she did, she wouldn't be crying her eyes out. Which means her brother wouldn't know this isn't real either, so the least I could do is have a little compassion. Poor guy, whoever he is, suffering over me like that, and his sister, suffering over all of us. Imagine a man daring to risk everything for love. Of me.

Then again, it's not for love of me, it's for love of this dark-haired woman's reflection I see in the mirror. Which makes sense, because a man's risking everything for love of me could only happen in a dream. Real life is populated with the likes of Frank, formerly known as fiancé, and Wes, formerly known as friend. Both currently known as pond scum.

I wonder if I'll see my alleged lover from the oppressed classes before I wake up. Much as I want to wake up and get back to my life, I can't help but be curious. Is he cute? Does he have some kind of blue-collar magnetism like Joe, the carpenter who spent a month earthquake-retrofitting my building and another three walking around my bedroom wearing nothing but a tool belt?

I realize Barnes is looking at me.

"Sorry?" I say.

"Do you forgive me, miss, for sobbing all over you like that? And you just recovered yourself."

"Don't give it a second thought. I hope you feel better soon."

"Oh, miss. You're so kind, you are. Always thinking of everyone else but yourself." She wipes a tear away. And with a curtsey, leaves me alone in this room. To think. And sleep.

Which I do within seconds, the last fuzzy thought being that I trust this will be all over when I awake.

Four

But it's not. I'm still here. Shit. It's morning. Birds singing. The scent of roses wafting through my window. Mrs. Mansfield in my doorway.

Like I said, Shit.

"Good morning, Jane. You look well."

I turn on my side, so that I am facing away from her.

"Are you well enough to come downstairs and have some breakfast?" She strips the covers off me; guess I don't have a choice. If this were really like a Jane Austen novel, someone like Captain Benwick would be at my feet reading me Scott and Byron as I recovered from my head injury. But instead I'm subjected to the whims of a frilly blond porcelain doll and her scalpel-wielding henchman.

"Here, let me." She helps me to my feet.

I take a few tentative steps and feel little of the weakness of the day before. Evidently the healing process in dreams is a swift one.

"Well? You seem infinitely better," she says.

"I guess so."

"Good girl. I shall send Barnes to you." She eyes my face and frowns, swiping her hand across my forehead and then examining her fingers, as if checking for dust on a dresser top. Then she leans over, her face close to mine, but instead of giving me a kiss, she sniffs at my skin, her mouth crinkling in distaste, before straightening her posture and gliding toward the door. "Your face could do with a good washing" is her parting endearment.

Barnes appears within moments, all demure and polite silence this morning. And for the next half hour she furrows her brow in concentration while she laces and buttons me into various layers of clothing and does my hair. I enjoy the pampering, which, come to think of it, is more necessity than pampering. After all, how could anyone get into these clothes alone, especially with the laces and buttons inconveniently located in the back of the garments?

I realize I have not brushed my teeth since God knows when, and I ask Barnes for a toothbrush, hoping that such a thing exists. Thankfully, she produces a reasonable facsimile, albeit a little ratty and with a metal handle, but nevertheless a toothbrush. There's even a tongue scraper. Using someone else's dental utensils is only the beginning of the unpleasantness, however. The tooth powder, which when I add a little water becomes a salty, chalky paste, not only makes me gag, but makes my teeth feel like they're being scoured with Comet. What I wouldn't do for a minty paste with fluoride. But I think of the doctor's brown and yellow smile and brush even harder.

After Barnes leaves me, I check myself out in the mirror and again experience that shock of seeing someone else looking back at me.

I arrive downstairs at the breakfast table, drawn by the aromas of freshly baked bread and hot chocolate, but I experience a brief, stomach-churning moment when the first thing I notice on the table is a giant ham glistening with fat. Mrs. Mansfield sees the look on my face and motions to a servant to take away the platter. "Your father," she says and rolls her eyes. "He plans to spend the day in his atelier"—she draws out the word "atelier" with a sneer—"and you know he will not emerge till dinner. Now, what would you like?"

I think of declining half of what Mrs. Mansfield presses on me to eat, but I decide it's best not to give her any cause to suspect a relapse. Besides, I figure all that delicious bread and hot chocolate has imaginary calories, another advantage of eating while unconscious.

While I eat, she talks. Mostly about someone named Mr. Edgeworth. "How refreshing," she says, "to meet with a man whose manners and person are as agreeable as his fortune." I gather from Mrs. Mansfield's monologue that the man in question is a widower who inherited his nearby estate from his aunt several months ago. "As if that sour old prune's death was not favor enough, it was very obliging of her to leave everything to him."

A young, broad-shouldered serving man briefly enters the dining room to deliver some dish or other, as if there isn't already enough food here to feed the population of twenty dreams. I think I catch him looking at me for longer than is likely proper for a servant, but I am so conscious of wanting to run into my alleged lover that I'm probably just imagining things. Still, as he bustles at the sideboard I check him out. Long legs. Dark brown hair, somewhat unruly despite the ponytail. He glances my way again—intense brown eyes, almost black—and I smile. He spills a basket of rolls all over the sideboard, his eyes darting to Mrs. M, who is too engaged in her monologue to notice. Definitely clumsy enough to be Barnes's brother.

He leaves the room, and Mrs. Mansfield asks me what I think of Mr. Edgeworth. I amuse myself by telling her, in perfect ladylike fashion, that I am in perfect agreement with her opinion of him. She opens her mouth as if to speak, her hand, having just dabbed her mouth with a napkin, suspended in its aborted trip back to the table.

She seems to recover and scrutinizes me, eyes narrowed. "It appears that knock on the head has done your mind some good." Then she launches into an account of the latest news of my siblings and their apparent concern for my well-being. I manage to glean from her talk that I have one sister, recently married to some rich guy and living in another county—"At least one of my daughters does not live only to disoblige me," she says while buttering her toast—and a single brother studying at Oxford, the mere mention of whom brings a softness to her voice and face that is almost maternal. I think I can guess who her favorite is.

Finally Mrs. Mansfield has exhausted her scintillating supply of family news and encourages me to "take a turn in the shrubbery."

I'll take anything I can get if it means getting away from her. This is also my first chance to be alone, other than in my bedroom, since I've found myself in this endless dream. Granted, I've had long dreams before, and one's sense of time is always questionable while sleeping. But I've never had a dream with such vivid details before. I can smell the herbs and the flowers in the garden, feel the sun and the breeze caressing my skin. And after what seems like at least an hour of walking, I also feel some tightness in my calves and little drops of perspiration on my back. These sensations feel every bit as real as the intense hunger I had last night.

And the touch of that quack doctor's knife. I shudder and test the bend of my arm, which is stiff and still stings a little. All I have to do is continue to play the part of the dutiful daughter, and it will all be okay till I wake up.

Five

Gravel crunches beneath my shoes as I head back toward the house. That same lonely sound my feet made on that night two months ago when I paced around the gravel path behind Wes's house, smoking cigarette after cigarette and wondering where Frank was. Or where Wes was, for that matter. Finally I settled into the little niche next to Wes's front door and waited.

I heard his sneakers slapping on the driveway before I saw him. "Where is he?" I said, startling him so badly he dropped his key with a clatter.

"Courtney. What are you doing here?" He ran a hand through his unruly curls.

"He's not answering his cell. You said he was on his way here hours ago."

Wes looked down at the key and picked it up.

"Do you even know where he is?"

Eyes still cast down, he mumbled something I couldn't make out.

I went all cold inside. "What the hell is going on?"

But all he did was shake his head.

"This is bullshit," I said, grinding my cigarette under my heel and turning to head back to my car.

Wes grabbed my hand. "Don't go."

But I did. I went straight to Frank's place and let myself in with my key. I searched through his desk drawers, his unmade bed, his piles of dirty laundry. I listened to the messages on his answering machine. I even played TV cop by rubbing the tip of a pencil over the pad of paper that was next to his phone until I could read the address on it, which was vaguely familiar.

When I pulled up in front of that address, I laughed until I had to wipe my eyes. I was in front of the showroom of our wedding cake designer. And there was Frank's '69 Mercedes parked across the street, "the last handmade car Mercedes made," as he always pointed out to anyone admiring it.

Not three hours before I'd been bitching to Paula about how Frank wouldn't do anything for the wedding, how I'd dragged him to a tasting appointment at this very cake designer's, how I'd begged him to bring her a deposit check with my written list of specifications, which he refused to do. Clearly he'd had a change of heart. It was times like these, when Frank would bring me takeout or massage my feet after a long day, that I'd remember why I fell in love with him. He tried to be all nihilistic and can't-be-bothered, but inside he was as sweet and vulnerable as anyone.

I parked my car and walked toward the shop with the white curlicue lettering on its double glass doors. Weymouth Wedding Cakes and Confectionery. I'd chosen it because Weymouth was where Frank Churchill and Jane Fairfax got engaged, and because this wedding and its reluctant bridegroom needed whatever bit of Austen-mojo I could muster. I had tried to tell Frank that Frank Churchill was this gorgeous guy from *Emma* who had a wicked sense of humor and a way with the ladies, but my Frank could care less.

The store was all lit up, though it was after business hours; I could see through the windows that a small elderly woman was vacuuming. I tried the door, which was unlocked, and smiled at the woman with the vacuum. “Is Amy here?”

Her worn face creased into a thousand wrinkles as she returned my smile and pointed behind her to swinging chrome doors.

Wait a minute. How would I explain my showing up here? Frank might not only be annoyed that I’d spoil his surprise; he’d know I must have dug around his apartment to find out where he was. Unless, that is, I said I was on my way home from Paula’s, passed by, and noticed his car.

I pushed open the swinging doors, revealing the length of a high-tech chrome kitchen—and at the far end, their backs to me, Amy and Frank, leaning over a gleaming chrome counter as if studying something on it. The list for the cake, apparently. They made no indication of having heard me open the doors; the vacuum cleaner drowned out every other sound.

And then, far away, the vacuum cleaner turned off, and I heard Amy’s low, throaty laughter as

Frank put his arm around her slim waist and turned his head to whisper something into her ear, his lips brushing against her skin.

I froze between the two swinging doors. The room got longer, the figures at the other end of it farther away.

Amy turned to face Frank. And then she removed his arm from her waist and slowly tucked a strand of her glossy black hair behind her ear. "It was fun, okay? But I'm not into anything serious."

"Don't flatter yourself," he said, running a finger down her bare arm, his full lips curving in a smile.

It was then that I heard myself gasp. It was then that he saw me.

It was then that I remembered Frank Churchill too was a liar.

They say the truth will set you free, but what nobody tells you is that sometimes the truth will also make you miserable. As I stood between those swinging doors, looking into the eyes of that man at the other end of that room, I saw the truth of what marriage to him would be like. I saw a lifetime of pretending I didn't notice when he flirted with the waitress at Ammo, or fed birthday cake to a woman at my party, or how his eyes inevitably followed the most beautiful woman in the room without even a perfunctory nod to how I might feel.

And so, within the space of a few hours, I was free. Free of my fiancé, and free of my closest male friend. I can still see that whipped puppy look on Wes's face when he admitted to me that he knew Frank was sneaking out to be with Amy that night yet agreed to lie for him anyway, and how pale he went when I told him I never wanted to see him again.

It was the same look Wes had two months later when I ran into him, just hours before I went to sleep and ended up in this dream. Funny that I haven't thought much about that day—yesterday, to be exact, despite the illusion of time passing. I haven't thought much about that day except for the end of it, when I was reading *Pride and Prejudice*. But now all I can think about is what happened earlier in the day. And the more I think about it, the more I understand why I must have conveniently shelved it.

I can still feel the hot, dusty, L.A. midafternoon stagnation, that airless heat that sent me into a new store off Vermont. I was cooling off in the central air—so much better than the AC in my car or the cheap window unit in my apartment—and looking at a skimpy leather top, wishing I had the right kind of body to wear it. That's when I felt his eyes on me. Wes, a few feet away, staring. He was holding hands with a petite, pixyish woman, but dropped her hand the second he saw that I saw him.

Then he rushed over to me, leaving her standing by a rack of overpriced tank tops.

"Courtney, I was just thinking about you—"

"How nice for you," I said, pushing past him toward the back exit, stopping only momentarily to feign interest in the sale rack and slow the pounding of my heart. I glanced behind me, and there he was, only a few feet away, mouth open stupidly, while the pixie remained at the cash register, throwing daggers with her eyes.

"Courtney, I am so sorry."

"Forget it."

"I can't." He caught up to me and put a hand on my shoulder.

I shrugged it away.

Silence. When I looked up, his gray-blue eyes behind his glasses were moist.

"I've been wanting to call—"

"Your friend's waiting."

"I have a lot to say to you."

"Not interested."

This time I made it to the exit without once looking back, not even as I walked through the parking lot, and not even as I drove off in my car, hands shaking, heart hammering in my ears.

But I couldn't stop thinking about him on the drive home, and I couldn't stop thinking about him as I rummaged through my refrigerator trying to decide whether wilted lettuce would do for a salad or if I should allow myself two spoonfuls of Cherry Garcia. And what was really weird was that I kept thinking about how Wes's eyes looked like they were filled with tears and how I could still feel the touch of his hand on my shoulder and why I'd never noticed how attractive he was before.

Attractive? I had never been attracted to Wes before, and I couldn't stand him now. So then why could I still smell that freshly scrubbed, citrusy scent of him that was so familiar to me as I brushed past him in the store?

I shakily eased myself into a kitchen chair, my stomach turning cold with fear. Was I so self-destructive that I found myself attracted to a man the second I knew he could hurt me? Frank had lied, and so had Wes. Granted, with Frank I had been willfully blind. But Wes? I never could have imagined it. If only he had told me what he knew, I would have been spared the humiliation of walking into that scene. Frank nuzzling up to Amy in that kitchen, whispering in her ear, running his finger down her arm. The way he looked at me when he saw me watching him. I'd spent two months trying to purge that image from my brain. I'd spent two months trying to stop picturing where they actually did it—against all that gleaming chrome? Or in the unmade bed I'd rummaged through in Frank's apartment? I'd finally achieved whole days in which I did not replay those scenes. And here I was again, standing in front of those swinging doors.

But even worse was the look in Wes's eyes. The naked sadness in them. I'd never returned a single one of his calls or emails.

I shot up from my chair, determined to do something, anything, to put Sub-Zero refrigerators, chrome counters, and Wes's gray-blue eyes out of my mind. That's when my vision started narrowing toward black and my hands gripped the edge of the kitchen sink. Dizzy, I sat down again. Poured myself an icy shot of Absolut. Much better. Perhaps all this emotional confusion was simply due to my not having eaten since breakfast, if you didn't count the bag of chips I got from the thief who owned the corner store.

That's when I decided to order myself a large clam-and-garlic pizza and reread *Pride and Prejudice*. I would self-medicate with fat, carbohydrates, and Jane Austen, my number one drug of choice, my constant companion through every breakup, every disappointment, every crisis. Men might come and go, but Jane Austen was always there. In sickness and in health, for richer, for poorer, till death do us part.

And so I curled up in bed with Elizabeth and Darcy and read until the familiar words lulled me into calm and peace and harmony, and the next thing I knew I woke up here. But didn't I also go for a swim, sometime after I ran into Wes and before I took *P & P* with me to bed? For some reason I seem to remember doing that, too, but now it's all fuzzy. Maybe I'm mixing up two different days. After all, when had I ever delayed my need for pizza with a trip to the pool? Certainly not since breaking up with Frank. Which was another thing I could say in favor of being single: At least I didn't have to deal with his disapproving looks.

Right now, I don't want to think about Frank or Wes. I don't want to think of all those hours I spent doing laps either, all in pursuit of a body one could only achieve through genetics or surgery or both.

I reach the house and consider standing up Mrs. Mansfield rather than join her in the sitting room after my walk, as she hath commanded. But I want a distraction from those dangerous thoughts, any distraction. A little poking around at the various rooms on the ground floor leads me to what is evidently the sitting room. There are a couple of sofas, several chairs, a massive fireplace, and a couple of tables in the sunny room. Mrs. Mansfield is seated at one of the tables, intent on some sewing she's doing. She looks up and smiles when I walk in, and indicates an embroidery frame on the table.

"Here you are. I knew you would be eager to get back to your work."

In your dreams, lady. And last time I checked, this is mine. I sit down at the table and pick up the embroidery, amused by the thought that anyone could think I am capable of doing anything that involves a high level of domestic skill. I can't even hem a skirt.

As I look at the embroidery (pretty, whoever had done it), Mrs. Mansfield says, "What is it, my dear? Are you not interested in your needlework today?"

"Just not in the mood, I guess."

"Are you unwell again?"

Again? This Jane person must be one of those fainting hypochondriac types, a Mary Musgrove, always loosening her stays and reaching for her smelling salts. Then again, with all this tight stuff around my torso it doesn't take much imagination to figure out why fainting might not be that far-fetched. "I'm hanging in there."

Mrs. Mansfield's brows contract. " 'Hanging in there'? You know that is a common way of talking I cannot abide. Have not I warned you about engaging the servants in idle conversation, Jane? Now pick up your needle. You have a bad habit of leaving things unfinished. Accomplished women do not leave work unfinished. And women without accomplishments do not make good marriages, especially women of thirty whose first bloom is a distant memory."

This woman is more and more resembling my real-life mother. The same put-downs masked as helpful advice, the same warnings about becoming an old maid. Okay, how about I show Miss Bossy-corset just how much I can fuck up that embroidery with my clumsy, home-economics-dropout fingers. So I pick up the needle. And watch in stunned disbelief as my long, tapered fingers (oh so different from the small and somewhat stubby ones of my waking life) fly over and through the cloth, creating lacy flower petals and leaves and delicate little borders. Who is this? What Martha Stewart–like demon of a Stepford wife is possessing me?

I think about stopping, but watching the effortlessness of my alien hands doing their embroidery thing sucks me in. Time stretches out, yet passes quickly. Before I know it, Mrs. Mansfield is telling me it's time to dress for dinner. I attempt to make sense of all this in the quiet of my bedroom. But what sense is there to be made of anything? It's a dream, where anything is possible. Even my ability to sew. And like it.

At dinner, a true carnivore fest, I finally meet my "father." He is a tall, thin, quiet man with strawlike hair in shades of brown and gray and the hollow-cheeked look of an ascetic, though he consumes more food than I can imagine he has room to put it. He's either a bulimic or blessed with the metabolism of a hummingbird. Clearly he likes me or, more precisely, likes who he thinks I am, as the only words he speaks other than those in response to his wife are when he tells me how happy he is to see me looking so well again and how his joy has inspired his painting the entire day. This is a welcome departure from my real father, a would-be writer who left when I was only nine years old, ostensibly to pursue his art, but who has not, to my knowledge, published so much as a greeting card, let alone ever sent one to his only daughter.

After dinner, Mr. Mansfield retires to his "atelier," the mention of which causes Mrs. Mansfield to arch her brows and make a sort of snorting noise, and leaves me consigned to sit with her in the drawing room.

I see a newspaper lying on a table. The date: August 12, 1813.

So what does one do for entertainment in 1813 England? Fortunately, conversation is not on the menu. The expected activity is my reading aloud to Mrs. M from the second volume of *Pride and Prejudice*—a first edition, no less. Hands trembling, I open the precious volume to the title page, which simply says, "by the author of 'Sense and Sensibility'." What I wouldn't give to take this treasure home with me, a real, impossibly new first edition. With my career prospects, however, a dream is about the closest I'll ever get to holding one of these puppies in my hands.

I open to the place Mrs. M has marked and read to her for hours. It's the most fun I've had since this whole thing began. And now it's time for bed. Strange, isn't it, to end a dream in exactly the same manner in which I began it?

That's it! That's all I need, this little bit of synchronicity. That's what will bring me back to reality. I know now that when I close my eyes to go to sleep, I will wake up where I belong, in my very own twenty-first-century bed.

I'm so pleased with that thought that as I kiss Mrs. M on the cheek and say good night, I nearly tell her how much I've enjoyed meeting her. But I decide not to. Not that I have problems lying, but I realize there is something truly fun about this play-acting I'm doing, and I don't feel like saying anything to spoil the moment. It's harder to keep quiet when I say good night to Mr. M, because I really do wish I had more time to get to know him better.

Within half an hour, I'm tucked snugly under the covers of Jane's luxurious four-poster bed, and my eyes are getting heavy. Odd, I usually can't go to sleep that quickly when I'm awake. I giggle at the absurdity of such a thought. I command my mind to focus and remember every detail, as I intend to write everything down in my journal as soon as I wake up back in L.A.

Seven

It's dark in the room, and my mind is full of the dream.

I can still feel the jagged softness of the grass soothing and slightly tickling my bare feet as I walked through the field. The moon in the night-time sky was round and full and bathed everything in a silver glow. As I crossed a section of grass that was damp, I wondered whether I would catch a cold. That's when I realized I wasn't just barefoot, I was naked.

I crossed my arms over my breasts and crouched down, scanning the landscape for observing eyes, for a place to hide, but I seemed to be all alone. I relaxed my muscles and stood; so what if I was naked? If no one was there to see me, why shouldn't I enjoy a moonlight stroll without clothes?

Soon I came to a miniature lake, more a swimming hole, really, its calm, mirrored surface reflecting the moon above. The water made me aware of how dry my mouth was, and so I knelt down to take a drink.

And then I caught sight of my reflection.

Looking back at me was the strange woman with the long dark hair and pale skin. The reflection smiled at me, and I felt my own face smiling. But inside my stomach was a chill.

"Don't be frightened," the reflection said.

"Don't be frightened," I said to the reflection.

That's all I remember. I lie here in bed, my heart pounding as I wait for the truth to unfold with the first glow of daylight coming through a gap in the curtains. I am not back in my apartment. I am still in the dream.

But wait a minute. I just woke up from a dream. Last time I checked, it's not possible to have a dream within a dream.

Am I really asleep?

A cold rock of fear settles on my chest. Dear God. I'm not going to wake up. I'm not going to wake up because I'm not asleep. My dream was a message, the reflection in the lake the messenger.

I am here, in the past or in some other reality, living out someone else's life.

But how could this be? Am I actually inhabiting the body of a real, live person? And if this Jane person is indeed real and alive, then where is she now? If my own body isn't sleeping and dreaming all of this, then what is it doing right now and where is it? Could it be that I'm living Jane's life and my own simultaneously? If so, where is Jane? Where is her essence, her spirit, her personality, whatever it is that inhabits a person's body?

Maybe I've gone crazy. Maybe my mother, my real-life mother, is standing over me right now and patting my hand in some mental ward, looking into my vacant eyes while I live out insane fantasies of being an early-nineteenth-century Englishwoman.

Was all Mrs. Mansfield's talk about insane asylums my subconscious mind's way of breaking the truth to me? But isn't the catch-22 of being crazy that if you really are crazy, you don't know you are?

If I'm not crazy, then how do I explain my presence here? Did I walk through some kind of rip in the fabric of space-time? Have I watched too many *Star Trek* reruns? If this is time travel, then how am I in someone else's body instead of visiting this time period in my own body? As if time travel would be any sort of explanation anyway.

Could this be a past life? No, a past life would have already happened, and I wouldn't be bringing my twenty-first-century persona into the mix. I wouldn't even know about myself in the twenty-first century if I were really having a past life. I'm getting dizzy thinking about this.

Wait. Could it be some sort of parallel reality happening simultaneously with my own? Okay, then why would I be in the body of a nineteenth-century woman but possessing the mind of a twenty-first-century woman?

Have I died and reincarnated? Can people reincarnate into the past? That would be a good trick. Is that what Buddhists mean when they say that linear time is just a mental construct? Are we actually overlapping into different times? Will I return to the twenty-first century to find a Roman gladiator sitting in the next booth at House of Pies or Mrs. Mansfield standing behind me in the checkout line at Target?

I'm not even so sure I believe in reincarnation. Why am I even engaging in these speculations? How is any of it going to get me my life back?

Don't be frightened, said the reflection in the pond. I can't get the image of that face, her words, out of my head.

I feel like I can't breathe. I open the window with shaking fingers and will myself not to hyperventilate. My breathing slows, and I feel the sun warm my face. I inhale the tang and sweetness of herbs and grass and flowers, hear the birds chirping in the vividly green trees. I pull up the sleeve of my nightgown, and there is the same healing cut on my arm from the doctor's knife. All of these sensations are undeniably real.

I'm here. In someone else's body. In someone else's life. And here, it appears, I will stay until—or if—I figure out how to get back.

Okay, so how do I get my life back? Willing myself out of here didn't work. Insisting I'm not who they think I am almost got me committed, not to mention nearly bled dry.

There has to be a way to get my real life back. I just haven't figured it out yet.

I hear a quick rap at the bedroom door, and then it opens a crack. It's Barnes, wanting to know if I'm awake. Damn. I really don't feel like dealing with anyone right now. Then again I'm not sure I can get into my clothes with all their laces and buttons in the back. Not to mention that horrible, stiff corsetlike thing that makes the simplest motion, like sitting down in a chair or bending over to pick something up, an exercise in creative problem-solving. Hasn't anyone ever thought of ergonomics? Or common sense? It's as if they purposely designed them for women who have hired help. Of course they did.

It's good that Barnes is here, that she can help me get dressed, that her very presence will stop me from curling into a fetal position or screaming until they cart me off to an asylum. Because—and I feel the blood drain from my face—being committed would be much worse than a nightmare. It would be a no-exit situation far more horrible to contemplate than life imprisonment in the higher echelons of a society that predates a woman's right to do more than embroider and keep house. I have to compose myself and get through this day. I have to believe that somehow it will all become clear. And that somehow I'll find my way back to my real life. I have to believe this. Or else I can't function. Right now I feel the familiar morning pressure on my bladder. And relieving that pressure is all the reality I can handle at present. That and getting dressed. And playing the role.

When I enter the breakfast room, Mrs. Mansfield appraises me, eyes narrowed. "Your complexion has improved, but that color is most unbecoming to it. Have not I told you so at least three times? After you take a turn in the shrubbery, Jane, I want you upstairs and in your new blue gown. We cannot have Mr. Edgeworth seeing you in anything but your best looks, can we?"

"Mr. Edgeworth?"

"You know perfectly well he is expected for dinner today. If you would listen to your mother she would not have to repeat herself."

Oh God. She is now referring to herself in the third person. This is a particularly annoying habit my real-life mother also has, especially when she imagines herself as being poorly treated by someone, which is actually most of the time.

I break off a piece of a warm roll. I stuff it in my mouth and reach for the jam. It's apricot. Delicious. And that chocolate smells irresistible.

"I must speak with Cook about the roast," Mrs. Mansfield says, putting her napkin down. She gets up from the table and walks toward the door, mumbling something about soup and fish sauce and the timing of each course and that she would not have a moment to herself until dinner. "Not that you would know anything about the matter," she says, addressing me for a parting blow before sweeping out of the dining room, her last words trailing behind. "You are incapable of household management."

When the door closes behind her I gulp down the rest of my chocolate and wrap another roll in a napkin. This is a perfect time to escape.

Eight

As I leave the breakfast room, that cute serving guy from yesterday is coming in. We do one of those awkward advance/retreat/advance dances in trying to avoid crashing into each other. He turns bright red and averts his eyes as we make it past each other. This has to be Barnes's brother. I turn my head to take a last look, only to catch him doing the same. We both turn away. Oh, well. If this is the guy in question, then I'm sure there's no reason to give him a second thought, not with things on such a junior high school level.

The air outside is sweet, the birds are singing, and the flowers are resplendent, but I will not allow myself to get sidetracked by the scenery. Walking always did clear my head, and even if this isn't my own head I am determined to clear it well enough to find a way out of this situation.

Maybe the key to getting home lies in figuring out what I'm doing here. Could Jane and I have swapped lives? Could she be living my life right now, walking around in my body and talking in my voice? Talk about culture shock. At least I'm here with some knowledge of history, sparse though it may be. Jane, whoever she is, could not possibly know the future.

I have a flash of some upper-class, nineteenth-century Englishwoman dealing with my twenty-first-century, left-coast life. If she could get past the aesthetic shock of my industrial-carpeted little apartment, which is slightly larger than the Mansfields' drawing room, complete with wrought-iron security bars on the louvered windows and graffiti on the front gate, the noise alone might give her a breakdown. Between the LAPD helicopters making their nocturnal circles in the sky, the old deaf guy next door with his crowing rooster and blaring Latino talk radio, and the ear-splitting conversational tones of my boss, it would be enough for any gently bred Regency girl to question her own sanity, just as I now question mine.

Wait a minute. I don't want some strange woman living my life. Maybe it isn't the best life, but it's mine, and I want it back. I want my crummy little apartment with its paper-thin walls and floors pumping god-awful power rock from the apartment of the hostile Russian downstairs, who will never lower his music no matter how often I ask. I want my lousy job and my loud boss and the unpaid bills that keep me there. I want my friends, all of them. Paula, Anna. Even Wes. Mostly Wes. I want my bottle of Absolut chilling in the freezer. I want my raggedy stuffed dog, the one Daddy gave me on my ninth birthday. I want my music, my movies, my books, and my clothes. I want dresses that I can put on myself. I want to wear pants, jeans, real underwear. I want a toilet that flushes.

And I want to walk into a room and hear people call me Courtney.

I think of some stranger inhabiting my body, just as I am inhabiting Jane's. I can just see this Jane person surveying my belly and criticizing my flabby thighs. Or the cellulite on my ass. It's not that I'm a bad-looking woman or anything. But I'm not the long, willowy beauty that Jane is.

I can't believe this. Here I am, stuck in some parallel reality or whatever and all I can do is obsess about whether some strange woman that might be living in my body is dissatisfied with her new home. Anna once told me that obsession is just the mind's way of avoiding the real issues. Well, what is the real issue here? That I'm a time traveler stuck in a stranger's life? Who wouldn't want to avoid such a thing?

Figuring this out is a hopeless business, and my head is starting to throb. I have to calm down. I left my migraine meds in another reality, and I don't think a bleeding would be quite the same thing.

The sound of a horse nickering alerts me to my surroundings; I am passing a paddock with two horses inside. The brown one has its head to the ground, intently chewing some grass, but the cream-colored one goes right up to the railing as if to greet me, its big gentle eyes framed by long white eyelashes. I stroke the side of its face, and it seems to enjoy the contact. Boy or girl? What do I know about horses?

I wonder if this is the horse that I supposedly had the riding accident with, and I shudder. The horse gently nudges my hand with its velvety muzzle, as if to reassure me. "Don't mind me," I say. "You're a good girl. Or boy."

A slight teenage girl in a drab brown dress and apron, a cap covering her hair, is walking toward the house with an empty pail. She comes closer, and stops to curtsey slightly before continuing on her way. She ducks her head as she walks by, but I can see enough of her perfectly defined brows and milky complexion to tell how pretty she is. And young—she must be all of sixteen. She should be hanging out with her friends at the mall and looking through college catalogues, not schlepping a pail in a drab brown sack of a dress.

I stroke the horse's muzzle one last time, then continue on my way, taking a cooling walk through a long avenue of shady trees. Things could be a lot worse. I could be a scullery maid like that poor young girl instead of a wealthy young woman in a mansion. Sure, there's Mrs. M, but other than subjecting me to dirty medical instruments and threatening to have me committed, she seems relatively harmless.

On the other hand, this all has to end eventually, doesn't it? I'm sure wherever the real Jane is, she's just as eager to get back to her own life as I am to mine. So why not just relax in the meantime, experience the sensation of living in another body and another time, Jane Austen's time, no less, and have faith that real life will return soon enough. What do I have to look forward to on a typical day anyway? Breakfast alone? Marking time at work? Lousy television to fill the evening? Or maybe dinner with Paula, who's in full energy-vampire mode these days? Sooner or later I'll return to a sink full of dirty dishes and an empty refrigerator. At least in this world someone else does the shopping and cleaning up.

Nine

When I return to the house and go up to my room, a pastel blue dress is all laid out for me on the bed. I hate pastel blue. This must be the one Mrs. M is so hot on having me wear for dinner with that Edgeworth person. Barnes, who's either psychic or has been lying in wait for my return, taps on the door and offers her services for changing clothes and doing hair.

I notice Barnes's eyes are red, and her face is blotchy. "Are you all right, Barnes?"

"Oh, it's my brother, miss. Understands your silence as proof that all is over and done. Which, I says to him, is the best for all concerned."

"My silence?"

"Don't you worry none, miss. I'll see to him."

My life is complicated enough, and frankly, I really don't want to know. I don't need to try and fix Barnes's brother's problems on top of trying to pretend I'm someone else.

"Well then," I say, eyeing the pastel blue thing on the bed. "There must be something else I can wear."

"But your mother is most particular, miss—" And poor Barnes looks so terrified at the idea of defying Mrs. M's directive on this point that I sigh and tell her to forget it.

I survey the array of hairpins and brushes on the

dressing table. I open a couple of jars whose contents look like they might be used to moisturize or perfume, but I see nothing that remotely resembles makeup.

"So Barnes, any chance I might have a little something to color my lips or cheeks, both, preferably?"

Barnes's eyebrows fly up, and her right hand grips her chest.

"Come on, Barnes, I'm sure there are women who at least wear a little color on their cheeks, even if they don't admit to it."

Barnes looks at her shoes. "You do not do such things, miss."

"But I'll bet my mother does." Actually, I'm bluffing. If Mrs. M is secretly wearing blush or worse, then she does it artfully enough so that it looks natural.

Barnes looks at me like she is about to become roadkill.

"I'm right, aren't I."

Barnes starts backing away, not looking me in the eye. "Now, miss, I am sure I don't know what you mean."

"Come on, Barnes. Be a pal and borrow some for me. It'll be our little secret."

Barnes has reached the door. Her voice quavers. "Please, miss. Don't make me. Your mother would—I cannot even begin to imagine what she would do to me."

I put my hand on her shoulder. "Sorry, Barnes. I'll sneak in there myself."

Barnes clutches at the doorframe. "Oh, please, miss. I beg you. If she sees anything like that on your face, she'll blame it on me, to be sure."

"God. What kind of fascist regime have I landed in?"

Barnes's eyes fill, and I force myself to calm down. "It's all right, Barnes. I'll be a good girl and leave you in charge of making me beautiful, as I'm sure you're well qualified to do."

I make her sit down for a minute, and after I smile at her encouragingly she recovers enough to start getting me dressed.

When she's done with me, I do (or at least the strange face in the mirror does) look pretty good. And I have to admit that deadly as that shade of blue is on my usual self, it does suit the coloring of this borrowed body of mine. I pinch my cheeks and bite my lips, a poor substitute for the arsenal of paints and powders I'm used to having at my disposal. Oh, well. At least I needn't worry about being the only woman without so much as a drop of lip gloss at a party full of painted-to-the-hilt beauties, which is my version of the classic nightmare of being naked in public.

When I go downstairs to the drawing room, Mr. and Mrs. Mansfield are waiting for me, along with a broad-faced, middle-aged brunette who turns her dimpled smile on me, and a much younger woman with pale pink ribbons wound into her fiery red hair, dark blue eyes, and a sneer on her face. I curtsey to the strangers and realize that since they aren't introduced to me, I'm probably expected to know who they are.

Mrs. Mansfield is doing most of the talking, which gives me the chance to gather that the broad-faced woman is her sister, Mrs. Randolph, and that the sneering redhead is Mrs. Randolph's daughter. Mrs. Randolph is not as superficially pretty as her sister, but her personality is definitely attractive. I can tell from her warm hug that this latest addition to my so-called family, a maternal aunt in the truest sense of the word, likes me a lot, and being an easy mark for any kind of positive attention, I immediately like her back. The daughter, Susan, on the other hand, kisses me on both cheeks, proclaiming her "vast relief" at her cousin's recovery, but her eyes are hard and her smile is merely a variation of her sneer.

Then a man walks in. I can't see much more than a silhouette, because the sunlight is behind him.

"Miss Mansfield," he says. "You look remarkably well. What a pleasure to see you again, all the more so because your parents tell me you are quite recovered."

He moves closer, and now I can see his features. "Yes, I've heard that, too," I say, trying not to stare.

He flashes me a broad smile. Not bad. Not bad at all.

So this fine specimen is Mr. Edgeworth. Certainly nothing approaching the elderly widower I pictured. Mid to late thirties at the most. Dark blond hair, large hazel eyes, and a little cleft in his chin, which reminds me of Wes. I didn't even know Wes had a cleft in his chin until he shaved off that silly goatee. Why would anyone cover up an asset like that? Speaking of assets, this guy's aren't too bad either. I tear my eyes away from his form-fitting knee breeches and am grateful that his eyes are on Mrs. M, who is, incredibly, giggling like a teenager.

"I quite agree with you, Mr. Edgeworth," she says. "Jane appears to be in the peak of health."

And suddenly it hits me that all this talk of Edgeworth, all this fuss about the dinner and what I should wear to it, isn't about her own crush on the guy; it's all been aimed at me.

I notice Edgeworth stealing glances at me, and suddenly I start wondering if I'm showing too much cleavage or if I've spilled wine on my dress. But when I let my eyes rest on him for more than a nanosecond I realize that these are approving looks. That he's trying through eye contact to get me to join in the conversation. A few sharp looks from Mrs. Mansfield encourage me to break in, but my throat refuses to produce more than a couple of unintelligible croaks and squeaks. My palms are sweating, and my throat is dry.

It's not like I've never been in blind-date situations before. But I'm one of those people who hates them and always has to be tricked into it by being invited to some gathering at which I just happen to be introduced (as if it hadn't all been planned) to the potential man of my dreams. These particular MOMDs have ranged from the computer nerd with the handshake that felt like a limp sea anemone to the performance artist whose magnum opus was licking dry a dozen opened cans of smoked oysters. Even though I usually feel not the slightest bit of interest in the man who has been summoned to the party, the dinner, or the art opening by the well-meaning friend, I always stupidly agonize over what kind of impression I've made on the would-be suitor.

These mental gymnastics were particularly horrid on the few occasions I allowed myself to be persuaded to go on an actual, one-on-one blind date. In fact, I spent many hours afterward depressed because some colorless twit seemed to want to end the evening as quickly as I did. After all, what kind of a loser couldn't even captivate a colorless twit?

Blind dates and setups of all kinds are completely useless, I long ago decided. Most intelligent men and women like to go forth into the world and stalk their own prey, choose their own mirrors of dysfunction, and repeat their own patterns of abusive relationships, without the well-meaning but futile efforts of friends.

What am I getting myself so rattled about? This whole scenario is only temporary at best, so who cares if this Edgeworth person likes me or not or is just being polite, or what my "mother" hopes for or expects. I have absolutely nothing to lose. I can look at the situation as just another interesting adventure. In fact, I can even turn it into a little experiment. What if I decided to be filled with self-confidence and poise? Wouldn't that be a refreshing change from my usual reality?

Sure, but what if he isn't interested in me?

What difference does it make? What if I decide to try on more than just a new face and a new body? What if I try on a new personality, too? Could it be any harder than trying on a new dress in a size larger than mine? Or, for that matter, trying on an empire-waisted, pastel-blue gown and facing the world without so much as a dab of lipstick? What couldn't I do now, having already committed such a breach of fashion logic and lived to tell the tale? Why couldn't I pretend to be a woman with a solid core of self-worth, who likes herself no matter what the nearest handsome man or evil mother thinks of her?

Ten

I turn to Edgeworth with a big smile and immediately join the conversation with entire words and sentences. However, I'm careful to follow his lead without asking too many questions, as I have no idea how much I'm already supposed to know about him. After all, I am an imposter in a borrowed body, and have no wish to expose myself and have to answer questions I can't possibly answer. Which would also ruin my experiment.

Edgeworth offers his arm to me when it is time to go in to dinner, and off we go in pairs. So odd, this buddy system for the field trip to the dining room, but I have to admit I could get used to the press of Edgeworth's arm against mine.

True to my resolution of trying out a new personality, I have no trouble talking to him throughout the meal. I don't even lose my cool when I drop a bit of soup on my dress; I just laugh it off and ignore Mrs. M's laser look.

Edgeworth says to me in an undertone, "Things do seem to have a way of turning upside down whenever we are in close proximity."

"Do they?" I say with a smile.

"I must say, though, I would not have expected you of all people to be positively cheerful after such a mishap."

He looks at me expectantly, but I am waiting for a clue to what he might mean.

"Have you forgotten how irked you were at Mrs. Randolph's party when I had the singular misfortune to spill tea on your gown?"

He grins mischievously, tilting his head slightly. A lock of hair falls onto his forehead, and instantly I have a mental flash of a spreading wet blotch on my dress, the angry heat on my face spreading just as rapidly. It was spilt tea on a white dress, a dress from another day.

The disorientation of having a memory of myself being in this body and this period-piece world is so dizzying that I feel my hands gripping the edge of the table to keep myself from falling over.

Calm down now. Of course it isn't an actual memory. It can't be.

"Do forgive me," he whispers, his hazel eyes full of concern. "It was most ungallant of me to mention it."

"It's not your fault. It sounds like I have some serious anger issues."

"I, ah—I did not mean for this subject to take such a sober turn. Allow me to make amends by giving you leave to repay my clumsiness. You may aim your next errant cup of tea at my coat, Miss Mansfield."

I laugh. "I appreciate your generous offer, but I'd rather you didn't tempt me. We rage-aholics must swear off such pleasures."

I see Mrs. Mansfield's ears prick up at the sound of the word "offer," and I smile inwardly, reminded of Mrs. Jennings believing she's overheard Colonel Brandon proposing to Elinor in *Sense and Sensibility*.

After some vigorous whispering between Mrs. M and her sister, who is sitting a little closer to me, Mrs. M appears to have got the message that Edgeworth's offer was not of the matrimonial kind.

As dinner progresses, Edgeworth continually asks what I think about things, small things like the warm weather or whether I like to take my time with a book or read it as quickly as I can. He seems to be genuinely interested in what I have to say, unlike most of the men I've been attracted to. Frank liked to hold forth to me on a regular basis; I called it his "lecture mode," but he couldn't care less about what I might think or say about the subjects of his lectures. Wes was different, though. With him I usually did most of the talking, and he was more attentive and solicitous of my opinions than just about anyone. Including Paula, who is often so caught up in venting her own woes that I'm lucky if I get to offer her thirty seconds of advice. But after Frank and I split, she was my self-appointed heartbreak doctor. She'd bring me takeout, force me to eat, drag me out dancing, fill me up with martinis, and hold my head as I vomited out everything I'd eaten and drunk.

Edgeworth interrupts this most inappropriate reverie for the dinner table by talking about art. I chime in with stuff about Renaissance painting that I learned from the two college art history classes I took, and I can tell Edgeworth is impressed. There isn't much I usually feel knowledgeable about, particularly current events. Which is why I often end up at dinner parties off in a corner playing with the family pet or baby, or helping out in the kitchen.

But here, in an environment without television, radio, or the Internet, I don't have to worry much about sounding ignorant of the latest crisis in foreign policy. Not that there's any talk of politics at this table; I'm pretty sure it wouldn't be considered appropriate conversation for the ladies. All right, I'll admit it. It's easier for me to try on my new personality of self-assurance in this reality than it is back in L.A. And yes, I'm aware that said self-assurance is purchased with ignorance and sexism. I am a sell-out. I might as well be one of those complacent veiled women from *The Handmaid's Tale*.

Edgeworth catches my eye and smiles, and I decide to stop inwardly composing the feminist world court's prosecutorial summation to the jury. I'd rather talk about art and gaze at that cleft in Edgeworth's chin when I'm not melting into his hazel eyes.

Speaking of eyes, I feel more than just

Edgeworth's on me. I look around the table and see that the heretofore poker-faced Mr. Mansfield has paused in his methodical shoveling of food to catch my eye and raise his eyebrows in what appears to be mild surprise. Susan Randolph is narrowly observing me, too. And Mrs. M is whispering to her sister, whose eyes dart in my direction as well.

But if Edgeworth is aware of all the observation, his conversation is no indicator. He segues from painting to reading, saying that he cannot understand why so many of his friends regard novels as an inferior class of writing; lately he has learned to fill many an hour absorbed in a novel, and he is eager to read more. I agree, of course, though I can contribute little in terms of knowing what is currently being read, except for *Pride and Prejudice*, that is. I mention *Sense and Sensibility*, too, because it is the only other Jane Austen book published to date. I decide not to mention Fanny Burney, because I found *Camilla* about as compelling as one of those eighteenth-century paintings of frou-frou femmes on a swing surrounded by fat-faced cherubs. As for Maria Edgeworth, I got through *Belinda* but was definitely underwhelmed, and for all you know she's one of his relatives. I loved *Tom Jones*—but that is already almost a hundred years old in 1813. The truth is, most of what I've read doesn't even exist yet.

Edgeworth asks me what I think of *Pride and*

Prejudice, and I expound, in true-believer fashion, on how exciting the story is and how realistic the author's portrayals of human nature are. Edgeworth hasn't read it yet, but says he now looks forward to doing so.

Susan Randolph, who's been eyeing us for some time, says, "Mr. Edgeworth, I counsel you against such pursuits, though your name may account for your tastes in reading."

"Thank you for your hints, Miss Randolph, though I bear no relationship to the Mrs. Edgeworth to whom you allude."

"Nevertheless," says Susan, "the authoress of *Pride and Prejudice* would have you believe that women think of nothing else but marriage."

"You do not approve of the book?"

"There is nothing to approve in a book wherein all the females spend their days dreaming of being married, scheming to be married, or lamenting because they are not married. That is a narrow and confining portrait of my sex of which I certainly do not approve."

I take a long swallow of wine to calm down. I don't buy this burst of sisterhood, not from a woman who could look at another woman with that reptilian chill.

Edgeworth glances at me and clears his throat. "Well, then. Did either of you ladies find *The Mysteries of Udolpho* amusing?"

I am unable to contain myself. "It is obvious to

me, Susan, that the author means to take a humorous stab at the cold and calculating marriage market for which women are bred, and at the same time acknowledges that marriage is actually one of the few career choices for women of her time. Nevertheless, I believe she prizes love, and marriage for love, above all else."

Susan laughs. "And I believe she condones a woman's right to aspire to a situation far above what she was bred to do. First there is marriage above one's level of fortune. Then there is marriage above one's rank."

I roll my eyes. "Dear me. What's this world coming to?"

"Exactly. The more silly novels young women read, the more silly notions fill their heads. If you ask me, cousin, I believe you read too many novels for your own good."

"And if you ask me, *cousin*, I'll tell you what a clever character in a clever novel I read once said: 'The person, be it gentleman or lady, who has not pleasure in a good novel, must be intolerably stupid.' As for that post-feminist Camille Paglia crap, you twentysomethings seem to forget that if it weren't for women aspiring to situations far above what they were bred to do, we'd still be pumping out a kid a year and squeezing ourselves into corsets. If I were you—"

Suddenly I realize the table has gone completely silent. I look around me, and everyone is staring. I catch the eye of Mr. Mansfield, whose wineglass has frozen halfway to his mouth. He clears his throat and raises his glass to Mrs. Randolph. "What spirited young women our daughters are, eh, sister?"

Mrs. Randolph laughs feebly, reaching for her wineglass but knocking it over instead. In the ensuing bustle of footmen mopping up the mess, and Mrs. Mansfield offering to tell a story of how she once got a wine stain out of a white gown, the tension is broken.

Ah well, *in vino veritas.*

I see Susan shake her red curls smugly at Edgeworth, as if to say, I told you so. As soon as her attention is elsewhere, however, Edgeworth whispers to me, "I cannot say I comprehend all your allusions, Miss Mansfield, but I do admire the spirit of your expression."

Looking into those warm hazel eyes is much more pleasant than sparring with Susan.

He is the last guest to leave, and when his carriage is finally announced, he bows his good night to me. As he raises his head, that lock of hair falls onto his forehead again, and I am gripped by a sensation I can hardly define. Suddenly I see him with different eyes. He is no longer an attractive man who shares my interests. He is a disingenuous flirt.

I fumble my way through the good-byes, the ceremoniousness of it all, through Edgeworth's promises to call on us the next morning and Mrs.

Mansfield's honeyed replies. After he leaves, I endure Mrs. Mansfield's regaling me ad nauseum with the various successes of the evening and the charms of Mr. Edgeworth, as if I weren't present to see it all myself.

"But," she adds, "I could hardly keep my countenance when my niece rattled on about women scheming to be married. We shall see how long her high and mighty airs last. Three seasons in London and still she is unmarried. Well, you have had more than that, yet here you are. No one quite good enough for you. I had almost given up hope until Mr. Edgeworth moved into the neighborhood. And then you nearly threw it all away. It is a wonder he has endured it. However, you were quite agreeable to him tonight. Though I am ashamed of you for indulging in that nonsensical outburst. Men do not find harpies attractive."

I roll my eyes and turn my back on her.

"Look at me, Jane."

I don't.

"Very well. But if I were you, I would take great care not to speak nonsense. You never know how it might be interpreted. And what might happen as a result."

I whip my head around, and the malevolence in her eyes makes my stomach drop.

"Good night, my dear," she says sweetly, closing my door. I tell myself her threats are idle; after all, what would she gain from bringing upon herself the shame of having me committed? But then I remember what she had said about telling everyone I died as a result of my riding accident, and I go cold all over with fear. I really must watch myself—especially around her.

After I hear her footsteps terminate at her own bedroom door, I sneak down to the drawing room to spend a solitary half hour musing over Mrs. Mansfield's threats, as well as her allusions to my past with Edgeworth and my odd reaction to him when he said good night.

Eleven

Actually, there's nothing surprising about the wave of distrust that came over me when Edgeworth said good night. After all, when have I ever trusted the opposite sex? My reaction was self-preservation instinct, pure and simple.

I want to say good night to Mr. Mansfield, whom I find in a room I would have missed completely, had I not been curious about the door at the other end of a small room filled with huge vases and baskets of cut flowers. When I open the door, Mr. Mansfield is looking at a canvas, one of dozens that are hanging on the walls, propped up on easels, or stacked against the walls. There are drop cloths on the floor, and a table filled with paints and various other containers of pungent-smelling paint supplies.

I have an instant sensation of disorientation when I realize that the canvases are filled with abstract shapes and broad strokes of color and are mostly nonrepresentational. Did people do this kind of art in the early nineteenth century? Then again, if I can be here with my twenty-first-century mind, then I suppose other incongruities of history and art are possible, too. Still, I want to ask Mr. M about his art; what he does seems so delightfully out of place here, but I cannot reveal my ignorance.

He smiles at me and covers the canvas he had

been examining. I'm overcome with curiosity, and I walk toward the easel and reach tentatively for the cloth that covers the painting.

"May I?" I say.

He raises an eyebrow, as if to gauge my seriousness, then removes the cloth, revealing a bold, cubist sort of work. Part of it looks semi-representational; I can make out something that might have been a self-portrait looking in several directions at once, and the rest just slashes and swirls of color.

"This is amazing." I wish I knew something about this kind of art so that I can say something more intelligent.

"You needn't try and spare my feelings."

"But I like it."

"Are you sure you are not experiencing the effects of breathing in the smells of this place? I do feel a bit strange sometimes myself, but then again it may be the flowers next door, the profusion of which is what sometimes turns my stomach, if truth be told."

"There are rather a lot of them."

"And still they do not do their office, for as you can see, or shall I say, smell, the aroma herein is every bit as forthright as it was before your mother hid me away behind an indoor garden. And my desire to immerse myself in it remains undiminished." He smiles sheepishly. "We all have our weaknesses."

Don't I know it. I have a rush of kindred feeling for Mr. M, whose shamefaced attachment to his painting and his studio reminds me of my own ungovernable addiction to Jane Austen novels. Like Mr. M, I indulge alone. None of my friends knows that most of the sick days I've taken from work are not sick days, but Austen days. None of my friends knows that the new bestseller they bought me for Christmas or my birthday has usually been put aside half-read because I needed to get back to *Pride and Prejudice* or *Sense and Sensibility* for the twentieth time.

Until recently, not one of my friends even knew that I had gone so far as to join an organization of other Austen addicts; i.e., the Jane Austen Society of North America. That is, until Paula noticed a JASNA newsletter, addressed to me, in my bedroom. She hooted with laughter at a photograph of some of the members in Regency dress at a meeting, and then stopped short when she saw my unsmiling face.

Not that I have ever once attended a meeting of my fellow addicts. I am too afraid of exposing myself to such a literary group, who would no doubt think me unworthy because my entrée to Austen was via Colin Firth prancing around in tight pants for the BBC. So what if I ran out and bought all the novels and read every single one before I saw another film adaptation. A woman with a Jane Austen action figure, still in the box no less (because the box is the best part), would surely be shunned by such scholarly folk.

The truth is, I am more concerned about being in the company of people whose eccentricities might even surpass mine than I am about their superior academic qualifications. I mean, after all, at their annual meetings they actually dance at Regency balls, many dressed in costume, no less. Would meeting such people in the flesh hold up a mirror to my addiction, and would I be afraid of what I saw? And what if—God forbid—I gave in to temptation and went to one of those balls myself? Would I not only be reading Austen in secret on sick days, but also find myself doing so in an empire-waisted muslin? Is all that self-conscious rejection and closeted longing—no pun intended—what landed me in this fractured-Austen-novel of a world?

"Jane?" Mr. M's voice snaps me out of my tail-spin; his face is filled with concern. "Are you quite all right, my dear?"

I muster a smile. "Oh, yes."

Mr. M replaces the cover on his painting. "Do sit down for a minute, if you can bear it." He motions to a chair. "So, Jane, it appears you have made a conquest of Mr. Edgeworth."

I let out an awkward laugh. "I would hardly call it a conquest."

"I know you, Jane. You are not the sort of girl who bestows her attentions idly. And there is a marked difference between your manners toward Mr. Edgeworth tonight and what I have observed on previous occasions."

"Oh really?"

Mr. Mansfield peers at me over his glasses. "I daresay you are not joking me right now."

"I would love to hear your perspective."

He smiles. "I am quite fond of you, Jane. And I am not of a mind, as many parents are nowadays, to simply give a daughter in marriage to the highest bidder, without any regard to her feelings and wishes. Your mother may be well satisfied with your sister Clara's marriage, but I am not. In truth, before I gave my consent I warned Clara against entering the marriage state without as great an affection for the man as she had for his fortune."

He looks at me and raises an eyebrow. "Do not affect to be shocked, my dear. You know this to be so."

"But what does any of this have to do with me?"

Mr. M takes off his glasses and starts polishing them with a cloth. "I am merely sharing my observations, which are that on previous occasions you spoke but little to Mr. Edgeworth, despite your mother's various hints to be more talkative. Instead, you took every opportunity to engage yourself in conversation or activity with others, and almost seemed to avoid Mr. Edgeworth's attentions. Your mother noticed this as well, and with great dissatisfaction, I might add. I can have no doubt that it is as clear to you as it is to me that your mother wishes to see you married to Mr. Edgeworth. And as I do not know you to be shy of conversation in general, I could therefore only conclude, until tonight, that is, that your manners while in company with Mr. Edgeworth were not the result of shyness but rather, at the very least, indifference."

"And to what did you attribute my indifference?"

He shrugs. "Perhaps you find it inconceivable that a widower who truly loved his wife could possibly form a second attachment. However, your mother believes that you did like him, at least at first, and then changed toward him, quite unaccountably. Far be it from me to pretend to understand what goes on in a woman's mind when it comes to matters of love. However, even I can see that your mind has taken a different turn tonight."

"You mean you think I'm in love with Mr. Edgeworth just because I talked to him at dinner?"

"Your mother will choose to think so. As may Mr. Edgeworth. So if you are not inclined to raise expectations among your friends as to your becoming the second Mrs. Edgeworth, I suggest you refrain from encouraging him." He pats my hand. "Not that I think there is anything improper in your behavior, my dear."

"This is unbelievable."

"Mr. Edgeworth appears to be an amiable, gentlemanlike sort of man. He is of a respectable family and from all reports appears to have a considerable fortune. These are important qualities, my dear, but unless you love the man, I fear you will never find happiness."

"How could I love this person? I hardly even know him."

Mr. Mansfield smiles and puts on his glasses. "I knew you would be open with me, Jane. Let us say no more about the matter. And let us hope that your mother's fancies have not carried her too far away just yet. Or that Mr. Edgeworth does not declare himself before there is any chance of your manners toward him returning to their former state."

"Oh, please. You've got to be kidding."

He winks at me. And I laugh with relief.

Afterward, I lie in bed, unable to fall asleep, unable to get my conversation with Mr. M out of my mind. This isn't another century; it's another planet. All I do is have a nice chat with a guy over dinner and everyone's ready to order wedding invitations. Talk about making assumptions.

If there's anything I've learned as a single woman in search of that holy grail, a decent relationship, it's that I have no right to assume anything. I have no right to assume I am in a relationship with a man, even if that man is someone I'm regularly sleeping with. I have no right to assume fidelity, not even from my fiancé. And if I were to sleep with someone new, I have no right to assume I'll get so much as a hey-I-had-a-good-time-last-night phone call. If I'm lucky, he might spend five minutes with me two weeks later when I run into him at a party. Even Frank took months to use the dreaded "R" word; the "L" word took even longer. And now I'm to assume that a man I talked to at dinner, an absolute stranger, could be a matrimonial object if I don't curb my conversational excesses? True, he isn't exactly a stranger to Jane, but he's certainly a stranger to me.

As is everyone else in this borrowed life. The thought makes me shiver, despite the warmth of the night. How can it be possible to inhabit a strange body, talk with a strange voice, and be saddled with the life history, environment, parents, and friends of that person, all of whom insist that you are not *you*? More important, how am I ever going to get back to who I really am?

Twelve

I am no closer to an answer at breakfast than I was the night before. Mrs. Mansfield is all smiles, which are only briefly interrupted when she comments that I look a bit pale. But when I eat a little breakfast, she tells me that my complexion is already improving. That's right, Mrs. M. Hot chocolate is the new revolution in skin care.

"Mr. Edgeworth is expected any moment, and when he comes I will remark on how fine the weather is today and how pleasant it would be for the three of us to take a walk around the grounds."

Yeah, yeah. Whatever. Maybe chocolate *is* good for the skin in this reality. And has no carbs. Perhaps there is a God after all.

Mrs. M dabs her mouth with a napkin. "Mr. Edgeworth will of course express his willingness to escort us. I will, however, develop a sudden headache. Quiet and solitude being the best medicine, I will decide to stay inside and insist that you and he go on without me."

She smiles smugly and spreads some jam on her toast. What an accomplishment, to get me alone with prime marriage material. If she only knew how many men I've been alone with. And what I've done with them. Ah yes, Mrs. M. I can just see you reaching for your smelling salts. I smile at the thought.

At which she says, "I am glad to see the idea does not displease you. You will, of course, be attentive to Mr. Edgeworth today and show him every courtesy."

"Whatever you say, darling." I get up and make a mock curtsey. "And now I would like to get a head start on that walk until our guest arrives. With your permission, of course."

"Saucy, aren't you," she says with a sneer. "Mind you keep to the house, Jane. I want you here as soon as Mr. Edgeworth arrives."

I salute like a good soldier. "Yes, ma'am."

As I stroll through the shrubbery, something Anna said keeps repeating in my mind. Something she gleaned from one of her creepy friends in her meditation class or from one of the endless parade of new-age practitioners she pays to dissect her aura, polish her crystals, or give her house an energy cleaning. Frankly, she'd be better off spending her money on getting her house cleaned the good old-fashioned physical-plane sort of way, because it's an absolute sty. What she said was something about trusting that everything, no matter how horrible it might seem at that moment, ultimately turns out to be a blessing. It's odd that I remember her saying what she did, because I usually tune out her well-meaning platitudes.

Now I know why I remember this particular so-called truth, because that's just what she said to me right after I discovered that Frank had slept with

Amy. It was a blessing, she proclaimed, that his infidelity came out before, rather than after the wedding. I know she was right, but at the time all I could think about was how I was going to endure the humiliation of informing everyone I'd invited that there would be no wedding, including returning wedding gifts to those eager guests who'd wanted first pick at the registry. But, she insisted, it was a blessing to be saved from an illusion; I mean, I could have married that illusion, right?

But how about the fact that I wanted my day of illusion—just one measly day; was that too much to ask? Was it too much to wish I'd been spared the truth until after the wedding, until after I got to be queen of the ball in a white satin dress? It was *my* illusion, damn it, and Frank had cheated me out of it. He had cheated me out of reaching that milestone in my life, that public proof of my worth. How much nicer it would sound if I could say, "I'm divorced. It just didn't work out," than, "I'm single. I've never been married."

That I am now attempting to derive comfort from Anna's words is proof of my desperation. How can it be a blessing to be stuck in some time warp where everyone thinks I'm someone I'm not and everyone who does know who I am hasn't even been born yet?

Blessing or no, I have to muster all the positive thinking I can. I don't have the luxury of retreating to my room and crawling under the covers like I do at home. They'd just think I'm "unwell" again and start sending for trout-faced doctors with dirty knives. I have to be positive. I have to believe I'll find my way back, even if right now I have no idea how. I will stop obsessing. I will enjoy this walk, I will enjoy the grass and trees and flowers and stop worrying about how long I'll be stuck here—oh God, what if it's forever?—I will not allow myself to entertain that thought. Yeah, right. I'm not only entertaining that thought, I'm taking it out to dinner and a movie. I'm here, for however long, real or unreal, time travel or insanity. It feels real, therefore it is. Or something like that. The goal is to focus on the now and figure out how to reclaim the past. Or the parallel. Or my sanity.

Too much thinking never solved anything.

A rustling on the path behind me makes me jump. I turn, and I am face-to-face with Edgeworth.

"Hello," I say, practically tripping over my hem in my confusion, then trying to act nonchalant by casually leaning on a tree trunk but missing it by a hair, the result being that Edgeworth grabs one of my flailing arms and narrowly stops me from falling on my ass.

"Well then," I say, checking my dress for tears, "that was elegant."

He bows. "I apologize for startling you. It was my fault entirely."

I smile at him. "I beg to differ."

I could just imagine Frank taking the blame for one of my blunders. Not in a million years, let alone two centuries. He was always telling me how clumsy I was, and delighted in recounting stories of my latest klutz-fest to anyone who'd listen. And his laugh, that condescending look, was nothing like the good-natured smile on Edgeworth's face. It reminds me of how Wes smiled at me when I dropped an entire tray of baked ziti on the floor. He not only helped me clean up the mess, he also told Frank he was a jerk for having a laugh at my expense.

"Are you hurt, Miss Mansfield?"

"Just my pride."

His eyes sparkle. "I am glad you are materially unscathed." He offers me his arm. "Shall we take a turn together?"

Why not. His hair looks more golden in the sun, and his eyes are now emerald instead of hazel. More like Wes's eyes. That's ridiculous; they're nothing like Wes's eyes.

"Your mother has charged me to tell you that she is suffering from a sudden headache. She asked that I accompany you on your walk so that she might recover in quiet and solitude."

"Poor Mrs. M," I say, hardly able to keep a straight face.

Edgeworth's eyes twinkle with amusement. My parting suspicions of him last night were probably just my defense mechanisms working overtime. It's no wonder my mind's confused; not only am I dealing with this time warp situation, but I'm also simply not used to feeling so at ease with a man I've just met, regardless of time period. Except for Wes, that is, but he was my boyfriend's friend when I met him, and not an attractive single man, so it's not the same thing. When faced with an available man I find attractive, I usually spend half the time planning my words in my head and the other half being hyperconscious of my body language. With Edgeworth there is almost none of that.

There is a stone bench on one of the gravel paths, and Edgeworth asks me if I would like to sit for a few minutes.

"Sure," I say, but when I meet his eyes I can see something is wrong.

He looks down at his boots. "I must speak with you."

I can feel the blood drain from my face. Why is my stomach doing flip-flops?

He raises his eyes to mine. "Allow me to express what is weighing upon my mind."

I nod, my heart pounding so hard I can almost hear it.

"For a time I hoped—no, I believed we had an understanding. But then your manner changed so markedly. And, as you would not speak to me of it, I was left to conclude that my sister had had a hand in it. I am well aware that Mary has never forgiven me for the service I did her, though I know to her feelings it was no service at all."

He pauses for a moment, wiping the palms of his hands on his trouser legs. I have, of course, no idea what he's talking about.

"And then your accident. You know not how I longed to speak to your parents. But I dared not divulge to them what you appeared no longer to acknowledge as true. Then, when you recovered, I was determined to make you see me differently. I know not what I hoped to achieve; to change your dislike to indifference, perhaps. If more was possible, I could not let myself hope for it. But now I see a change; I mean, I hope I am not mistaken in believing that you do not dislike my company. That is a beginning, is it not?"

"I—"

"Yes?"

"I guess I'm not sure what kind of misunderstanding—and I'm sorry if I was . . . I mean, I'm not sure I understand what—"

"Let me be clear, then," he says, enfolding my hands in his. "If you consent to be my wife, Jane, I promise to devote every waking moment to being worthy of your trust."

He looks so intense, so serious. What am I supposed to say? What do you say to a man you are supposed to know but don't but he proposes to you anyway and he lives in a different time period? I peruse my mental catalogue of Jane Austen dialogue for possibilities. Emma's *I have no thoughts of matrimony at present* might lead Edgeworth to attribute it, like Mr. Collins, to my *wishing to increase his love by suspense, according to the usual practice of elegant females.* And Emma's *Believe me, sir, I am far, very far, from gratified in being the object of such professions* is far too harsh. As is Lizzy Bennet's *You could not have made me the offer of your hand in any possible way that would have tempted me to accept it*. Even if I wanted to say yes, I couldn't expect Jane Austen to do all the work. After all, what did Emma say to Mr. Knightley? *Just what she ought, of course.*

Edgeworth's squeezing my hands snaps me out of search mode. "Allow me to interpret this interesting silence as a favorable reply?"

Oh my God. He is practically quoting Mr. Elton verbatim, and *Emma* hasn't even been written yet.

He raises my hands to his lips, but I extricate them before he can seal the deal. "I don't mean to be rude, but—are you out of your mind?" And with that I am rushing down the gravel path as fast as I can without drawing attention from any of the nosy servants who might be working outside.

What freaks me out more than Edgeworth's anachronistic quoting of Austen is the fact that I've just been passionately proposed to. When has any man ever spoken to me like that? Not Frank, whose drunken mumblings of "Okay, you win—let's get married" could hardly count as a proposal, let alone a declaration of love. But I was so starved for a commitment that all I could feel was gratitude the next morning that he didn't plead temporary alcohol poisoning. As for any talk of wedding plans, "Just leave me out of it," he said. "I'll show up, but that's where my participation ends."

Understatement. When not affecting the demeanor of a condemned man on his way to the gallows—or hooking up with the cake designer—Frank took every opportunity to condemn the institution of marriage as an affront to free will and a means of subjugating women. These professed attitudes were, of course, entirely inconsistent with his habitual manipulations that I fold his laundry, unclog the milk steamer on his espresso machine, or upgrade his software. "You're so much more computer-literate than I am," he'd plead, though as I discovered one night while checking my email on his computer, he had no problem bookmarking and presumably logging on to longlankychicks.com and various other tall-thin-naked-girl websites, which were all in a neat and tidy folder.

Boots crunch the gravel path behind me. "Have I offended you?" Edgeworth says, out of breath.

"Absolutely not. I just . . ." Suddenly I am unable to form words. There's so much vulnerability in those emerald eyes, so much pent-up emotion in that clenched jaw that for a moment I am actually tempted to say yes, I'll marry you. Just take me right here and rip my bodice from my heaving bosom.

Suddenly I am seized by an explosion of laughter, complete with snorts and gasps and doubling over. I'm not stuck inside someone else's life. I'm stuck inside a romance novel with pretensions to Jane Austen.

"Dearest, sweetest Jane," says Edgeworth, raising my hand to his lips. "You have made me the happiest of men."

Apparently he's interpreting my mirth as an affirmative.

"Whoa," I say, still giggling at the thought of Edgeworth posing on the cover of a romance novel with embossed gold lettering, like the ones my mother always had on her nightstand. "I won't deny I'm attracted, but don't you think this is way too fast? I mean, I haven't even slept with you."

Edgeworth drops my hand, his face instantly red.

"That is cruel, Jane."

"What?"

The ensuing pause feels endless.

"You're angry," I say.

"I am *not* angry." He paces back and forth, shaking his head, and then kicks a tree trunk with his boot. He winces in pain, clenching his fists.

Definitely not angry.

"This is madness. Absolute madness."

My mouth goes dry. Calm down, he doesn't mean it literally. Nevertheless, laughing like a hyena and making lewd jokes is clearly not the safest mode of behavior for someone in my position.

"Can you tell me, Jane, how two people who once understood each other perfectly could come to this?"

"I wish I could tell you," I say, struggling to sound like the Jane he knows. Or thinks he knows. "But the truth is, sir, that I have not the honor of understanding what you mean."

"Ah. I will not pretend I do not understand you."

"And I will not pretend that I do."

"You do me a great injustice. Granted, I am a man of eight-and-thirty, and I am no saint. But can you truly believe such a dishonorable portrait of me?"

Trying to figure out this conversation is like trying to do the *New York Times* crossword puzzle with half the words in Swahili. But I don't have to understand it. I just have to sound like I do.

"I don't—I do not know what I believe. Nor do I know what 'dishonorable portrait' you are talking about."

His brows lift, then his eyes scan my face, searching for what? The truth? I watch as his face shifts from distrust to puzzlement, and finally, a relaxed sort of calm. "I must confess I do not understand you, but I am relieved that you do not seem to think ill of me."

I am so moved by the naked vulnerability in his eyes that I find myself touching his hand. He looks away, his other hand quickly swiping at his eye. Was that a tear?

I fight the urge to gather him in my arms and cradle his head against my breasts. And rip off his clothes.

What difference would it make if I changed my mind and said yes? Who would it hurt? After all, this parallel reality, or whatever I'm in, is only temporary.

Wait a minute. Am I that starved for a commitment, that desperate to be married? Wherever I am may be temporary, but how long is that? It could be days, hours, weeks, or years. Do I really want to gamble whatever "temporary" is on marriage to a stranger, whether or not I am passing up the chance of a lifetime? Or a reality? Or even two realities?

Guess I'll just have to take that risk.

Edgeworth clears his throat. "May I still have the honor of calling on you again when I return from town?"

"You had better."

He smiles. "You are a mystery that I am determined to solve."

"That makes two of us, Mr. Edgeworth."

And two of something else as well: a pair of white butterflies are suddenly dancing in the air, right in front of my face. They take off and are replaced by a lone orange-and-black spotted one, which promptly lands on my dress. I move my hand to touch it, but Edgeworth gently stops my hand with his.

"Its wings are too fragile to be touched."

Instant déjà vu. Where did I hear that before? Suddenly I'm shivering in my thin dress. It was warm and sunny just a moment ago, but now the light is muted and dull. I look up and see that steel-gray clouds have moved across the sun. A chill breeze makes me wish for a shawl. My feet take me back to the house, and Edgeworth walks beside me in silence.

When we enter the drawing room, Mrs. Mansfield has miraculously recovered from her headache. Her eyes above the dimpled smile are diamond hard, narrowing as she scans my face for information.

When Edgeworth leaves within fifteen minutes of polite chitchat—and without returning to the drawing room after he goes off to Mr. Mansfield's atelier to say good-bye—she scrutinizes me but says nothing. But as soon as she spies through the window Edgeworth riding off on his horse, she rushes off in the direction of the atelier.

I escape to my room, but Mrs. Mansfield is soon outside my door.

"Your father tells me," she says, "that Mr. Edgeworth bade him good-bye and promised to call on us when he returns from town."

I say nothing.

Mrs. M puts a hand on her hip. "Well?"

I sit at the dressing table and pick up a hairbrush.

"Did Mr. Edgeworth make you an offer of marriage?"

I can't do much with the brush, as my hair is up.

"I asked you a question, Jane."

"He did, and I said no."

Her eyes bore into me. "You what?"

I smile at her sweetly. "I said it nicely."

Mrs. Mansfield's face is an alabaster mask. "Tell me, Jane. Do you really think anyone else as amiable or rich will ever make you an offer of marriage? You are thirty years old. And your portion, while not insignificant, is nothing to what a man of Mr. Edgeworth's fortune might rightfully expect. Yet you dare to refuse him. You dare to disoblige me."

I choke back a reply, my stomach tightening. Why do I care what this woman thinks?

"And when your father dies? What will become of you? Do you wish to live out your days in this house, the maiden aunt who looks after her brother's children—may God grant him a son and heir—because you were too obstinate to marry when you had the chance?"

I look at her with the same level gaze she has trained on me. I will not let her get to me.

"Well?" she says.

I shrug my shoulders. "You have it all figured out already."

"Except why you refused him. I demand to know why."

"No reason at all. Only that I don't love him."

"What has love to do with it?"

"You know, that might make a good title for a song." I'm tempted to launch into my best Tina Turner rendition, but I think better of it, especially because Mrs. M is already looking at me like a cockroach she is debating whether or not to grind under her heel.

"I hope you realize what you have done. He will never pay his addresses to you again." And with that, she turns on her heel and leaves.

"He'll be back," I say to the empty room.

Actually, I'm not so sure. He may have left intending to return, but who knows what might happen. His bruised male ego might not want to risk any more rejection. And he could meet someone else in the meantime.

Oh well, too bad then. If he doesn't come back, I'll deal with my regrets, if by then I feel any. Or if I'm even still here. Edgeworth will be gone for two weeks; this whole charade has to end by then. I will not allow myself to think otherwise.

Which is easier said than done.

Thirteen

It is now day five of the hostage-in-another-body crisis, and this particular body is starting to smell ripe. No wonder; not only has my sole option for daily ablutions been a pitcher and basin, half the contents of which ends up on the floor rather than on my skin, but in place of deodorant I've been resorting to dousing my armpits in a flowery perfume. But not today, I decide, flinging off the covers and ringing the bell for Barnes. In typical Barnes fashion, she appears at my door within seconds.

"Barnes, I need a bath."

She looks rather flustered. "Now, miss?"

"Would you rather hand out perfume bottles to place under the noses of all who approach me?"

"But you'll be late for church."

"Church? Barnes, I stink."

She wrings her apron between her hands. "But your mother is most particular about the time—"

"Please don't tell me I have to go."

She looks at me plaintively. "I'll give you a good scrubbing, I promise, and you'll be clean and sweet-smelling quicker than you can eat one of Cook's ginger puddings. And then I'll lay out your favorite yellow gown, and first thing tomorrow you'll have a steaming hot bath."

"What about when we get back from church?"

"Your mother is most particular—"

"Don't tell me. I don't think I can take any more bad news before I have my tea."

"Shall I send up a breakfast tray?"

I sigh. At least I wouldn't have to look at Mrs. M before I have my tea. "A tray sounds perfect." I point to my right armpit. "And please help me do something about this, will you?"

In no time I am semi-deodorized, dressed, and Mr. M is handing me into a real, honest-to-goodness horse-drawn carriage, which clip-clops its way to an ancient little stone church. This isn't bad at all. Here I am, just like Lizzy Bennet or Jane Austen herself, all dressed up in costume, trooping into the church's hushed interior with the rest of the bonneted women and waistcoated men who are filing into the pews, just like I belong here.

Aside from the period-piece novelty of it all, it's been ages since I've been to a church service; maybe it will calm my mind and give me some perspective on my situation.

But then the minister, a blubbery bald man with a dirty neck, opens his mouth. And in a high, castrato-pitched voice, begins pontificating on the loose morals of women in modern society. Instead of providing any juicy details, however, he punctuates his vague generalities with lengthy readings from the Bible. He goes on. And on. And on. I glance next to me at Mr. M, whose eyelids are sliding down and head is rolling back. He quickly jerks back to attention, wipes a bit of drool off the side of his mouth, and gives me a sheepish half-grin. The old ladies in the opposite pew, on the other hand, are gazing at their man of the cloth with rapt attention and affirmative nods of their heads.

There's not much I can do in the way of people watching to keep the boredom at bay, as every time I try to turn around in my seat to see who else is in the church, I catch at least half a dozen people in the act of staring at me. Do I look that much out of place here? Is my nose running? Then I realize that they probably want to see for themselves if my brain is addled from the fall I've supposedly taken. It's got to be a lot more interesting than listening to the minister. I spot Mrs. Randolph and her daughter, who appears to be sneering at what's written in her prayer book. As for Mrs. M, she keeps hissing at me to face forward and act like a lady.

Finally, I manage to escape by staring off into the middle distance and picturing myself on the worn leather sofa in my apartment, at my cluttered desk at work, in my clothes-strewn bedroom, gossiping with Paula and Anna while fixing my makeup and trying on outfits for a night out, then sipping a dirty martini with two olives while flirting with my favorite bartender. I picture myself looking like myself, talking like myself, feeling like myself.

My reverie is rudely interrupted, however, by the

sound of—can it be? Someone is actually farting in church. And not some sheepish, just-slipped-out mistake of a fart, but several trumpeting bursts. And not once, but three times, and from different directions. Holy mother of—this last one is close enough for me to smell. I pull out a bottle of lavender water from my bag and spend the rest of the service with it under my nose, well aware of the irony of my worries earlier this morning about offending others with my own odor, and wondering if Elizabeth Bennet, or Jane Austen for that matter, ever had to endure such assaults on their weekly devotions. No wonder Mary Crawford was so horrified that Edmund Bertram was going to become a clergyman. I am appreciating *Mansfield Park* more every moment.

The next morning Barnes is true to her word. No sooner do I haul my unwashed body out of bed and ring the bell than Barnes appears at my door with promises to "start the process directly."

Process indeed. First comes a huge copper tub, carried into my room by two maids and laid out over a few layers of thin towels. About an hour and two cups of hot chocolate later, the buckets begin to arrive. Huge, steaming, and by all appearances, heavy buckets are handed in by unseen hands to the two maids who had carried in the tub and are now sweating from the labor and the steam, and all of it is supervised by Barnes.

I realize that every one of those buckets has been hauled up to the third floor of this house. All for a single bath. For me. I look at the maids sheepishly and start apologizing for all the trouble I'm putting them to, but they merely curtsey and mumble and duck their heads while casting what look suspiciously like "get a load of the madwoman" glances at one another. So I shut up. Besides, my need to have this body clean trumps my empathy for the proletariat.

Finally, the last bucket is lugged and poured, Barnes mixes the perfect amount of cool water in with the hot, and her sweating assistants depart, wiping their foreheads with corners of their aprons and looking as if they could do with a chiropractic adjustment.

Barnes helps me out of my nightgown and gives me a floor-length, long-sleeved, shiftlike garment to put on, then lays a thick layer of towels over the backrest part of the tub, which makes me realize that I'm supposed to get in the bath wearing the shift, presumably to prevent my skin from burning off on contact with the hot metal surface of the tub.

I dip in a toe—perfect temperature. Within seconds I am luxuriating in a total immersion experience, head leaning against the padded back of the tub, eyes closed. I will never again take for granted indoor plumbing of any kind, even my tiny stall shower with the perpetual mildew problem. But this is much, much better.

I'm roused by Barnes's throat clearing; would I like to wash my hair? Why not; let's go for broke. But when she massages a gloppy mess, which smells suspiciously like a rum and Coke, into my scalp, I wonder whether I am actually going to end up with cleaner hair.

But once I am toweled, dressed, and sitting before a mirrored dressing table, Barnes brushes the shiny, soft, and untangled tresses this body is blessed with, and I figure it's best not to know what's in that shampoo. Nevertheless, I decide to limit the washing of hair to a once-a-week schedule. As for baths, I manage to negotiate two per week with Barnes, despite her worries that such frequent bathing could be hazardous to my health.

When Barnes leaves the room, I shiver, not from my damp hair, but because I realize I've just finished creating a schedule for myself in a place where I'm not supposed to be.

Fourteen

As the carriage once again clip-clops its way toward the little stone church, I realize I have, in the space of only a week (if time can be reckoned in such a place), fallen into a routine. Hot rolls and jam every morning, roast meats in the late afternoon. In between are embroidering, walking in the garden, and various scoldings from Mrs. M, accompanied by snide comments on my single status. The days end with reading aloud while Mrs. M sews, then visiting with Mr. M in his atelier, and snuggling up in bed with the two things that keep me sane, *Pride and Prejudice* and *Sense and Sensibility*.

Tonight is no different. As my bedside candles illuminate a page in the precious first edition I hold in my hands, I understand, as I have long understood through my own insatiable appetite for readings and rereadings of Jane Austen's six novels, why children want the same stories read to them a thousand times. There is comfort in the familiarity of it all, in the knowledge that all will turn out well, that Elizabeth and Darcy will end up together in Pemberley, that Anne Eliot will pierce Captain Wentworth's soul, and that Mr. Elton will be stuck with his *caro sposa* for the rest of his life. It is so unlike the unpredictability and unfairness of real-life endings and the half-life stasis I inhabit.

Yet I cannot pretend that the pristine, first-edition volume in my hands constitutes my only pleasure in these days and nights. Yes, the "reality" of this world is certainly smellier and less sanitary than I ever considered when I used to fantasize myself into one of those quiet drawing rooms pretending to do needlework while a hottie in skintight trousers sent me meaningful glances from across the room. But why would I have considered such things; after all, with the exception of Fanny Price's slovenly family in Portsmouth, and Sir Walter Eliot's snobbish ideas of what Anne must meet with at Mrs. Smith's, no one talks about dirt and smells in the novels. Certainly no one talks about chamber pots and what it takes to have a bath. Nor does anyone do so in the Hollywood-sanitized film adaptations, the most unorthodox of which limits its commentary on the earthiness of the era to an image of a prodigiously endowed farm animal meandering into the Bennets' house. Thankfully, nothing of that sort intrudes into the reality in which I find myself, nor in the two-DVD set of the BBC's *P & P* that I've watched so many times I could practically act it out end to end, all five hours of it.

Could all those viewings, combined with all those rereadings, have resulted in my current state of affairs? When Frank caught me watching the *Pride and Prejudice* DVD in the middle of the night for the umpteenth time, he sneeringly referred to my fascination with Jane Austen's world as postmodern nostalgia. Not that I have the faintest idea of what "postmodern" means, despite Frank's having spent many hours lecturing me on the topic.

Sanitized simulacra, lack of indoor plumbing, and oppressive mothers notwithstanding, there is something about the simplicity and quiet of this world that not only does not disappoint, but which exceeds any expectation. I don't have the constant noise in my brain from all the Internet, iPod, and radio signals streaming all those sounds and words and pictures into my consciousness practically every waking moment of every day. I never even noticed that noise in my brain until I realized I didn't have it anymore.

Yes, I miss my friends, but there are a few things I do not miss. I do not miss waking up crying yet again over Frank's betrayal—somehow being here has dulled that pain. I do not miss having to face my mercurial boss for yet another day of reading scripts that will never become movies, thank God. And I do not miss answering his perpetually ringing phones, being berated one minute for forgetting to stock the fridge with some obscure bottled water from Norway, and the next minute counseling him on what to buy his girlfriend as an apology gift.

I do miss Wes, though. I miss amusing him with accounts of my boss's random acts of clueless egotism, which always makes me find the humor in them myself. I miss sipping vodka and doing the dishes with him after his dinner parties, while everyone else practically passes out in the living room from too much good food and wine. And I miss his unconscionably divine cooking, which has no apparent effect on his lanky frame. It's as hard to stay angry at Wes here as it is to feel more than an abstract sense of heartbreak over Frank.

As for Mrs. M, she has lately limited the worst of her venom to my unmarried state; there hasn't been a single allusion to madness or asylums in several days. I'm sure that's due to my concentrated efforts to sound authentic and to confine my twenty-first-century verbal snideness to the diary I've begun.

Something else to look forward to doing tomorrow. That and bath day.

"Miss?"

I bolt up from my semi-reclining position in the tub, sending surges of bathwater toward Barnes, who is towering over me, holding a towel in front of her.

"Sorry, Barnes. I must have dozed off."

"Not at all, miss." She dabs her forehead with a corner of her apron, and again proffers the open towel. I stand up and she enfolds me in it, followed by a robe, which I tie around my waist, dropping the towel to the floor.

It is then that I feel a trickle down my leg, and I see that it's not water, but blood.

It isn't my usual time, but then again, this isn't my usual body.

"Barnes?" She whips her head around, disengaging herself from the task of deciding which of two gowns I should wear this morning.

"It appears I have my period. Do you have anything I can use?"

She looks at me blankly. "Begging your pardon?"

"I'm menstruating, Barnes."

Still a blank.

I point to the carpet, which now has evidence of my condition. "Sorry, Barnes. But if you don't get me whatever you have that might resemble a tampon or a pad, there's going to be a bigger mess than this."

Barnes's cheeks flame. "Oh, dear." She drops the dresses on the bed and scurries over to a drawer, retrieving from it a couple of rolled-up lengths of linen and an odd beltlike contraption with strings, which she deposits in my hands before bustling out the door, cheeks flaming, stammering something about fetching a fresh basin of water.

I am stumped by the belt, but I'm not about to ask Barnes to show me how to use it, as she appears to have regained no part of her composure when she returns with a basin of water and an empty bowl that she places under my bed, presumably to hold the soiled linen. Fortunately, I will not be expected to get through the day clenching a wad of fabric between my thighs, as Barnes replaces the two candidate dresses for the day in the armoire and pulls out a fresh nightgown from one of my drawers. Mumbling something about telling my mother I am "indisposed" today, she tugs the nightgown over my head and puts me right back into bed. Quite a different experience than what I'm used to. No shoving of tampons and then scurrying off to go about business as usual, no matter how bad the cramps or bleeding are, and mine are usually bad enough to legitimately keep me in bed.

"Now what would you like me to bring you for breakfast?" Barnes seems to have calmed herself a little, now that I am settled in bed and she has dabbed at the carpet with a wet cloth, apparently to her satisfaction.

"Surprise me."

Barnes half-smiles her relief, then bobs a curtsey and begins to head out the door.

"So Barnes, what do you call this?" I point vaguely in the direction of my stomach.

"Miss?" The flush has returned to Barnes's cheeks.

"What do you call the reason why I'm back in bed today—you know; woman to woman?"

She glances toward the partially open doorway, perhaps wishing to escape, and then turns back to face me.

"You mean your . . ." she stage-whispers, furtively glancing behind her as if checking for eavesdroppers, then closes the door to make sure, her back against it. "You mean your monthly courses?"

"Yes. Thank you, Barnes."

She stands there for a moment, looking at me uncertainly. "Will there be anything else?"

"Just breakfast."

And with that, she flees.

Fifteen

"Barnes, don't you think a day and a half in bed is enough already?"

Barnes deposits a tray on the table next to my bed. My mouth waters at the sight of cold roast beef, thick slices of bread, and a pot of mustard. Being confined to my room has made the arrival of my meal trays an unusually welcome break in the dullness.

"But you are unwell, miss."

"I am not. In fact, I believe I've even stopped bleeding."

Which is enough to send the blood rushing to Barnes's face. She looks down at her shoes, twisting her apron between her hands. "Your mother is most particular . . ."

If I have to hear that one more time I'll scream. "Can I please get out of this room tomorrow then?"

"Of course, miss. If you are not indisposed."

I sigh and settle back into bed. It seems that while giving way to the grosser bodily functions seems to raise nary a blush in the Lord's house, having one's period makes one a social outcast in one's own house.

"Thank you, Barnes. That will be all."

Guess I'll stretch my legs and have something to eat, then write in my journal.

The roast beef is delicious. I didn't realize how

hungry I was. Plate cleaned, I allow myself a little walk around the room, now that I've finally figured out how to use that odd menstrual belt contraption. Not that I seem to be bleeding anymore, but just in case. Funny how in this body I've bled for only a day and a half with no cramping whatsoever. This is the mildest period I've ever had in my life, and it actually seems to be over.

I look out the window at gray, overcast skies and a green expanse of lawn glistening with moisture. At least I'm not being kept from good weather. Never did like walking in the rain. Nevertheless, I'll blow off some steam in my journal about the position of women in Jane Austen's world. I certainly don't have anyone to rant to but myself. What did Anne Eliot say in *Persuasion*? *We live at home, quiet, confined, and our feelings prey upon us.* That's right, Anne. And it sucks.

I unearth the slim leather-bound volume from its hiding place inside the depths of a hatbox that resides in the very back of my closet. Can't be too careful with the likes of Mrs. M under the same roof. Funny how with all my searching of this room for letters or a diary that the real Jane might have kept—something that might give me a clue to her life before I arrived—the only thing I came up with is this slim, blank book of pages, hidden, or forgotten, in this very hatbox.

I retrieve the lightweight, portable writing desk from the top of the bureau and settle myself into an armchair covered in dark pink watered silk. Inside the lid of the desk are packets of blank stationery, sealing wax, quill pens, and a pot of ink. But no letters, of course. I still can't get over how quickly I've taken to writing with a quill pen. Not a single blot of ink, neither on clothes nor on paper. Just flowing script, which, as I flip through the pages of the journal, I realize looks almost nothing like my own handwriting. Yet I recognize the words I wrote.

I shudder and turn more pages to get to a blank one, when near the end of the filled-in pages one of them catches my eye. *Courtney Stone*, it says. *Courtney Stone Courtney Stone Courtney Stone.* Over and over again, evenly filling every imaginary line, spilling onto a second page.

But wait a minute. Around three quarters of the way down that second page it says *Jane. Jane Jane Jane Jane Jane*, over and over until it spills onto the next page, where about a third of the way down it says *Jane Mansfield Jane Mansfield Jane Mansfield*, again and again until the page is filled. And instead of the amusement at the anachronism that I tell myself I should feel, the flesh rises on my arms, and I shiver, slamming the journal shut.

I have no recollection of having filled in those pages full of names.

I shove the journal back into the bottom of its hatbox, my desire to write killed. All I want to do is crawl back into bed and will myself to sleep, so that I don't have to think about any of this. But as I lie here unable to sleep, forehead sweaty, covers balled into a tangle at the corner of the bed, my mind spins with the vision of those pages of names.

My not remembering having written those names is only a symptom of a larger problem: Despite my daily sense of culture shock, I cannot deny that I am starting to feel like a different person. After all, how can I really think of myself as Courtney when no one around me does, when no one calls me by my real name, shares my memories of who I am? How can I even be sure of who I am when the voice that comes from my mouth is as alien as the face that looks back at me in the mirror?

I will not think about this. I will not. I will read *Pride and Prejudice.* In fact, I will open it at random for guidance and wisdom. I array the three volumes on my bed, spines facing away from me, and choose one. Then I close my eyes and open the book, letting my eyes fall on the first line I see:

She was wild to be at home—to hear, to see, to be upon the spot . . .

And instantly I am comforted. If Lizzy could get home, and if all would turn out well for her, then there is hope for me, too. I will read myself into a state of calm, and then in a few hours I will sleep, and who knows where I might wake up tomorrow?

Sixteen

The good news when I awake is that I have indeed stopped bleeding, and that means even Barnes won't be able to come up with a reason to extend my house arrest. I still can't get over the good fortune of a mere day-and-a-half-long period. One more reason to admire this borrowed body, aside from its glossy hair and slim figure. Anna would say, "I told you so," she who's always talking about how women make their periods lengthier and more uncomfortable than necessary by ignoring their biological need to let the blood flow freely and to take it easy for a couple of days while reveling in their womanly power. But normally I don't have the luxury of taking a few days off to revel in my womanly power, and I doubt that Barnes or anyone of her class does either.

I get so involved in thoughts of feminism and class struggle and the unfairness of it all that I don't realize Barnes is standing outside my open door until I hear her gently clearing her throat. I motion for her to come in, as I have done every morning, and I nod my approval, as I usually do, at the dress she chooses for me to wear for the first part of the day. Funny how easily I have fallen into that routine, too.

I'm so happy to get out of this room that I feel positively sunny at the sight of Mrs. M at the breakfast table, despite her arched eyebrow and laser eye. The sun itself shines through the French doors, and with that the promise of a turn in the shrubbery. I can't believe I'm actually thinking in terms like "turn in the shrubbery." I giggle and turn it into a smile, which I bestow on Mrs. M as I spread strawberry preserves on my toast.

"Stop giggling, my dear. It is most unbecoming in one whose age suggests the tutoring of schoolgirls rather than the manners of one."

I put my knife down so that I won't be tempted to fling it at her.

She stares at me as if daring me to take the bait.

But I only smile and dab my lips delicately with a napkin. "Thank you for your kind hints, Mama."

Her eyes narrow in skepticism, but I am unmoved. "Well." She throws her own napkin on the table and stands up. "When you have had your walk, I shall expect you in the sitting room."

Round one of the day goes to me.

How lovely to be outside again, the sun warm on my face, the knots in my limbs untangling with the joy of a long walk. As I make my way back toward the house down the gravel path, the pretty cream-colored horse spots me and trots over to the fence that encloses the paddock, nodding its head as if in greeting, irresistibly drawing me to it.

I stroke her velvety nose and, without thinking, snuggle my cheek against hers. And in that moment I am swept into split-second sensations—the sound and feel of pounding hooves as I ride the horse, wind whipping through my hair, the sweep and crunch of narrowly missed branches, and a lurch in my stomach as I sail through the air—

I gasp, realizing I am holding fast to the mane of the horse; Belle, that is her name—how do I know that? Her luminous brown eyes with their long white eyelashes regard me with concern. I pat her, my hand shaking. "It's all right, girl."

Is it really? My legs wobble slightly as I continue toward the house. Get a grip on yourself. You're imagining things, no doubt wondering what Jane might have felt when she fell off her horse before you realized you were wondering it. Your mind is playing tricks on you. Anyone would be disoriented in your position. Calm down. Mustn't let Mrs. M suspect you're feeling anything but in top shape.

By the time I reach the house and make my way to the sitting room, I am a thousand times better. Mrs. M nods to me as I enter, and I take up my embroidery frame with more eagerness than ever before. I need the clear-minded, meditative calm that sewing gives me.

Once again I find myself marveling at the slender fingers of these alien hands as they draw the needle through the cloth and create intricate designs without any thought or effort. It's as though I am simply allowing the fingers to do their work, hold the needle, choose the colors of threads, fashion flowers and birds and leaves on the cloth. And like all the other times I have sat here embroidering, a detached sort of calm comes over me as I observe these fingers—my fingers—doing their work. *I* have nothing to do with it.

As I sit here, absorbed in the movement of my fingers and the ticking of the clock, I have a split-second mind flash, an image of Edgeworth emerging from his stables, bits of straw clinging to his hair and clothes. That is all, but it sends a chill up my arms. It isn't like an imagining, it's like a remembering. But how can I have a memory that isn't mine, that I couldn't possibly have access to?

Yet I *know* it is a memory. As disturbing as the sensation of being thrown off that gentle horse. Or of seeing the dark, spreading stain of spilt tea on my white gown.

The problem is, they aren't *my* memories.

The next day, I'm stalked by that same, split-second image of Edgeworth coming out of the stables. Why does it flash through my mind when I walk in the garden, or sew, or drift off to sleep? Why, when I wake up the following morning to the sound of birds singing, is it there again?

A walk before breakfast will clear my mind, I decide while Barnes buttons me into my dress. But I barely make it to the first gravel path when I realize what I have not allowed myself to know: My mind, my very identity, is tied up in all the memories of the life I called my own, my life as Courtney Stone. Yet that bundle of memories, that thing I call my self, is residing in Jane's body. And that body has a physical brain of its own. And that brain has memories imprinted on it—visual, experiential, sensory memories. Perhaps the more I become used to living in Jane's body and using her brain, the more I am starting to access her memories.

A chill runs up my arms despite the warmth of the sun, and I wrap my light shawl tightly around my shoulders. What did I think the embroidery thing was all about anyway? Or the accent? Or the way I *know*, without thinking, just how to curtsey when I enter a room? Or how to pour the tea? Or how to walk in to dinner? And that doesn't mean just putting one foot in front of the other. A part of me instinctively understands that body language is everything in a place where so little is actually said out loud. The placement of people, who enters a room first, who follows next—it is all an unwritten communication of who is more important than whom, and it is as potent as anything spoken. How could I, who have done little more than read a few novels of the period, have such an intimate knowledge of this language?

The embroidery is what stood out in my mind because it's so pronounced, but the fact of the matter is that it isn't just luck or some kind of fluke. The pure scientific explanation, if anything about this situation could possibly be called scientific, is that I am reaping the benefits of memory, cellular and kinesthetic, in playacting this role of Jane. With all this help from Jane's brain, which contains her body's memories of embroidering, curtseying, speaking in a particular way, and God knows how many other things, it's no wonder I am so apt at playing the part. Without those unspoken memories, I would stick out as an anomaly to even a casual observer. But I haven't. Everyone is fooled. They were fooled even when I was insisting to them that I wasn't Jane.

So what will become of who I really am? What will become of that bundle of memories called Courtney, my real self that resides, hidden from view, inside this body? Will I/it slowly disappear, inexorably surrender to the onslaught of synaptic activities, the cumulative effect of cellular memory that is now evolving into conscious thought?

Is this mental image of Edgeworth coming out of the stables just the first of an avalanche of memories not my own, memories that will take up space in my mind until I finally forget who I really am? Or will my mind be split up, a storage space for two different lives? How will I manage it all without going insane?

Can I consciously stop the flow of memories so I can hold on to my self? Would this compromise my believability as Jane, and would I then be exposed as an impostor, or worse, insane?

Then again, do I really want to stop the flow of memories? After all, this unconscious, second-nature sort of memory gives me a decided advantage. I needn't worry about appearing clumsy or have to relearn physical things Jane already knows how to do, things that if I could not do I'd never be able to explain why to anyone.

Given that kind of logic, why then can't the thought-memories also give me an advantage? Why should I assume that allowing Jane's memories in would necessarily mean having to empty my mind of my own memories? Why should I entertain the thought that the brain's hard drive lacks space for two lives' worth of memories?

And what might I discover if those memories really do come back fully? Everything. I'd know everything about the woman whose body I'm in, everything about her family, her life, her friends, even Edgeworth. Everything that her letters, her diary, anything she might have written or received in writing, might have told me, if such papers exist. I'd no longer have to watch my conversations when I meet new people. I'd no longer have to fear exposing myself as not knowing something I should already know. What a relief that would be. It's exhausting to be always vigilant against exposing my ignorance.

But where, in a world devoid of land lines, cell phones, or email, are those damned letters? Why does Jane's room, and indeed her entire house, appear to be devoid of anything she might have written down? Or received in writing?

Despite rummaging through every drawer and potential hiding place I could think of in my room, and in every other room whenever I've had an opportunity to snoop around, I've found nothing.

I realize I've reached the house and am struck with an idea: What if Jane put her journal or letters or even both in her father's atelier? That's one place I haven't looked, haven't even considered looking. But wouldn't that be the perfect hiding place, since Mrs. M's delicate sense of smell cannot abide it? I could even search through it now, since Mr. M will be gone for at least another half hour on his morning ride.

Keeping an eye out for servants, I slip into Mr. M's sanctum sanctorum, which he, thankfully, leaves unlocked.

Taking care not to get paint on my clothes, I open every drawer and cupboard in the room and rifle their contents. Nothing. Then I spot, under a table in the far corner, almost completely obscured by a tall standing vase of flowers (Mrs. M refuses to give up), an odd-looking wooden box. Could that be it? If I were Jane, that would be the very place to hide my precious papers.

Heart racing, I move the vase to the side and scramble under the table, pulling out the box, which has a heavy lid with a strange-looking, sticklike handle. There's something solid in there;

I can feel the weight of it shifting as I place the box on top of the table. Maybe a thick packet of letters? A heavy journal? I try to lift the lid, but nothing happens. I jiggle it a little and realize it slides open. I hold my breath as I slide it back.

Inside a brown rat lies on its back, glassy eyes staring, paws curled up stiffly.

I hear screaming before I realize I am the one doing it. I practically collide with Barnes, who is flying into the room as I am flying out of it.

"Heaven help us, what is the matter?"

But all I can do is point toward the box, which lies open on the table. Barnes rushes over to it.

"Barnes, don't!"

But she's already looking inside. "Never you mind, miss. That there rat is dead as can be. He can't do you no harm, I swear it."

She rushes over and pats my arm, a kind smile on her face. "There, there, miss."

Thank God. Of course it's dead. Why else would it be lying on its back with its paws in the air? I shudder.

"Why don't you go upstairs and throw some cold water on your face?" Barnes says.

I manage a nod and lean over, suddenly dizzy. "Barnes?"

"Do we have many of those"—I gesture in the general direction of the evil rat trap—"in the house?"

"Yes indeed, but thanks to old Jack, the best carpenter that ever was, they've been empty for years. I'm as surprised as you to find what you did today, but I guarantee old Jack will sniff out the place this one came in through and patch it up before you can finish your breakfast."

My stomach lurches at the thought of food. "And Barnes?"

"Yes, miss?"

"You won't say anything about this to Mrs.—I mean, my mother, will you?"

Barnes's eyes are full of empathy. "Of course I won't do anything of the kind, miss. Now you go upstairs and take care of yourself."

"You're a real friend, Barnes."

"Aw now, miss." She curtseys and ducks her head, the frills of her cap only partially obscuring a face glowing with pleasure.

Sure enough, after throwing some cool water on my face and lying down for a couple of minutes, I am not only calm, I am also hungry. That's about all the excitement I can take for today. And then, as I head down the stairs toward the breakfast room, I remember that tomorrow is when Edgeworth is expected to return from London.

Seventeen

I am stuffing myself with hot rolls and strawberry jam in an effort to stop obsessing over whether or not he will come to see me, how soon after his return that might happen, and whether or not I even want him to, since Mrs. M will no doubt whip herself into a frenzy if it happens, when the woman herself sweeps into the breakfast room.

"I shall send your father to pay his respects to Mr. Edgeworth the day after tomorrow. And I shall dispatch an invitation to dinner for as soon as may be. Otherwise Mrs. Moore will get to him first."

I put down my roll, appetite destroyed, and go off to cut roses in the garden. My basket is almost filled when the image of Edgeworth at the stables comes back again, but this time instead of a quick flash, it is an entire scene. A scene in which I am a participant as well as an observer. I see myself (or, more accurately, I see myself as Jane) watching Edgeworth as he emerges from the stables. My/her stomach tightens and my forehead perspires as he walks toward my hiding place behind a bush. I/Jane have not been deliberately spying on him per se, but nonetheless I dread the possibility of his finding me here. When he suddenly changes direction and walks off without discovering me, my body relaxes in a huge release of tensed muscles and cautiously exhaled breath.

And there the image ends.

I look down at the half-filled basket of roses in my hands, the soft pink of their velvety petals and the sweetness of their scent as real as the soft breeze that caresses my face and carries the scent to my nose, as real as the image of Edgeworth coming out of the stables, and as real as the bodily sensations I had as I watched him do so. There's no use denying that this is a memory—Jane's memory—and that it has become my memory. A memory that is recurring so frequently, and becoming so detailed, that it has to be significant.

I retreat to my room, hoping for some quiet time to think. But less than half an hour has passed when Barnes knocks on my door and tells me that the man himself is waiting downstairs in the drawing room.

My throat goes dry and my palms start sweating. He's not even supposed to return until tomorrow. But I force myself downstairs, where Mrs. Mansfield is offering him food, drink, a comfortable chair. Edgeworth turns to me, his hazel eyes sparkling with warmth and friendliness, his hair golden in the sunlight coming through the gap in the curtains. There is no awkwardness to stumble past.

Mrs. Mansfield wastes no time in inviting him to dinner.

"Thank you but I cannot," he says, "for I came here intending to ask you and your family to dine with me on that very day. My sister Mary is come from London, and since she and Miss Mansfield," he adds with a significant look at me, "took so much pleasure in their acquaintance when Mary was last here, I had no doubt that the prospect of meeting again would be desirous to both parties."

Not a bad idea, meeting this sister of Edgeworth's. If I play it right, she could be a valuable source of information. As for her brother, he is even more appealing now than he was the last time I saw him. I'm even starting to appreciate his clothes, or at least how he looks in them. Of course, what's not to like about the tight trousers, and the long tails on his coat are kind of cute. But to me even the more outlandish parts of his outfit look sexy, like the immensely tall hat, and the collar of his shirt, which almost meets his jawline.

A timid knock on the door announces Barnes, who glances at me almost sheepishly before addressing Mrs. Mansfield. "Begging your pardon, ma'am, but you asked me to let you know—"

"Yes, yes, I remember," says Mrs. Mrs. M, rising out of her seat and shooting Edgeworth a look of exasperation. "I do not have a moment's peace. If you will excuse me, Mr. Edgeworth."

Edgeworth is already standing, and makes his bow.

Mrs. M says, "Till Sunday, then, when we shall have the pleasure of seeing you and Miss Edgeworth at church."

"My sister and I shall be with our aunt tomorrow, and thus shall accompany her to church there."

"Well, then. I hope you will not be in a hurry to leave now on my account." Face turned away from Edgeworth, she raises an eyebrow at me and sweeps out of the room. I can just imagine whose idea it was for Barnes to have such a well-timed need for her mistress.

Edgeworth takes a chair much closer to mine this time. "My sister desires me to beg your forgiveness for being unable to wait on you herself today. She is most anxious to see you. As was I." He gazes into my eyes with such intensity that I feel the heat rising up my neck.

"I need not ask if you are well, as your looks tell me everything." He looks down at his hands, then meets my eyes again. "Forgive me, but I cannot help saying how happy I am to see you. If business had not detained me in town, I would have returned even sooner."

He reaches out his hand to me, and I place mine in his. He turns my hand over and grazes my palm with his thumb, and my whole body tingles. I look up into his hazel eyes, and—in stalks Mr. Mansfield on his spindly legs.

Edgeworth drops my hand and leaps to his feet, and I don't know how much Mr. M saw, but Edgeworth looks as flustered as I feel, and Mr. M scrutinizes us for a moment before launching into a polite welcome.

I hardly hear the exchange of courtesies and Edgeworth's stammering something about having some pressing business with his steward. Within a couple of minutes he is bowing his good-bye and wishing us a good day.

I mumble something to Mr. Mansfield about needing something from my room, and escape.

I am sitting on my bed reliving the touch of Edgeworth's fingers and the magnetic pull of his eyes when Mrs. Mansfield barges in with barely a knock.

"Jane, I expect you to visit Miss Edgeworth on Monday morning. After all, it is incumbent upon her neighbors, especially a neighbor singled out as a particular friend, to welcome her."

As it turns out, there's no need for me to make any such effort. Just as I am about to leave the house to meet my so-called friend, I hear the clatter of carriage wheels and the subsequent sound of two female voices in the entrance hall, one of which is Mrs. M.

I steal down the stairs to get a look before they see me, but Mrs. M's radar is up, and she instantly turns around and sings out to me, "How delightful, Jane! Here is Miss Edgeworth!"

Mary Edgeworth, a round little brunette, rushes to my side and kisses me on each cheek before enfolding me in a hug. "Thank God you are well, dearest Jane." She pulls back to look in my face. Her eyes are chocolate brown, and her face is round and soft. Not the sort of girl to turn heads at first glance, but when she smiles, she has deep dimples in each cheek, and the light in her brown eyes reveals flecks of gold. But best of all is her voice, a surprisingly deep, cigarette-sexy sort of voice that does not go with the rest of the package, but which instantly becomes absolutely and totally Mary Edgeworth.

Mary proposes to Mrs. Mansfield that she take me out in her carriage. "An airing would do us good, Mrs. Mansfield, as the weather is so abominably hot that walking would be insupportable."

Perfect, I think, until she asks Mrs. Mansfield to join us. But, thankfully, Mrs. M declines; her motive, no doubt, to promote the friendship between me and the sister of the most prized bachelor in the neighborhood.

No sooner does the coachman close the door behind us when Mary's face turns grave. "I was beside myself when I heard of your fall. And furious with my brother for not having told me sooner. Thankfully he gave me swift news of your recovery. But I could not rest till I laid eyes on you myself."

I squirm as her eyes examine me, wondering if she will notice her friend is not quite the same. "So what do you think?"

But she just keeps regarding me steadily. I try to act nonchalant, glancing out of the carriage window at the passing trees and fields. But I keep returning to those gentle brown eyes. A couple of times it looks as if she is about to say something. Finally she says, "You are too good to reproach me, but this alteration in your manners—I know the cause."

"You do?" That makes one of us.

"My dear Jane, it took all the self-command in my power not to write again after you failed to answer my last. I assumed you were angry or shocked. Or maybe both."

She sighs. "What a fool I was to have waited. Had I written again, no doubt your mother would have told me of your fall, and I would have come instantly, instead of weeks later."

She searches my face again. "You do not seem angry with me now. Have you forgiven me for what I wrote you?"

"What you wrote me," I parrot, trying to buy time because I have no idea what she's talking about.

"Good God. I never once considered—did you not receive it? It should have reached you at least a week before your accident."

"I don't know; I mean, I don't think so."

"I cannot imagine how this could be."

"Was it important?"

"Oh, dear," Mary says, twisting her handkerchief in her hands and looking out the carriage window. "Somehow writing such things is less unpleasant than speaking them out loud."

She blinks fast and bites her lips; she's trying not to cry.

"What is it, Mary?" I find myself squeezing her hand.

"Has my brother any hope of securing your affections? If so, then I am persuaded it is my duty to tell you what I know. But if you are still as set against him as you appeared to be when last I was here, then I will have no need of repeating to you now what was so painful for me to write. Had I not heard from Susan Randolph that your feelings for Charles seemed to take a turn again, I would never presume to burden you now with what was in that letter. Which, it seems, has been no burden at all because it never arrived."

Apparently Jane had either burned that letter or hid it too carefully for someone like me to find it.

"Perhaps your brother and I were not the best of friends in the past," I say, watching her carefully, "but he seems like a decent human being."

"I see."

"Then again, I don't know him very well."

"Oh, but you will know him," Mary says. "You will know exactly what he wishes you to know. And nothing else. Which is precisely what I fear."

"Am I missing something? This is your brother we're talking about, right?"

"And you are my friend Jane, are you not? You know how it is between Charles and me. Have you forgot everything?"

While I contemplate a plausible answer, Mary shouts to the coachman to stop the carriage.

"Jane, would you walk with me in the lane? If we reach the village we are sure to meet with some of our acquaintance, and there will be little chance of continuing our discussion."

The coachman hands us out of the carriage, and Mary and I walk arm in arm in the heaviness of the heat for a few minutes. Thankfully, she's not pressing me for an answer to her question.

And then I remember that it's she who wants to tell me something about her brother, something she's supposedly written to Jane.

Either she tells me now, or I'm going to wilt in this heat. I steal a glance at her, and her face is as red and sweaty as mine feels.

"Please," I blurt out, "tell me what you wrote in that letter."

She turns to me, answering my smile with a flicker of one, then gently disengages her arm and takes another couple of steps. She stops again, taking off her bonnet and smoothing a sweaty strand of hair off her forehead.

"Very well," she says, her voice a raspy whisper. "I fear that my brother is not a man to be trusted. In short, it has come to my attention that he is . . ."

"Yes?"

She won't meet my eyes. ". . . a libertine. There. Now you know everything."

She looks at me for a moment and bites her lip before casting her eyes down again.

"Is that all? You don't expect your brother to have lived like a monk, do you?"

Mary draws herself up to her full height, which is about a head shorter than I am. "No, but neither do I expect him to seduce a servant in our household."

"You know this for a fact?"

"On more than one occasion I came upon them conversing most freely, and once I even saw them kissing. Then, when I discovered she was in a condition certainly not suitable to continue in our service, I confronted Charles."

"A condition." When was he kissing this other woman, is what I want to know.

"Yes, Jane. She was with child."

"Don't tell me you made her leave."

"I gave the poor girl ample money so that she could return to her family for her confinement, and I supplied her with references that would enable her to secure another position. But I could not let her remain in the house. Nor did she wish to do so."

"And your brother?"

"He denied he was the father of the child. And insisted he had never taken liberties with her."

"Obviously, you don't believe him."

Mary's eyes widen and her mouth opens as if to speak, but at first nothing comes out. "I saw them kissing!"

I force myself to take on a neutral tone. “And how long ago was that?”

She hesitates for a moment. “At least eight months ago.”

I realize I’ve been holding my breath. “So what does that prove?”

“You cannot be serious. A girl who is in his service? Who is under his power? Even if she were his equal, no respectable man kisses a woman to whom he is not even engaged.”

“If there were coercion or intimidation, then I agree he should be strung up. But it doesn’t sound like that was the case. And the fact that she’s pregnant doesn’t mean your brother was the doer. Did she say he was?”

Mary sputters but nothing comes out, then looks at me as if I really am a stranger. When she does speak, her voice is practically a whisper. “Of course she said nothing of the kind. To me, his own sister?”

We walk on for another minute while I contemplate the prudishness of a society that can hardly admit to the means by which the human species reproduces itself, let alone that those same humans actually participate in the process.

“Of course I suggested that Charles marry the girl, despite the fact that all our friends would shun her society. And his.”

“And?”

“He said he was sorry for her but had no intention of taking on another man's duties. He is the most unfeeling creature I have ever known."

Mary is almost shaking with rage.

I say, as gently as I can, "Why do you hate him so much?"

She looks at me uncomprehendingly. "How can you ask such a question? You know as well as I that he has ruined my only chance at happiness."

She swipes at a tear and pulls out a handkerchief, dabbing at her eyes. I don't dare ask her what it was her brother did, or supposedly did, as it's clearly something I'm supposed to know.

The winding path we've been following has led us to a pond. There is a wisp of a breeze, the first hint of a respite from the heat. "Why don't we sit for a minute?" I say. "The grass looks dry here, and I'm about to drop from this heat."

Mary silently assents, and we arrange ourselves on the grass, no small task with tightly laced stays forcing my upper torso into an unbending position.

For a while we sit looking at the sparkling water and listening to the singing of birds. There is not another person in sight. The air is soft on my face, and a delicate breeze begins to cool my skin a bit, though it would take a much cooler and stronger wind than this to penetrate the damp, lace-up contraption around my middle.

Mary suddenly squeezes my hand.

"Jane, do forgive my outburst. Only you know what has disposed you to give Charles the benefit of the doubt, despite all evidence to the contrary. But do take care, dearest friend. Be observant of Charles's behavior, not just to you, but to others. Let your observations of him—past and present—be your guide."

There's nothing unreasonable about that piece of advice. And I have to admit there is something about her (despite all the sexual prissiness, which really isn't her fault anyway) that I find genuine and artless.

"Don't worry about me, Mary. I can take care of myself."

"Oh really?" Mary gives me a playful tap on the arm. "Is that why you tumbled from your horse after that dreadful fortune-teller warned you against riding in summer?"

"Fortune-teller?"

Mary's eyes narrow. "You cannot have forgotten. You were pale as a ghost when you left her tent."

There must be something I can say that will satisfy both her and my curiosity. "It *was* a bad fall, you know. I've been forgetting things lately."

"My dear Jane!"

"Nothing to worry about. The doctor says the memory loss is temporary."

"So you really do not remember that fortune-teller at the fair?"

"Just bits and pieces . . . nothing of any substance."

I'm evidently becoming a skilled liar, for Mary looks convinced.

"Do tell me what she said, Mary. I love that silly stuff, don't you?"

Mary shivers slightly, despite the heat, and looks me straight in the eyes. "Not anymore. You only consented to see her because I particularly urged you. What a good joke it would be, I said. And you replied that you would think so, too, but only if the good woman fulfilled your wish to be someone else. Which, it almost seems, has actually come to pass." Her words choke off in her throat, and she hides her face from me.

I move to put my arm around her shoulder, but she waves me away.

"Do forgive me, Jane. Of course you are not yourself right now."

"Don't apologize. You're right. More right than you can ever know. I wish . . ."

No. No way.

"What is it, dearest friend?" At this moment, her eyes are like Anna's were that night I found out about Frank.

"I can't tell you."

"But you want to, I can see it."

Can I trust her?

I take a deep breath and look at her face, and see only concern in her brown eyes. "Promise me you won't repeat a word."

Mary raises an eyebrow. "My dear, you insult

me. But you are serious, I can see it in your face. Of course I promise. But you make me anxious indeed with all this ceremony."

"I warn you. You might not believe what I have to say."

"You torture me, Jane."

I take a deep breath. Here goes. "I know I look like Jane and talk like Jane, but I am not Jane. I know this sounds absurd, but I am actually someone else. I woke up one day, and I was literally in a different body, and in a different life. I have no explanation, but it is the truth. I swear it."

Mary eyes me narrowly, searching my face. "And what of this memory loss you mentioned? Could that not be the explanation?"

"I only said I lost some memories because I couldn't think of a better way to explain my lack of knowledge. Jane's entire life is a blank to me. My memories are of a different life, of a different person."

Mary is silent for a few moments.

"I believe you think you are telling the truth, Jane. But might not this indeed be a severe case of memory loss, which, I understand, is not uncommon after such a fall as yours? And might not the rest be a product of your own confusion? And a most understandable confusion at that?"

"No, I don't see it that way, though I understand why you would. And if you're wondering about my sanity, I assure you that I'm perfectly rational, though I understand that to your ears my words must sound like the very definition of irrational."

I watch Mary for her reaction. She sighs and looks puzzled, but there is still warmth in every look and gesture. "I will not insult you with anything less than the truth," she says. "I do believe you are sincere. And for that I am sorry for you. I also believe that in time, your memories will return in full, and your confusion will be at an end. Until then, and forever, if you wish it, I remain your friend."

I tear up, overcome. "You cannot imagine how I've felt these past weeks. No one to confide in. Afraid I'd be locked up in some asylum."

"My poor dear girl." She puts her arm around my shoulder.

"May I talk to you about this from time to time? Ask you about things Jane would remember?"

Mary smoothes her dress and gives me a sly look. "Provided you do not refer to yourself in the third person. It is too strange. Agreed?"

I nod my assent, and I can't help but smile.

"I promise I will try to help you remember everything. It will all turn out well. I know it will."

I hug her, my heart swelling with gratitude.

As we walk back toward the carriage, arm in arm, I'm energized in a way I haven't been since my arrival. To have a friend here, someone in whom I can confide without fear of betrayal or ridicule. It's beyond anything I've allowed myself to hope for.

Still, the demon voices who have always second-guessed anything positive in my life begin to clamor for my attention. What if I'm wrong? What if she turns on me, decides to report what I've told her to Mrs. Mansfield? What if she decides I'd be better off in an asylum? Maybe even does it out of some misguided feelings of friendship?

No. I won't worry about that happening. Besides, it would be her word against mine. No one else will know of our talks. And I don't ever have to put anything down in a letter.

She did warn me to take care, didn't she?

Eighteen

In preparation for Edgeworth's dinner party, Barnes laces and hooks me into a filmy white gown that makes me look like a virgin bride, something I never thought I'd say about myself. But then again, as I regard my reflection in the mirror, I am anything but myself.

The carriage ride to Edgeworth's estate takes us through a long, shady lane with dense woods on either side. As we round a curve in the road, Mrs. Mansfield nudges me and raises an eyebrow, and a monumental house is revealed. It's Pemberley, for God's sake.

"Fifteen thousand a year, my dear," says Mrs. M. "Can you imagine such riches?"

"Uh, that would be a big negative." But that, of course, is a big lie. I feel like Elizabeth Bennet when she sees Darcy's house after having turned down his proposal. *And of this place, thought she, I might have been mistress!*

Mrs. M opens her mouth to speak, but Mr. M cuts in. "I may not have fifteen thousand a year, but I daresay our daughter hardly lives in deprivation."

"That is not what I meant at all," Mrs. Mansfield huffs. "Nevertheless, it is a daughter's duty to marry well, thus ensuring the welfare of future generations."

"With such a burden to shoulder, it is a wonder that young girls choose to wed at all."

At this, he catches my eye with a little wink, and I try not to laugh.

Mrs. M fumes. "Your daughter is hardly a young girl."

I press my hands against my temples. "Would you two kindly refrain from disparaging my advanced age? You're making my head throb."

"Now, Jane, mind you not ignore Mr. Edgeworth and pay all your attentions to his sister," says Mrs. M, apparently heedless of the possibility that her daughter could be suffering the after-effects of a near-fatal head injury. "Though I do suppose she must be lonely without parents and only one brother. But with such a plain face and masculine voice, her chances of finding a husband who is amiable as well as rich are slim."

"I happen to like her voice. And so do a lot of men, I imagine."

Mrs. M snorts her derision. I steal a glance at Mr. Mansfield, who keeps his gaze on the green expanse of Edgeworth's lawns. Thankfully, we reach the house in another minute.

A liveried footman with a powdered wig shows us through a marble entryway and into an elegant drawing room decorated in muted shades of yellow and blue. Edgeworth and Mary are waiting for us with welcoming smiles and no apparent tension between the two of them.

We are the first, but not the only guests to arrive. Their cousins, a nondescript, thirtysomething man named Mr. Talbot, and his sister, Anne Talbot, a pretty girl of about seventeen, all arms and long neck in her pink puff-sleeved dress, enter the room a few minutes after our arrival. They are with their mother, a bustling woman in a peach silk gown whose fluttering eyelashes as she greets Mr. Mansfield make him clear his throat and look down at his shoes. In my world she'd be one of those fiftyish Beverly Hills matrons who dress like their daughters and still turn heads, but minus the airbrushed Botox freeze.

"Miss Mansfield," she says as she crosses the room to the butter-yellow sofa where her daughter has gingerly placed herself next to me, and maneuvers herself between the two of us. "You are every bit as pretty as my niece said you were." Her smile reveals a gap between her slightly protruding front teeth, which is sort of girlishly sexy.

Before I can open my mouth to reply, she says, "What a pleasure it is to be once again in the quiet of the country, after enduring the rushing about of Anne's first season in London. They say it is a trial for the girls, but I dare say it is far worse for their poor mothers, who must sacrifice every hour to the endless crush of parties, dinners, and balls. I am sure you can hardly imagine having to endure such exhaustion at *your* time of life, Miss Jane."

My shoulders stiffen. "Actually, I love to party."

Her mouth opens as if to speak, then she purses her lips. "I see."

She fans herself rapidly, then flashes me another smile. "A party of respectable people is always a delightful thing, especially when the host is an angel. Do you not agree, Miss Mansfield, that my dear Charles is such a man?"

Edgeworth, who is standing by the massive marble fireplace talking with Mr. M, overhears his name and bows in our direction, then catches my eye with a slight roll of his own.

Mrs. Talbot begins speaking in a sort of stage whisper. "Why, I only had to mention how knocked up with the gout my poor husband is, and dear Charles insisted on riding over to Hargrove Court."

"Oh, is that a retirement home?"

"I suppose its situation might be called retired, but Hargrove Court is my dear Mr. Talbot's ancestral home. Mr. Talbot, of course, is too proud to ask anyone for advice, but I know he will be gladdened at the sight of his favorite nephew, who has offered his services in some matters of business. You know how men can be about business, always shutting themselves up in the library and talking about I don't know what for hours." She gives me a conspiratorial look.

Another bewigged footman appears in the doorway to announce dinner, his voice as somber as that of a mortician greeting mourners arriving at a funeral. As we troop into the dining room, Mary sidles up to whisper in my ear. "Do forgive me for seating you next to my aunt Talbot; she insisted upon it." To which I can only sigh. I've barely had a chance to observe Edgeworth, let alone spend any time with him.

The meal itself is staggering in its sheer proportions. By now I'm used to seeing a ridiculous number of dishes on the table at the Mansfields'. At first I was shocked by the sheer waste; the table and sideboard were always filled with more dishes than five times the people there could possibly consume. I was relieved when I realized that no one was expected to eat every dish. Otherwise, everyone would be hopelessly obese and constantly drunk, since the quantity and variety of wine served is also remarkable. As it is, I can hardly believe the capacity for alcohol these people have, even the women, though they usually water down their wine. As for the food, I stopped fooling myself about imaginary calories and began to watch my own intake after I noticed this body was the not-so-proud owner of a burgeoning pot belly.

Nothing prepares me, however, for what we're served at the Edgeworths'. I lose count of the number of dishes, which are changed at least three times. I also lose count of how many times Mrs. Talbot either brags about her daughter's accomplishments or praises Edgeworth for his many fine qualities. It's almost as if she has a crush on her own nephew.

She reminds me of Frank's mother, who, at our engagement dinner, talked to me incessantly about what a catch Wes was. Not her son, whom I was going to marry, but Wes, his best friend. Did I understand why such an extraordinarily good-looking young man such as Wes was still unattached? Did I know Wes had once saved her husband's life when he choked on a piece of steak? And did I know that Wes used to carry her grocery bags to the car when he had his high school summer job at the Safeway?

Poor Wes, looking like he was about to crawl under the table, while Frank just continued to throw back shots of tequila and pretend there was nothing odd about his mother's praising his best friend to his bride-to-be, rather than praising her own son.

The scrape of the chair next to me brings me back to the present; Mrs. Talbot is standing, as are the other women, and I scramble to my feet for the after-dinner exodus to the drawing room. Just what are the men going to talk about when we leave the room? Discuss sexual exploits? Tell dirty jokes and guffaw through clouds of cigar smoke? Give me my after-dinner cigarette any day over a stinky cigar.

Which is another thing. Though there are moments when I imagine putting a cigarette between my lips and taking in a soothing lungful of nicotine, I haven't had any actual withdrawal symptoms since being here. The other times I quit, and voluntarily at that, I was so edgy I bit my cuticles until they bled and felt myself fully capable of committing indiscriminate murder with the nearest sharp object. Here, however, not smoking has been easier than I would ever imagine. And that's a good thing, because even if there were a cigarette available, I imagine lighting it up would be out of the question.

In the drawing room, Mary extricates me from Mrs. Talbot's grasp by luring her into a conversation with Mrs. Mansfield about the latest fashions in London. I gather that dresses with a waistline are not yet in the cards, however, and my eyes glaze over as Mrs. Talbot describes the latest sensation in ribbon trimmings.

By the time Mary sinks down next to me on the sofa, she hardly has time to apologize for my situation before the men join us.

"Do join me for a drive in my carriage tomorrow," she says. "We can really talk then."

As soon as Mary makes sure all her guests have coffee or tea, she sits down on the sofa next to me again, only to be called from it this time by her brother.

"Would you favor us with some music, Mary? I am sure our guests would enjoy hearing your new pianoforte."

Which I suppose was a special gift he bought for his sister? Like Darcy did for his sister?

I can see that Mary isn't pleased, but when the rest of the guests add their own entreaties to her brother's, she shifts gears and heads toward the pianoforte as if she has no other desire in life. The Actors Studio could take a few lessons from her.

Edgeworth now heads over to me, where he takes the place Mary vacated. I catch a poisonous glare from Mrs. Talbot, upon which she instantly morphs her face into a display of teeth and dimples. What's up with that woman?

My stomach flutters as Edgeworth settles into his seat and smiles at me. He smells like soap and freshly washed linen. His lips and cheeks are reddened, perhaps by the wine. His eyes are more brown than green in the candlelight.

Mary's fingers strike the first note on the keyboard and I look up at her; she quickly casts down her eyes, in the way that one does when caught staring.

Edgeworth whispers in my ear, "I believe a commendation for bravery is in order for you, Miss Mansfield. It is said that the wife of an émigré French nobleman volunteered for the guillotine rather than be seated next to a certain lady at dinner."

I muffle an explosion of laughter and have to take several deep breaths before I can allow myself to look at him. His sly smile almost sets me off again.

Then a lock of hair falls over his forehead, and as he reaches up to smooth it back into place, the music fades and I see him making this same gesture as he leaves the stables. Again, he walks toward my hiding place, my heart pounding as he comes closer, and at the last second he turns. My face burns as a slim young woman emerges from the stables, strands of auburn hair falling down around her face, her apron flecked with bits of straw. She catches up to Edgeworth, her hand reaching out for him, her smile confident. He stops her hand, then brings it to his lips in a courtly gesture. He rushes off, brushing straw from his clothes and looking around as if to make sure he is unobserved, while I tremble in my hiding place, leaden and hollow.

The applause from the dinner guests brings me back to where I am. I am the only one who isn't clapping, and I realize that Edgeworth is staring at me. I give him a cold glance and clap dutifully.

"Are you unwell?" he asks in an undertone.

"Is that all you people ever ask?" I spring out of my seat and go to Mary at the pianoforte to tell her how much I enjoyed her playing, even though I heard almost none of it. While the others chime in with their own praise, I steal a glance at Edgeworth, who is trying to put on a brave face but keeps glancing at me with wounded eyes.

Thankfully, the evening is soon over, because I can barely allow myself to look at him. In the carriage, I am silent while Mrs. M rhapsodizes over Edgeworth's coming to sit next to me in the drawing room. All I want is to be alone and quiet so I can figure out what I'm feeling.

Nineteen

It's betrayal, I realize. That blindsided, gut-punched feeling I had when I saw Frank with Amy. The double whammy of it when I learned that Wes knew all along and lied for Frank.

I get that what I saw in my mind at Edgeworth's was Jane's memory, not mine. What I don't get is why I'm feeling Jane's feelings. Or are they my feelings?

What difference does it make? The truth is that Edgeworth is not a man to be trusted, and the truth is that finding him attractive should have been my first clue. Haven't I always been attracted to men who can't even refrain from flirting with other women at my birthday parties? Don't I possess a finely tuned radar that picks out the worst of the gender in a mob of thousands and finds him irresistible? Why would I think a change of era, body, or even brain would make a difference?

I lie down in bed, my body leaden. I want something to take my mind off everything. So, I creep down to the drawing room and find *Pride and Prejudice*, and I open the first volume to page one. Ah, yes. This is just what I need. This is my drug of choice.

When Mary comes by the next morning, I am puffy-eyed and stupid from lack of sleep but happy to see her. Here is someone on whose judgment and honesty I can depend.

Today Mary is coachman-less, driving me herself in a little open carriage to the pretty spot where we first got acquainted. The weather, which is considerably grayer and cooler than our last outing, is perfect for this nineteenth-century version of a convertible, which is too slow for a breeze but also merciful to my hairstyle, which is already protected anyway with one of the horrible, *de rigueur* bonnets I'm forced to wear—it's either that or battle with Mrs. M, and I'm learning to pick my battles.

As we settle ourselves and our dresses on a linen tablecloth Mary lays on the grass for that purpose, she says, "Do you forgive me, dear friend, for that horror of a dinner? You look pale today."

"I'll admit it wasn't the best evening I ever spent, but that's not your fault."

Mary smiles. "You are very good. But my aunt Talbot—how tiresome she is with her talk of Charles as the rescuer of my uncle."

"Oh?"

Mary brushes a leaf off her dress. "My uncle is in no more need of Charles's services with his estate than my aunt is in need of a new gown. No, it is for quite another purpose that Charles's presence is desired."

She looks at me to gauge my reaction. I avert my eyes and focus on the pond.

"Have you not guessed it?"

"I guess not."

"Well, my dear. She is determined to have him as a son-in-law."

"What?"

"The 'pressing matters of business' of which my aunt spoke have been pressing for many years. The truth is, she is an expensive woman whose disdain for economy has all but ruined my uncle, and she hopes an alliance between Charles and Anne will set all to rights again."

I need to stand up, move my legs. I can't sit another moment and listen to her. Why should I care anyway? If Edgeworth wants to marry Anne, let him.

As I move to get up, Mary stays me with a light touch on my arm, her golden brown eyes wide with concern.

"I have not upset you, Jane?"

"Of course not."

"Oh dear. He has no partiality for her. Anyone may see that his interests lie elsewhere."

I stand up and stretch to hide the hot tears that spring into my eyes. What's wrong with me?

"I couldn't care less," I say.

"I see your feelings have taken a turn. Very well, I shan't attempt to hide mine. Jane, if you have finally opened your eyes to his character, then I am happy for you."

Mary rises and puts her hand on my shoulder, but I move away.

"I'd rather not talk about it."

"Let us walk for a while then and enjoy the silence."

"Something I had precious little of last night."

She laughs. "Jane, you are a wicked creature to torment me about that disaster of a party," she says, linking her arm through mine. "My aunt gave us no hint of her intention to return our visit with such alacrity. Had I known, I should not have inflicted her company on you."

We walk without speaking for some time, and the soft grass and waving breezes, the play of muted light on the ripples in the pond, and the twittering of birds do a lot to ease my agitation and clear my mind. Mrs. Talbot wants her nephew as a son-in-law? It's one thing to read about Lady Catherine wanting her nephew Darcy as a son-in-law, and for her daughter Anne, no less; it's another thing to encounter it in real life, or whatever this no-exit land is supposed to be.

"It's so peaceful here," I say when we return to our little spot on the grass.

"In a few days my own peace shall be restored by the departure of Charles and our guests for my uncle's estate. And I have a notion to go to Bath; that is, if you would do me the honor of being my guest. Charles has engaged Mrs. Smith, who was my governess, to be my companion, thus providing me the means to go. It may not be the most fashionable watering place, and it will likely be rather thin this time of year, but compared to the retirement of the country I daresay there will be amusement enough to suit us both. More important, I am convinced Bath will do Mrs. Smith's rheumatic complaints a world of good."

Would I hesitate for a second to see the Bath of Catherine Morland, or even of Anne Eliot? Not to mention a chance to escape Mrs. Mansfield?

Mary interrupts my thoughts. "I can see from your face that the idea does not displease you. Oh, will you come, Jane?"

"Yes," I say, hugging her and laughing. "Of course I will."

Twenty

As our carriage draws near the place I have visited only through Jane Austen novels, one of which has not even been written yet—must stop thinking about time the way I used to think of it—I glance at Mary, who has fallen asleep, her head on the shoulder of the dozing Mrs. Smith, a plain, motherly looking middle-aged woman who is not at all disabled like Mrs. Smith from *Persuasion*, despite all Mary's talk of "rheumatic complaints." It didn't take much to get Mrs. M's permission for my trip, especially because Mary is traveling with not only her big-brother–sanctioned companion, but also an additional carriage for our luggage, her personal aid, and a contingent of servants to make sure no harm comes to us on the journey. Besides, my so-called aunt, Mrs. Randolph, is due to arrive in Bath within a week of us, which, as Mrs. M put it, will ensure us "the most desirable chaperonage" to parties and balls.

The fact that Edgeworth would be nowhere near us did not seem to make a difference to Mrs. M. If he wasn't in her neighborhood, her daughter was free to be gone as well.

I usually get stressed out when I leave town, which isn't very often. The biggest stress factor is what to pack and how to fit all of it in my suitcases. But this trip involved none of those decisions. All

I did was stand by on the day before my departure and watch while Barnes packed my trunks and Mrs. Mansfield told her what to put in them.

When the last trunk was filled and Mrs. M finally left my room, I noticed Barnes furrowing her brow more than usual.

"What is it, Barnes? Are you tired?"

"Oh no, miss. I was just thinking how this week is a week of good-byes, what with you off to Bath and my brother gone as well."

"Your brother?"

"Ever since Mr. Dowling forbade him to wait at table, James was moping about and Mr. Dowling was this close to dismissing him. Anyway, James finally took matters into his own hands, and 'tis all for the best that he be as far away from Mansfield House as his legs can take him."

She sighed again as she removed a perfectly folded shift from the trunk and refolded it.

"But how will he support himself?"

"James has long had an offer of employment from a boyhood friend who made his way as a draper, but he always found one reason or another not to take it." She looked down at her shoes.

"I—I'm sure he will be very successful."

"Thank you, miss."

I sat down on the bed while Barnes fastened the trunks. I had only barely noticed James's absence in the dining room; I'd been too caught up in my own situation to waste a moment wondering why.

Oh, well, he was better off without someone who couldn't even remember having had feelings for him. Besides, my life was complicated enough without adding to it a forbidden flirtation, let alone a serious relationship, with a servant. I guess I was becoming a class snob after all.

"Barnes, when you hear from your brother, would you tell him I'm sorry if I caused him any pain? I hope you know I never meant to hurt him."

Barnes turned to me, her eyes full. "Dear miss. You are so good. God bless you."

Now, as the carriage comes to a stop before a long row of eighteenth-century townhouses, I wonder about Barnes praising me for my goodness. If I'm such a good person, or if Jane is, for that matter, then why do we get our hearts bashed in by men like Frank, or Edgeworth?

Mary opens her eyes and smiles sleepily, and I remember how fortunate I am to be here in Bath, far from the restrictions of the country, far from the dangers of falling into a depression.

"Do you like it?" Mary asks as I ease my stiff legs out of the carriage and survey the expanse of elegant, honey-colored stone buildings, on one end of which are green trees fronted by a neoclassical sort of building, and on the other far end is a stone fountain. The sun is low in the sky, turning the buildings a pinkish gold. Across the street, carriages are letting out women in feathered turbans and men in tails and knee breeches.

A door opens, and the couples glide past a footman in a powdered wig. I hear snatches of violin music and laughter. Following the sound, I glimpse glittering chandeliers through the upstairs windows.

"Are you joking? I can't believe what I'm seeing." And that's no exaggeration; as if everything about my life here isn't surreal enough, the scene across the street is so eerily familiar that I'm unsure as to whether I am having another one of Jane's memories or if what I'm looking at is right out of a movie version of *Northanger Abbey*.

But whether this is a memory or not, and regardless of which life it's from, I can't deny that this place is all that I could wish for, short of going back to my real home. From the palatial elegance of the house belonging to Mary's aunt, but which we have all to ourselves, to the bustling staff ready to cater to my every wish, from the inviting comfort of my room, which is actually more like a suite, to the absence of Mrs. Mansfield lurking about, I feel like I'm in heaven.

Being here with Mary also means having some distance from Edgeworth. Despite my telling myself that he's only a temporary part of this borrowed life, I can't deny that it's just too dangerous to be around him. I can't reconcile that disturbing image/memory of him and the auburn-haired woman with the effect he has on me in the here and now. I can't trust myself to be cautious around him. That was clear when he came to Mansfield House to wish me a good journey.

His visit to me was no more than fifteen minutes, and with Mr. and Mrs. M close by the conversation was hardly intimate. Until right before he left, that is.

When Mrs. M said, "How we shall miss the young ladies, Mr. Edgeworth. I hardly know how I shall do without Jane," I had to restrain myself from rolling my eyes.

And then Edgeworth said, "Perhaps only Shakespeare has words to express what it means to part with one's friends." And then, with a gentle look at me he said, " 'When you depart from me, sorrow abides, and happiness takes his leave.' " He returned his attention to Mrs. M with a smile. "Is that not so, Mrs. Mansfield?"

"You are fond of a play, are you not, Mr. Edgeworth?" said Mr. M.

"I believe Miss Mansfield is as fond of plays—and of poetry—as I." Again, he glanced at me as if trying to say something with his eyes, before smiling at Mr. and Mrs. M and making his parting courtesies and compliments.

I don't even know what I managed to mumble, if anything. I was so flustered by the time he left the house that I had to go off and walk for an hour just to calm my breathing and stop my palms from sweating.

As I lie in bed, attempting to mold my pillows

into a more comfortable shape, I once again thank heaven that Jane Austen's world has no phones, PDAs, or computers. This is the one time in my life that my happiness won't depend on the leavings of my voicemail and email. As for snail mail, there's little chance of that from Edgeworth. Thank goodness for archaic courting rituals. The farther away from him I am, the better.

No, I couldn't ask for a better situation. Without Mrs. M to annoy me and Edgeworth to confuse me, I can focus on what's important: getting back to where I'm supposed to be. And maybe even having some fun in the meantime.

Twenty-one

Everyone seems to be on vacation here in Bath. Come to think of it, life, not just Bath, appears to be one long vacation for just about everyone I've met; except for the servants, of course, who could definitely use a labor union. But even for women of the privileged classes, unmarried women, that is, life as a vacation is not exactly a refined concept. It's like one of those vacations where you've fantasized about going somewhere like a Caribbean island or Paris or even Las Vegas, but instead you were guilt-tripped into spending your meager vacation time visiting your parents. The big difference here is that the so-called family vacation is a life sentence. There's never any job or apartment of your own to go back to, just an endless basket of sewing and endless days with Mom in the drawing room.

No wonder the woman whose life I'm in was desperate for a new one. If her only possible career option, i.e., marriage, offered such perks as constant pregnancy and child-rearing, and submission to a philanderer, no less, who wouldn't? Which is why being in a new city, with my new friend, and without the restrictions of Mrs. M, feels like my first true taste of freedom.

Bath, with its elegant buildings of stone that look white in some lights, golden or pink in others, is a charming concoction of meandering streets, pedestrian bridges, and pleasure gardens. After the isolation of the country, people watching is as fascinating a pastime for me as admiring the architecture and the shops. How could anyone not prefer the variety of Bath to the sameness of the country? I am beginning to doubt the biographer I read who claimed that Jane Austen hated Bath. How could anyone hate Bath? Laugh at it, yes. But hate it?

There is much to laugh at in Bath, like the curious, daily ritual of promenading in the Pump Room, which is the social nexus of Bath. The Pump Room has the self-important architecture of a Greek temple, although it's directly next door to a massive Gothic cathedral. Everyone who's anyone appears in the chandeliered Pump Room to walk the floor, hear the band playing from a little balcony, note who else is in town, and, even more important, observe what they're wearing.

When we first arrived, there was the entering of our address in a big public book in the Pump Room, so that anyone we knew could find out where we were staying. There was the leaving of calling cards at the houses of the acquaintances of Mary's who were listed in the book. Unfortunately, there also was the enduring of tedious visits with said acquaintances, mostly female, whose idea of scintillating conversation consists mostly of the weather, the lace they're using to trim their gowns, and choice bits of gossip, such as the woman who danced five dances in a row with the same man when they weren't even engaged. Stop the presses.

But the Pump Room does much more than ensure Bath tourists access to such companions; it also purports to dispense a mineral water with curative powers. At first I was curious about the water, which a sort of bartender dispenses to the faithful who belly up and take their daily glass or two with ritual solemnity. But after my first and only sip, I could see it would not be an acquired taste. In fact, I decided it would never again pass my lips unless there were a loaded gun to my head.

There are those for whom drinking the water isn't enough, or perhaps the taste disgusts them as much as it disgusts me. In any case, they prefer to immerse themselves in the steamy baths that I can see from the Pump Room windows. So when one gets bored with watching the dry folks walk around the room, there's always a view of sopping wet bathers downstairs in their clinging yellow bathing outfits.

When we tire of all things Pump Room, we stroll the wide lawns of the Crescent, with its curve of sparkling white buildings, or we meander through the streets of the town. That's what I like most, just walking around and window shopping, making frequent stops in pastry shops for tea and sticky Bath buns with crunchy currants on top. There's so much walking that I don't even worry about the extra calories.

Of course, we can't resist going inside other shops as well. As Mary put it best, it would be shocking if we were to leave Bath without having visited her favorite dressmaker in Milsom Street and running up a considerable bill. Spend it, girl. Besides, Mrs. M insisted I get myself a couple of new dresses, and Mr. M seconded that dictum with plenty of money. Not to mention we've been invited to a ball and want to look our best.

I find, however, that a visit to the dressmaker is not nearly as much fun as a visit to the pastry shop. Aside from the inevitable sameness of waistlines and hemlines, dress shopping in the early nineteenth century requires an imagination my twenty-first-century brain doesn't possess. There is no such thing as fingering racks of finished garments, let alone trying on anything, not to mention the impossibility of walking out with a dress right then and there, the comforting heft of it wrapped in tissue in a trendy little shopping bag. Nevertheless, I surrendered to the dearth of immediate gratification and let Mary help me choose fabrics, colors, and patterns. I can see that this type of clothes shopping, which is really all about finding the right raw materials, imagining the end result, and having faith in the fashion sense of one's shopping companions, would take some getting used to. At least I can be grateful for the fact that this borrowed body looks passable in an empire waist.

It is now our fourth full day here, and Mary

decides that a dip in the hot baths is just what we need after our latest exhausting round of shopping and walks. The weather has cooled off, she points out, so the heat of the water will not be unpleasant.

"Besides, my dear," she adds, "the waters are not only healthful for those with poor constitutions, they are quite beneficial for the complexion."

"I am not about to float around in a fishbowl, with wet hair plastered against my face, for every bored soul in the Pump Room to see."

"We shall go to the Cross Baths, my dear, and you shall see how delightful the waters are."

How Mary can reach such a conclusion is beyond my comprehension. As we enter the sweltering pool in preposterous yellowish bathing attire that covers us from neck to ankle, my nostrils are assaulted by a potpourri of body odors rising from the boiling flesh around me. Spiced-orange pomanders, which sit in floating bowls tied on ribbons around our necks, lose the battle against the stench rising from the steaming water before it even begins.

But even the smell of this human soup is not as revolting as the sight of some of our fellow bathers. Just a few feet away from us, a stout woman grimaces as a younger female helps her unravel soiled bandages from her legs and then submerges those legs, open sores and all, into the water. Her companion isn't in much better physical shape herself. She has a loud, phlegmy cough that she makes no attempt to shield from the breathing passages of anyone within ten yards. The proximity of this pair is enough to make me scramble out of the water and stand shuddering at the edge of the pool.

Mary looks up at me from the steaming water. "It is hot, to be sure. But do give it a few minutes. You will see how comfortable it becomes."

I kneel down beside the edge and say in a low voice, "Didn't you see those people behind you? No, don't look yet."

Mary turns her head in the direction of the two women, then back to me, her face as serene as before. "And . . . ?"

"And if you don't get out of that water you're going to catch whatever horrible diseases they have!" I hiss.

"Foolish girl," she whispers. "This place is a preserver of health. In fact, I cannot help but think that if only we had brought my poor mother here to take the waters, she might not have succumbed to her final seizure."

Or succumbed sooner, I imagine. "I can't think of anything less healthy than this place."

Mary looks around her and then back at me, clearly not getting it. "Dear. They say the waters can cure a number of distempers. Perhaps it might help restore your memory?"

"I think I'd prefer amnesia—and some dry clothes."

"Very well. But would you mind terribly if I spend a few minutes here and then meet you outside?" She glances over to Mrs. Smith, whose eyes are closed and who appears to be blissfully unaware of the filth she is floating in. Mary whispers, indicating her friend. "I will of course persuade Mrs. Smith to stay as long as she wishes."

"For your own sake, and hers, I wish you wouldn't."

Mary waves me away, and as I hurriedly dress, I pray I haven't exposed myself to something that only a future of overly prescribed antibiotics can cure.

No sooner do I get outside the building into the bracing freshness of a brisk but sunny day than I see a vaguely familiar figure crossing the street in my direction. The light is in my eyes so I can't quite make him out. He moves a little out of the glare; it's James, Barnes's brother.

Our eyes meet, and he freezes in midstep, apparently uncertain as to whether he should approach. I pull myself together and make him a little nod of acknowledgment, and he hesitantly walks toward me, tipping his tall hat and straightening his coat. He is much more elegantly dressed than I imagine a typical servant in civvies would be. In fact, he looks just as gentlemanly as any so-called gentleman I've seen in Bath, and he's much easier on the eyes than most.

He stands before me, shifting nervously from one foot to the other and barely meeting my eyes.

What am I supposed to say to him?

I force myself to smile. “James. What a nice surprise.”

He starts, “Do you mean that?” then turns red and bows. After a moment, he looks more in command of himself. “I trust you are well, miss?”

“What are you doing here in Bath? I thought you went off to work for a friend of yours.”

“True, miss. And the best piece of luck it was. The very first thing my new employer did was advance me enough money to buy these clothes.” He sheepishly fingers the edge of his jacket, as if he has no right to wear it. “And to make sure I put them to good use, he sent me off to Bath to see to a small matter of business for him.”

“I’m happy for you.”

“Thank you, miss. It is most kind of you to say so.”

He can hardly meet my eyes for more than two seconds at a time. Could it be possible that I had some sort of relationship with this guy?

“Must you be so formal? There’s no one watching, you know.”

“Forgive me”—and at this he dares to meet my eyes—“Jane.”

The intensity of his gaze makes me catch my breath. “Aren’t I the one who should be asking for forgiveness?”

He puts his gloved hand around mine and squeezes my fingers gently. His brown eyes search my face, which suddenly feels hot.

"Jane, I didn't dare—I have so much to say. Will you meet me tomorrow? Outside the labyrinth in Sydney Gardens? Would two o'clock suit you? I'll look for you at the northwest corner."

His eyes dart past my shoulder, and he drops my hands as if his were burned. I turn around to see what's unsettled him. It's Mary.

She takes in the sight of me in a tête-à-tête with James and frowns slightly. "There you are, Jane."

"Mary, may I present Mr. Barnes. Mr. Barnes, this is my friend, Miss Edgeworth."

James's eyes widen, but he quickly bows to Mary, who barely nods in return.

"If you will excuse me, ladies," he says. "I must be on my way. Good day to you." And with a bow to both of us, he turns and walks off down the street.

"That was rude," I say to Mary.

"Indeed," she says archly, "to introduce me to a servant in your house as if he were a gentleman worthy of my acquaintance."

"He is no longer a servant in my house. He happens to be a draper. And since when did you become such a snob? Not that I would remember anything about you anyway."

"That is cruel, Jane."

"As was making him feel like a piece of dirt. Is

it a breach of etiquette to show common courtesy to someone who worked in my own house?"

"I have never thought the words 'common' and 'courtesy' belonged together."

I try to stare her down, but she won't budge. Instead, she turns on her heel and begins to walk toward home, with me following sullenly a half step behind.

When we reach the house, Mary stops to examine the visiting cards that have been left on a silver tray in the vestibule. I rush past her, taking off my bonnet and heading toward the solitude of my room.

"Jane," Mary says, her voice gentle again. "May I talk to you?"

"I'm not in the mood for a sermon."

"It won't be."

I nod and hand my bonnet and shawl to Mrs. Jenkins, the housekeeper, then follow Mary into the drawing room.

She settles herself on a sofa and pats the seat beside her. I sit down, as far away from her as I can manage, when Mrs. Jenkins sweeps in with the tea tray. The little privacy that exists in this world is even more diminished by the almost constant presence of servants. Not that I would mind having a housekeeper in L.A., hovering or not.

As soon as the door closes behind Mrs. Jenkins, Mary clears her throat. "Jane, I apologize for speaking to you sharply before. And for my coldness to your friend. Do understand that my only concern was for your reputation. Bath is full of gossips, and if but one of them had seen you holding the hand of a common tradesman, one who had been a servant in your own home, your life would be reduced to the most acute misery."

I roll my eyes. "Isn't that a bit dramatic? You weren't so concerned with your brother's reputation when you suggested he marry a servant in *your* home."

"But that was a matter of duty and honor, which must always outweigh any consideration of marrying beneath one's rank. How can you make such a comparison?"

I take a sip of my tea.

Mary gasps. "Do not tell me you are in love with this Mr. Barnes?"

"Absolutely not. No. I mean, why would I be? I don't know. Actually, I don't remember a thing about him."

"I see," she says, her forehead creased with worry.

"And what if I were in love with him? Do you think I would tell you after the way you reacted?"

Mary sighs heavily. "I do not blame you for being guarded."

I suppose it isn't her fault she was raised to be so tight-assed, but I'm not going to let her off that easily.

"Tell the truth, Mary. Would you still be my friend if I loved someone you didn't approve of?"

"I will always be your friend. But I have to say that though your loss of memories is certainly a disadvantage in general, in the particular case of your friend Mr. Barnes there may be some benefit to it."

"Less complicated for you, I suppose."

"And for you, dearest friend. I would be lying if I told you that such an alliance would be easy for you and your friends. Besides, while it is true you do not remember your connection with Mr. Barnes, would you not remember love? No, I do not believe you were ever in love with this man."

Suddenly the truth of Mary's words strikes me. "I suppose I'd have to attribute that sort of amnesia to a lot more than a fall off a horse."

Mary sputters with laughter, almost choking on her tea, and I start giggling, too. And with that, the mood shifts between us. Still, I decide there are some things better left unsaid. In particular, my determination to keep my appointment with James tomorrow. I can't help but believe that the more I learn about Jane's past, the better chance I have of getting home.

Twenty-two

As I sit before the dressing table in my room, brushing my hair before bed, I am struck with the absurdity of it all. Here I am, having a hypothetical debate with Mary about the types of men I should and should not consort with, when I don't belong here in the first place.

The more I stay here, the more difficult it is to have some semblance of detachment. After all, I'm doing more than just wearing a costume. I'm wearing another person's life. And face. And body. I'm looking at that face in the mirror, brushing that hair. Even the nightly ritual of brushing my hair and looking at my face—and yes,I am more and more thinking of what I see in that reflection as my face—has become second nature, even though at home, in my real life, I'd fall into bed with unbrushed hair every night without a thought. But here, living Jane's life, it's a challenge not to get sucked in; how could I function on a daily basis otherwise? Especially when Mary is the only person who knows I'm not who everyone thinks I am. But she, of course, puts her own construction on that. Nevertheless, I have to keep my distance somehow. I have to train my focus on reclaiming who I am. All of these distractions are a trap.

I put the brush down and get into bed. Lying here, in the dark, without a mirror, without another person to call me Jane, I can imagine being my old self, being Courtney, looking like Courtney—I mean, like myself. What is happening to me? When did I start referring to myself—to my real self, my Courtney self—in the third person?

It is a long time before I calm my mind enough to fall asleep.

The next morning is so rainy that it almost ruins my plan to sneak out and meet James. Navigating my way through puddles and mud is not appealing, especially in the long dresses and unwaterproofed shoes that comprise my wardrobe, not to mention the prospect of a rainy chill penetrating the thin fabrics of every dress I own. And I'm pretty much determined that only desperation will make me wear pattens, hideous contraptions meant to elevate one's shoes from the wet ground. They remind me of horseshoes.

But by the time Mary and I settle into the drawing room after breakfast, the rain has slowed down to a drizzle. By noon, it stops completely, the sun makes a tentative appearance, and I announce my intention to go shopping and walking. Mary is reluctant to go anywhere on such a "dirty morning," as she calls it, which suits me just fine. It'll make my two o'clock rendezvous easier to pull off, and I'll have plenty of time before that to walk and clear my mind. But as I get a pair of gloves and a shawl from my room, Mary appears in the doorway. She's changed her mind, she says; would I mind terribly if she comes along?

What can I say? I'll figure out later how to ditch her.

Our first stop is the Pump Room, where Mary peers at the book of books and then turns away from it with a wry face. "As promised, Susan Randolph and your aunt have arrived."

"I suppose this means we'll have to see them."

"We can hardly avoid it."

"Well, at least Mrs. Randolph, I mean my aunt, seems to be a good person."

Mary raises an eyebrow and smiles. "Seems to be? Have you not had sufficient time in her company to form an opinion of her character?"

"Yes, but that assumes I remember having spent that time."

Mary's expression turns serious, and we walk silently out of the Pump Room.

When we've walked down the street for a couple of minutes, Mary says, "Forgive me, dear friend. I now realize to what extent you have lost your memory, and it shocks me exceedingly."

I shrug, and Mary links her arm through mine. "Still, I am encouraged that you seem to remember Susan is not to be trusted. But I will do my best to help you remember everything."

"Just how untrustworthy is she?"

"Susan has long been jealous of you. Whenever any young man would pay you the slightest attention, Susan was sure to endeavor to make herself look good at your expense. A most unbecoming attribute in a woman."

"I'm sure she'll rejoice in seeing me safely single, with not an eligible young man in sight."

As if on cue, two young men in striped trousers and high collars, one with a mop of dark hair and the other a blond, turn the corner in our direction, pass us on the street, and stare.

"Indeed," Mary says with a sly smile, "not a young man in sight."

"Ah, but if they knew of my advanced age, they would cross the street instantly."

"Nonsense. I happen to know of two women who married in their thirties."

I turn to her with mock seriousness. "That many?"

"Hush," Mary says. "Now, what were you planning to buy today?"

"Nothing special. In fact, I thought I might just forget about shopping and spend the rest of the afternoon walking."

"Anywhere in particular?"

"I thought I might just meander and clear my head."

I can feel Mary's eyes on me while I develop a sudden interest in examining the architecture of the building we're passing.

"But," I say, "I would be happy to walk you home first."

"Before meandering to Sydney Gardens?"

I stumble and nearly step in a pile of horseshit. "How did you know?"

"Jane, I heard him."

I get hold of myself and continue walking.

"Of all places, Jane. You will be seen. And it will be a fine piece of news to be canvassed by those with nothing better to do."

"Listen, Mary. I didn't come here with you to be placed under house arrest. I am an adult. A thirty-year-old adult, I might add. And if the town gossips think I'm too young to meet a man in a public place, then you can thank them from me for the compliment. Let them shout it from the Crescent and print it in the newspapers, for all I care. Because this stops, right here, right now."

She has been staring at me, her mouth open in astonishment. She looks like she wants to say something but thinks better of it. That's fine with me, because it takes me several minutes to calm down. By then we've reached the house.

Mary starts toward the door, and ventures a look at my face. Hers looks almost frightened.

I say grudgingly, "I know you have my best interests in mind."

"Do let me accompany you at least," she says, her tone wheedling. "This way I can keep watch for any, shall we say, troublesome people and distract them from you and your friend."

"Thank you but no."

Mary sighs. "Oh, Jane. What will become of you?"

"I will be careful, I promise." I pat her hand, unable to stay angry at her. "Besides, I would rather not risk involving you in any potentially compromising situation."

"But—"

"Stop worrying. I'll be back before dinner."

"Do wear this instead of those bright colors," she says, taking off her large brown shawl and replacing mine. "You will be far less conspicuous." She looks at the effect of her shawl. "And that bonnet, the ribbons are too—here, wear mine instead." Her bonnet, a straw color with buff-colored ribbons, would, I imagine, make me blend into a crowd more than what I had on.

She nods approvingly at my transformation. "And will you still wish to go to the ball tonight?"

"Would I miss an opportunity to show off my new gown?"

Mary smiles her relief. And I escape.

Even I cannot get lost going to Sydney Gardens, which begins at the very end of the street where Mary and I are staying. About a block from the approach, a piece of paper lying on the ground catches my eye. It's a verbose advertisement for an upcoming fair, complete with "Delightful Wares, Puppet Shows, Magickal Spectacles, and a Fortune-Teller."

I zero in on the "Fortune-Teller" part of the notice and stuff the paper into my purse. Perhaps being in a similar atmosphere to what Jane experienced with her fortune-teller could give me a clue, to what I have no idea. I only know I have to go to this fair.

Fortunately for me, as I enter the Gardens I can see that the prospect of walking through mud has apparently scared many people away, despite the sunshine. There are only a few scattered groups of determined strollers wandering about, and I take care to keep my distance lest I run into someone who knows me. I've been here once before with Mary, and I know where the labyrinth is. I find what I believe is the northwest corner, but with my screwed-up compass it could be the southeast corner. In any case, there's no sign of James.

I hear a quick step behind me and turn around. It's James. He bows and quickly leads me into the seclusion of a grove of trees. We walk deeper into the grove, and I spot a bench that is half hidden by overhanging branches.

"Shall we sit?" I say, pointing toward the bench.

"I fear this was not the wisest idea," James says, "to bring you out here after such a heavy rain. If you should catch a chill sitting on that cold bench—"

"Don't worry," I say.

He frowns, unconvinced.

"See?" I pull out a handkerchief to wipe the few drops of rain from the hard surface.

"Allow me." He snatches his own handkerchief from a pocket and lays it down on the bench for me.

We sit, and as he adjusts the tails of his coat I notice that his hands shake slightly.

Through a small gap in the trees, I can see a well-dressed, middle-aged couple taking a leisurely walk in our direction. James glances at them and then turns to me. "What was I thinking? If folks should see us together, it would be very bad indeed."

"I assure you I couldn't care less what anyone thinks."

James's face registers his surprise. "But I thought that's why you—well—stopped talking to me."

"James, you have to understand that after that fall I wasn't myself, I didn't know—oh, the hell with it—"

I see the look of shock on his face and don't know whether to laugh or feel sorry for him.

"I wish everyone would stop treating me like a porcelain vase. Including you."

He looks at me with wounded eyes, and suddenly I'm not upset anymore. I'm just plain numb.

"What is it, Jane?

"Okay. Here it is. Straight out. I don't remember

anything. About you. About us. About a lot of things."

At the stricken look on his face I forget all about getting everything straight out. "It's because of my fall. It's temporary."

I wish he would stop looking at me like that.

"I'm sorry, James, but there's nothing I can do about it. I came here today because I want to know what happened. With us. How it started. How—serious it was."

His eyes widen. "Good God. You mean you don't remember?"

I meet his eyes. He looks down at his hands.

"I'm so sorry, James."

"It's all right, miss."

"Would you stop calling me that? I can't stand all this ceaseless formality."

"But it doesn't seem right. Especially now."

"James, you mustn't buy into all that Lady Catherine nonsense about rank and fortune."

"Lady Catherine?"

"Just plain old nonsense then."

James's face releases into a broad grin. "You always did talk like that. I remember all those times you said that someday it wouldn't matter what a man's mother or father was, that someday a man could do whatever he wanted, be whatever he wanted. And that women too would have a say in how the world was run."

I swallow hard. "I did?"

"And you'd make up all those stories. Like the one about the man who lived in a house made of logs and grew up to rule a country. And the black lady who refused to give up her seat in the coach to the white gentleman who demanded it. Which changed the way her people were treated in her country."

The flesh rises on my arms. Abraham Lincoln? Rosa Parks?

"You made those stories sound real," he says softly.

"Tell me more."

"I remember the day we first talked. Mr. Dowling was fleaing me good for dropping a plate, and you heard how he said I would never be anything approaching respectable, that I was a good-for-nothing common lout who had no right waiting on folks of rank and fortune. And afterwards you said, 'James, I've seen little of the world. But I've seen enough to know that rank and fortune do not a respectable man make. What is in a man's heart is what makes him respectable. This I know,' you said, 'from experience.' And then you began to cry so pitifully, like a little child whose heart is broke. I put out my hand and then—"

"Yes?"

"And we—"

"Go on."

"Perhaps it is better we both forget."

"Did we—spend much time together?"

He shakes his head. "It was dangerous."

"But you told your sister?"

"Never. She happened upon us once and never ceased to plague me about it until the day I left your father's house. She said I would ruin you."

"Ruin me? Do you mean we—"

He frowns in confusion, then his eyes widen as comprehension dawns. "No. Good God, no." He flushes and stares at the ground.

"But did I ever tell you—did I ever say that I loved you?"

He shakes his head slowly. "You love me? You always said how I was a kind man, a good man."

He clears his throat and glances to his left, toward two young women walking up the path in our direction. "We should walk."

We set off down a more secluded path, walking in silence for a couple of minutes. Then he reaches into his pocket and pulls out a watch. The way he holds it looks oddly familiar.

He pauses and meets my eyes. "Might I show you something?"

I nod.

He opens the pocket watch and from inside the cover extracts a slim coil of braided dark brown hair, almost black.

"Do you remember?"

I touch the hair, and in a split-second flood of sensations and images I see/feel myself in his arms, crying into his shirt, which is damp with my tears. I'm giving him the braided hair, watching the quiet glow of his face as he puts it in his pocket. And I'm kissing him, hearing him breathe hard, hearing the little moan that escapes as he tightens his arms around me but there's something wrong; it's not how it was with Edgeworth, when my whole body trembled with the force of my need as I held his face in my hands, touching his lips with my own, feeling him pressed against me through my clothes and aching with newly awakened desire. And so I'm pulling away from James, tears stinging my face, a cold knot of shame in my chest. I'm reaching for his hand and holding it to my cheek. *Forgive me*, I say.

"Jane?"

I come back to myself and Sydney Gardens and feel the hot tears running down my cheeks. James's face is full of concern.

"I think I'm remembering something."

Then, I realize I'm holding his hand and, as in my memory, I hold it against my cheek. "Forgive me," I say, and run, without knowing why.

Twenty-three

I half run, half stumble my way out of Sydney Gardens, vaguely aware of scratching my arm on a branch and almost crashing into a woman who seems oddly familiar but whose bloodred ribbons on her bonnet are the only thing about her that make an impression on my brain.

All I can think about are those mind-flashes; no, memories, which is what I have to call them. With every passing day, the lines are becoming less distinct between Jane and me.

I have no idea how I end up in front of the print shop, which is just a few blocks from Mary's aunt's house, but recognizing it is what brings me back to some sense of my surroundings. I realize I'm looking, or at least going through the motions of looking, at the same placid landscape I've seen in the window every day since my arrival, and I can taste a salty trickle of sweat from my upper lip. Yes, the print shop, like the one where Anne Eliot and Admiral Croft had their chat. Connecting where I am to *Persuasion* calms me down somehow, makes order out of chaos. I realize I am parched with thirst, no doubt from running so fast. Suddenly I notice passersby looking at me curiously, and I realize my bonnet is not sitting straight on my head and I'm breathing heavily.

It suddenly strikes me that Jane's almost-affair

with James has a chilling familiarity to it. Didn't I do something similar myself within days of learning about Frank's infidelity? That is, after spending the first two days in an immobilized stupor on Paula's futon. But on the third day, when she managed to drag me to an art opening, I proceeded, with vodka-fueled confidence, to flirt with the nearest young guy who happened to smile at me.

His baby face, tousled hair, and gangly frame made him look suitably harmless. What caught me off guard was his wicked sense of humor. "Someone should really clean that up," he whispered to me as we stood in a crowd trying to make sense of an installation that consisted of what looked like a couple of horse turds and a broomstick lying on a sheet of Mylar. I exploded in laughter, which set us off on a giggling fit that took me right back to junior high school, when teachers would separate me from my friends for laughing in class.

To escape the disapproving looks of our fellow art lovers, Evan—that was his name—and I sidled outside to laugh unencumbered, share cigarettes, and flirt. I agreed to go back to his apartment for a drink, when drinking was clearly the last thing on our minds.

At his place, a rabbit warren of Ikea castoffs, beanbag chairs, and laundry strewn over mattresses on the floor, Evan gazed at me in wonderment when I casually mentioned living alone in my one-bedroom apartment. Apparently a woman who actually had a roommate-less, parent-less living situation was a new kind of experience for him. He, on the other hand, had left his mother's house in Portland to crash in the already overpopulated apartment of a high school friend. Said roommates were out at a big party that night. Evan was only twenty-three, so that explained his perspective somewhat. He was also amazing in bed, which I wasted no time discovering that same night.

Drunk on a surge of ego gratification, I fell asleep with a smile on my face. I didn't need Frank. I was an empowered woman, free of encumbrances. But when I woke up the next morning and stumbled into Evan's bathroom, almost tripped over a pile of scuzzy towels on the floor, and then looked in the mirror, the pasty skin and bloodshot, mascara-smudged eyes of the woman staring back at me looked anything but empowered and free. I still had that gaping hole inside where my certainty about Frank used to be. And so I retreated from Evan's place as fast as I could, promising to call but knowing I wouldn't.

I realize my breathing is now back to normal, and after retying my bonnet and blotting my face with a handkerchief, I'm ready to walk the last few blocks to Mary's aunt's house.

When I enter the house I manage to ward off Mary's anxious questions. "Don't worry," I tell her. “We just had a little chat; he only wanted to ask about his sister.”

After a fortifying cup of tea, I go upstairs to dress for the ball in the assembly rooms, and Mary sends Hortense, her maid, to help me dress and fix my hair. But first, a hot bath, which entails the usual heaving, sweating servants hauling buckets of steaming water up the stairs and then hauling the used water down the same route. Once again, I swallow my guilt, refusing to join the ranks of the unwashed whose bodily odors, inadequately camouflaged by perfumes, assault my nose on a daily basis.

Learning to like living in such an odiferous environment, I suppose, must be an acquired taste, not unlike those rare, expensive cheeses that my high school boyfriend, the German exchange student who was the first guy to cheat on me and break my heart, used to favor for breakfast. The one he loved the most, I remember, smelled like unwashed feet. He used to hold it in front of my face and laugh when I wrinkled my nose in disgust. He claimed that he too used to hate the cheese as much as I did. But one day he surrendered to its smell, and it had been true love ever since.

I didn’t stay with Gerhard long enough to fall in love with his cheese. Nor do I intend to stay here long enough to fall in love with body odor.

After I am laced and buttoned into underclothes and gown, Mary helps me choose accessories.

"The pearls, dear; they make you look like purity itself." If she only knew. However, I have to admit that I look pretty fabulous. Or more accurately, that the face smiling back at me from the mirror looks fabulous, the pale skin accented by the flush of excitement that has rushed to my cheeks, and the frothy fabric of my off-white gown falling in folds that are about as flattering as an empire-waisted dress could ever be.

For a moment I wonder if I have the right to take pride in this appearance, but before I allow myself to fall into the spiraling abyss of that thought, another, more disturbing one, takes over: How in the world am I going to dance?

I put a lacy wrap around my shoulders and focus on making my way down the steps without tripping on my train, right hand firmly gripping the polished wood of the banister. And I decide that tonight will be another adventure into the exotic unknown, even if I can't dance. After all, no one can make me get on the dance floor.

Mary is already waiting for me in the entrance hall; I've been too caught up in my own vanity and worries to notice how pretty she looks.

"Your hair, Mary. It really suits you."

She half moves her hand toward her shiny brown hair, which is woven through with cream-colored ribbon, and then busies herself with arranging her shawl. "That is Hortense's work. Today she was most insistent."

"I love it."

Instead of moving toward the door, Mary sits down on one of the padded benches in the entrance hall.

"Aren't you ready to go?" I say. "Or is something wrong?"

"Mrs. Randolph and your cousin should be here at any moment."

"You're not serious."

"Jane, do you not recall my promising your mother that we would certainly not consider venturing to any balls or parties without Mrs. Randolph?"

"Mrs. M—I mean, my mother—won't know who does or does not go to the ball with us. I never thought for a moment you took that promise seriously."

Mary, who has been removing her fan from her bag, freezes in midmotion. "Upon my honor, I cannot believe you are of such an opinion."

I sit down on the opposite bench and take a deep breath. "You mean to tell me a thirty-year-old woman is not old enough to be a chaperone herself?"

"Not a thirty-year-old woman wearing ribbons in her hair and a white gown that makes her look three-and-twenty. Even if I were to agree to such a scheme—which I would not for reasons of propriety as well as honor—can you imagine what your mother would say if she were to hear of your pretending you were on the shelf in order to go unchaperoned to a ball?"

"Did you do everything your mother told you to do?"

Mary looks thoughtful for a moment. "I believe I tried to do so."

If I did everything my mother wanted me to do, I'd be an MBA married to an MD and driving to PTA meetings in an SUV. As if I would ever have an interest in corporate finance, let alone be caught dead owning a gas-guzzling instrument of global warming.

At that moment, Mrs. Randolph and Susan arrive, the former kissing me on both cheeks, holding my face between her gloved hands and telling me how pretty I look, and the latter wearing a fake smile that I return in kind. I suppose there's not much I can do about the chaperone situation. Not that I mind spending time with Mrs. Randolph, but the daughter—I have only a moment to grumble inwardly, because before I know it I am being led to a bona fide sedan chair. It's an upright rectangular contraption just big enough for one person, something right out of a book on ancient China, and manned by two men, one squat and bowlegged, the other of storklike proportions, who evidently expect to carry me to the ball in it. Assuming this must be some kind of joke, I hesitate at the door, if it could be called such, of the chair, but I see Mary, Mrs. Randolph, and Susan stepping into their own individual chairs as if they do such things every day. And not a smirk among them.

Mary notices my hesitation. "Do not trouble yourself, Jane. You shall be perfectly safe."

She smiles at me encouragingly, and I can do nothing more than acknowledge her with a nod. I feel the gloved hand of one of the footmen on my elbow, and I enter the chair and sit on its padded cushion. Before I know it I am lifted off the ground as if I weighed nothing and carried through the streets at an alarmingly fast pace.

The chair carriers must be even stronger and far more agile than they look, as there is surprisingly little jostling, especially considering the disparity of their heights and builds. I alternate between guilt at being carried by servants, like some potentate, and rushes of excitement as I delight in the sensation of what almost seems like flight.

When we pause at a street corner, I hear the labored breathing of the bowlegged, shorter chair carrier, and I am tempted to insist he stop the chair so that I can apologize for my disgusting bourgeoisieness and ask if the chair carriers have a union. But the chair begins moving rapidly through the streets again, and before I can become the first chair-union organizer in Bath, I am set down beside a building where dozens of other chairs are sitting, passengers are alighting, and scores of gowned and gloved women are taking the arms of men in light-colored knee breeches and white stockings, all moving toward the entrance of the building, which is of the customary light golden Bath stone, a smaller version of the Greek temple style of the Pump Room. My companions join me and I can barely make an intelligible reply, caught up as I am in the spectacle before me.

We enter through the wood-and-glass doors and make our way down a carpeted entrance hallway flanked by marble pillars and illuminated by crystal chandeliers. I am surrounded by the conversation and laughter of the other arrivals and am almost swept away by the crush of the crowd. I feel Mary's hand slip through my arm and her warm breath in my ear as she shouts into it that such a crowd is quite unusual for this time of year.

When we enter the ballroom, the sight of all the dancers sends fresh fear through my veins. What was I thinking? How could I imagine I could pull off this evening? I, the person who never dances at parties and has to be dragged to the floor at clubs—especially after that New Year's Eve party when I danced with Frank (I'd had so many Grey Goose martinis that I would have danced naked in the center lane of the 405 during rush hour). How could I ever forget him backing away from me, mouth twitching, eyes bulging, and collapsing on the floor in convulsions of laughter. "A scorched chicken attempting flight" was how he characterized my efforts. Even a gallon of martinis couldn't soften that particular humiliation.

Even so, as I look around the ballroom at the grandeur of the vast columned space and its sparkling chandeliers, the soft candlelight glowing golden on the gowned and waistcoated dancers, my worries fade. So what if I can't imagine being able to duplicate their steps without tripping over my skirt or wrap or both. I never thought I could embroider either.

Mary squeezes my hand. "It is lovely, is it not?"

It is. The candlelight casts a flattering glow on everyone in the room, from the servants and old gentlemen in their powdered wigs and the young men with their hair *au naturel*, to the women, octogenarians and rosy-cheeked teenagers alike, clad in the uniform empire waistlines and long gloves, necks glittering with diamonds, gold, and pearls. This is the perfect light for a woman forced to appear in public without makeup.

Even the smell of body odor has lost its usual overpowering quality tonight, heavily laced as it is with the mingled scents of soaps, perfumes, and the wax of a thousand melting candles. I can almost understand for a second, even in all my twenty-first-century fastidiousness, that one could come to like the scent of a ballroom. Is that Jane's sensibility, I wonder, that's responding to this particular mélange of scents? Or am I, my real self, responding to something else? Certainly I don't need a nineteenth-century frame of reference to pick up the erotic charge underlying the formality of the curtseys, bows, and nods of this elaborately stylized mating ritual.

Mrs. Randolph stops to talk to a woman who is all dark-green feathered turban and jutting bosom, and Susan is snagged by the woman's daughters. After enduring a quick introduction, I steer Mary deeper into the crowd and farther away from our chaperone. Mary cranes her neck as her eyes search the crowd. "I am determined to find you a partner."

"Mary, I don't think—"

"Jane. It would be shocking if I were to allow you to leave this assembly without putting that new gown to the use for which it was intended."

The musicians strike the first note of the next song from their perch above the floor, and I watch as a young man with sandy brown hair and a dimple in his cheek leads a shy-looking woman onto the floor. Long lines of couples form on the floor and begin turning and crossing one another in graceful, carefully choreographed figures, and I am so mesmerized by the synchronized elegance of the dance that I forget about Mary, that is, until she half falls against my arm and I grab hers to steady her.

"Forgive me," she says, her face bleached of color. I follow her gaze but see nothing out of the ordinary. Not from her perspective, that is. For me, being in a ballroom in Regency-era Bath is about as out of the ordinary as it gets.

"What is it, Mary?"

Mary looks down and shakes her head slightly.

"Some fresh air?" I take her arm and lead her toward the door.

Mary allows me to usher her through the crowd and outside the assembly rooms, where the air is crisp.

After a few minutes, Mary gives me a thin smile. "I am perfectly well again."

"Then why do you look like you just saw a ghost?"

"I thought I saw Will."

"Who's Will?"

Mary's eyes narrow, and she looks at me as if I'm a stranger, which of course I am. "Such a question. And from you, to whom I have confided everything."

"I have no memory of it, Mary."

Mary's expression softens. "Of course you do not. Forgive me." She looks off into the distance.

"But I would like to hear about him now. If you would like to tell me."

"Suffice it to say that Will Templeton was the man I was to marry; that is, until Charles drove him away."

"Your brother?"

"I was not yet of age, I had not yet the independence I now enjoy."

"And Will? Was he underage, too?"

Mary shook her head.

"So why didn't you elope?"

"Will was poor, Charles threatened to cut me off, and it would be three more years until I came into my own money." Mary fans herself vigorously.

"So Will just left."

Mary says nothing.

"Did you ever hear from him?"

She looks down at her shoes.

"How long ago?"

Her voice is a raspy whisper. "Six years."

Mary's hair is a bit mussed from all the fanning, and I smooth back a long strand from her face.

"Mary. Sweetie. Your brother may have been a tyrant, but your man was, I'm sorry to say, a loser. He didn't stand up to your brother. He never wrote to you. Don't you think it's time you moved on?"

Mary glowers at me. "Jane. You look like my friend, but I have no idea who you are."

"I'm only trying to help."

"You are cruel."

"And you are still in love with a man who deserted you six years ago! If I were in that kind of denial over Frank, I hope my friends would talk me out of it."

"Frank? Who is Frank?"

Whoops.

"No one. Absolutely no one. I meant Charles. Your brother. He reminds me of someone—a distant cousin named Frank. I did not accuse you of being cruel when you warned me about your brother, did I?" I put my arm around her shoulder, expecting her to repulse me, but she doesn't.

"Oh, Jane, was I cruel? I did not mean to be." Her brown eyes are imploring.

"Not at all. You said what you thought was necessary to say. As did I. If I weren't your friend I wouldn't talk to you this way. And risk losing your friendship. Which means more to me than you can possibly know."

Mary looks into my eyes, tears running down her cheeks. "I cannot deny that Will was weak. But I shall never forgive Charles."

I hug her, and I feel her relax into my embrace. Then she disengages herself with a sigh. "In truth, I hardly ever think about the matter. Charles and I spend little time in each other's company, and he is invariably civil and attentive to me." She dabs her eyes with a handkerchief and gives me a mischievous smile. "Which I bear as well as I can."

There is a light mist in the air, and I shiver.

Mary takes my arm. "Let us go inside, Jane, for I have not forgot my promise to find you a partner."

I am just about to open my mouth to protest when behind me I hear a familiar voice.

"And I, Miss Mansfield, would be honored to offer my services to you."

Twenty-four

I wheel around to see Edgeworth, who bows and gazes at me with such warmth in his hazel eyes that my knees turn to water. I'm not sure if my inward gasp is actually audible, but I certainly cannot form a syllable of anything intelligible.

"Charles," says Mary, displeasure written all over her face. "This is most unexpected. I had thought your business at Hargrove Court would require a longer stay."

I try not to stare at him in his cream-colored knee breeches and dark blue jacket. I never thought I'd have a crush on a man wearing knee-length white stockings. Actually, before waking up in this place I never imagined seeing a man in any kind of stockings whatsoever. I'm glad he's looking at Mary now and not me, because I'm sure I look like a slack-jawed idiot.

"I find I have more pressing business here." Edgeworth meets my eyes, sending a rush of heat to my face. "And since my uncle informs me his affairs are as disentangled as someone in his situation could ever imagine them to be," he says, lifting an eyebrow, "I passed much of my time being of no more use than a shooting companion to my uncle and a card player for my aunt."

"And do you plan to stay long in Bath?"

"That depends on how long it takes to conclude

my business." He looks at me pointedly, then turns his eyes back to Mary. "I have taken rooms at the White Hart, but Stevens insists I remove to his father's house in the Crescent."

He inclines his head toward a dark-haired, serious-looking man in his late twenties or early thirties, who seems to have been hovering a few steps behind us awaiting his cue.

"You remember Mr. Stevens, do you not, Mary? The younger brother of my old friend Captain Stevens?"

"Of course." Mary smiles on Edgeworth's friend with real warmth. "What a pleasure to see you, Mr. Stevens. It has been many years, I believe."

Stevens bows, stammering something.

Edgeworth turns his face to me, and I notice his smile creates expressive little lines around his eyes. "Miss Mansfield, may I introduce you to my friend, Mr. Stevens?"

Stevens and I dutifully perform our bows and curtseys, and Edgeworth offers me his arm. "Since I collect you are not otherwise engaged, may I have the honor of the next two dances?"

I open my mouth to speak, hoping an excuse will come out, but without waiting for my answer Edgeworth turns to his sister.

"Stevens is most anxious to dance with you, Mary, and only wanted to be assured that you remembered him before he put himself forward."

At this, Stevens turns almost scarlet and bows

again to Mary. "Unless you dislike the idea, Miss Edgeworth."

"Of course not." Mary manages a cheerful smile, though I can tell she feels backed into a corner. However, one look at Stevens's pained expression makes her manners click smoothly into place. She thanks him politely, and with no time for more than a worried glance at me, she allows herself to be led into the ballroom.

Edgeworth extends his hand. "Shall we follow their lead, Miss Mansfield?"

My stomach tightens. How can I possibly imitate the complicated steps and turns of the dancers?

"I can't dance," I manage to murmur.

Edgeworth frowns, puzzled.

"I mean, I don't know how."

His face relaxes. "And I suppose all the times we danced together are evidence of this deficiency? As well as all the times I marveled at how any creature could move with such grace?"

What the hell. If this body remembers how to sew, it probably remembers how to dance as well. And if it doesn't, I'll find out soon enough.

I shrug and give him my hand. As he leads me into the ballroom and across the floor toward the other dancers, the music and conversation and laughter become a soft blur of sounds, and nothing is distinct except the feel of his hand and the beauty of his face as he turns to me and says I have no idea what. It is as if I am an observer of myself as we take our place in the long line of couples.

Then, the music and the conversation and the couples and the room move from the periphery of my consciousness into sharp focus, and I laugh aloud at the realization that I'm dancing as well as anyone around me. I, the most uncoordinated and rhythmically challenged woman in the world, can dance. And not just a freestyle, move-your-body-to-the-music, fake-it sort of dance. But a highly choreographed, stylized sort of dance.

What is even more surprising than the fact that I know how to execute this elegant set of turns and moves is what I feel while performing them with Edgeworth. Every time he faces me, every time he turns me by the hand or crosses shoulders with me or performs any of the figures of the dance with me, it is with an unbroken gaze into my eyes. At first I feel almost too exposed, and I find myself breaking his gaze, only to be drawn into it again. And then I realize this is the way it is supposed to be done, for the gentleman standing diagonally across from me smiles and makes eye contact whenever the dance requires him to turn me or change places with me. But of course it is not the penetrating, I-know-everything-about-you way that Edgeworth looks at me. I can feel him watching me as the other man turns me. I am conscious of displaying the movement of my body as Edgeworth watches. And I observe him with equal intensity as he turns the lady diagonally across from him; she too smiles into his eyes. I am as heated by Edgeworth's gaze as I am by the exertions of the dance itself.

Here is an unbroken space in which a woman and a man may, with the full sanction of society, practically make love to each other with their eyes, their fleeting touch, and the display of their bodies. *Emblem of marriage*, indeed.

As I complete a figure-eight and face Edgeworth, he smiles at me admiringly. "No, Miss Mansfield, I see you cannot dance at all."

That is how Wes looked at me when I told him I was afraid I would never be able to dance at my wedding, that I wanted to take a few lessons to build up my confidence, and that Frank laughed at me for even suggesting it. "I know you can do it," Wes said, and there was no hint of mockery in his face, only admiration.

"How do you know?" I said.

"Because I have faith in you, Courtney. In fact, I'm taking those lessons with you. And we'll see who can't dance."

"Miss Mansfield?" Edgeworth's voice and playful smile bring me back to the dance. "Such a faraway look on your face. May I accompany you there?"

He is so beautiful, his hair golden in the candlelight and his cheeks flushed with the dance, that I say, "I wish you could."

"Ah. A secret place. Perhaps one day you will do me the honor."

What would he say if I told him the truth? He'd never believe it. Mary doesn't, and who could blame her. I look over at Mary, who is dancing with Mr. Stevens a few couples down the line from us. She appears to be enjoying talking to Stevens, who actually breaks into a smile that transforms his face into something animated and almost attractive.

"It appears my sister has an admirer," Edgeworth says, "and I could not hope for a more respectable and good-natured sort of person. Stevens is of a good family, and though he is but a younger son, he has a tolerably handsome income."

"And I suppose you know better than your sister what sort of man is right for her."

Edgeworth's hazel eyes widen. "No more than any caring brother would, I imagine."

What presumption. "I imagine your sister would see it differently."

My own anger surprises me, as does the sharpness of his answer.

"I imagine my sister and I differ on a number of matters."

"Such as her own ability to gauge the worth of the men in her life?"

The look on his face is almost sorrowful as he passes by my shoulder. "Is my sister still nursing the fairy story she told herself six years ago? If so, I am sorry to hear it."

Then he nearly turns the wrong way. "Good God. Is that what caused you to change toward me?"

He looks at me searchingly, but I tear my eyes away. I have no answers. Only other people's versions of events and fragments of memories that aren't even my own. Most especially my borrowed memory of him with the auburn-haired woman at the stables. None of which I can reconcile with how much I want to acquit him of whatever he may have done.

Of course I want to acquit him. Aren't I always willfully blind when I'm attracted to a man? I want to ask Edgeworth if the scene in question really occurred, but how can I? I/Jane obviously wasn't supposed to have witnessed that scene, or even to have been where I/she was at the time. Who knows what the circumstances were? It's so frustrating to not even know if it's real. Here I am, already existing in some half-life as someone else—how can I get my mind around the idea of trying to verify a half-memory?

The second dance ends, and Edgeworth is still waiting for my answer. All I can say is, "I don't know."

"From one minute to the next, you go from friend to executioner."

Mary and Stevens are walking toward us. Just before they reach us he whispers urgently into my ear, his warm breath sending a tingle down the back of my neck, "For even *the kindest and the happiest pair will find occasion to forbear; And something, every day they live, to pity, and perhaps forgive.* Do you remember, Jane? Are you not tempted to hear the accused testify before pronouncing your final sentence?"

The kindest and the happiest pair will find occasion to forbear. I know those words. But how?

He holds my gaze so deeply that it is almost unbearable. Of course he must be innocent. Mary herself had no excuse for why Will Templeton deserted her. But there still remains that image of Edgeworth with the woman at the stables. I know what I saw.

And then, all at once, another piece of the puzzle falls into place. Could this memory have any relationship to Mary's story of Edgeworth's affair with the servant in her house, a story I initially dismissed as exaggerated prudishness on Mary's part?

Why didn't I put the two together before?

Everything in me is shouting a warning, yet it's all I can do to stop myself from saying that I don't even want to know what he did, because I don't want him to be guilty. I can't remember ever having been so viscerally attracted to anyone in my life, not even to Frank. Not even close. And that makes my stomach turn cold with fear. It's the same sensation I had after I ran into Wes on Vermont—which was right before I ended up here—that realization of how attracted to him I was. I can still see the pain in his gray-blue eyes as I rushed past him to get out of that store. "Courtney," he said. "I am so sorry." I have to get away before Wes—I mean, Edgeworth—turns my powers of reason into mush. As if they aren't already.

Someone rings a bell, and Mary decides we need tea. I go through the motions of searching with my little group for a table in the tearoom without actually being in my body, which, I must bear in mind, isn't really my body anyway. For once I find that thought comforting. I need the distance it provides. I nod and smile at all the right moments, or maybe not, because I catch Mary as well as Edgeworth looking at me strangely a couple of times. I just want to get out of here, and though I don't like the idea of making Mary leave when she's obviously enjoying being with Mr. Stevens, who's paying a lot of attention to her, in the end it's she who suggests, and then insists, that we go home early. As she puts it, I am "too easily knocked up from all the exercise."

Pursing my lips to keep from laughing, I can't help but think that only a horizontal type of exercise is likely to render the effect she mentioned. And how unlikely I am to participate in such an activity when I can't even go to a ball without a chaperone.

Mary whispers to me that we should find Mrs. Randolph and Susan, whose bright red hair I easily spot on the other end of the room. I catch Mrs. Randolph's eye and wave, and Mary and I make our way to their table, Edgeworth and Stevens in tow. Susan immediately latches on to Edgeworth, hinting broadly that she wants to dance. Edgeworth mumbles something about needing to escort us home if Mrs. Randolph and she are not yet ready to leave, but that he would be honored if she would be so kind as to stand up with him when he returns.

Mrs. Randolph kisses me on the cheek and says into my ear, "Oh, well, my dear. She will have her way, you know. Better to give in to the small things, I always say."

The ride home in Edgeworth's carriage is short and silent. He sits opposite Mary and me, and I can barely meet his eyes. I only look into his face for a second when he hands me out of the carriage, and all I want to do is say something, anything that will make him smile at me again and make me feel how I felt when we were dancing, before I ruined everything. Wait a minute. I didn't ruin anything. I'm only trying to protect myself, which is what any sane person would do in my situation.

On the other hand, the word "sane" coupled with my situation is debatable.

Later, I lie in bed looking out at the stars, the covers balled up on the floor, sleep an elusive concept. And I realize that I might never know the truth about Edgeworth. Even if I confronted him with what I or Jane saw, and even if he came up with the best explanation in the world, it would still be his word against my fears, his promises against my experience with the most accomplished liars and cheaters in the world.

Twenty-five

Over the next few days, Mary makes sure that she and I are out when Edgeworth calls, though she never once admits this is what she's up to. But it's not difficult to figure out why she just has to get to the Pump Room an hour and a half earlier than we usually do, or why she tells Mrs. Jenkins to have dinner ready for us an hour later than she usually does, or why she has an urge to worship in a different church on Sunday. I know it's best that I keep my distance, but every time we enter the house I scan the table in the entrance hall for visiting cards. And every time Mrs. Jenkins tells her mistress that Mr. Edgeworth called I catch my breath. I wonder how long this can go on before we run into him—or before he leaves Bath. If only I could see him once more before that happens. No. I will not engage in such absurd behavior. I have had quite enough betrayal.

On the fourth morning after the ball, I'm getting ready for breakfast and can't find my tortoiseshell comb. I rummage through a blue knit purse and pull out a crumpled piece of paper. It's the handbill for the fair that I found on the ground the day I met James in Sydney Gardens. I'd completely forgotten about it. I look at the paper more closely: Good God, today is the day of the fair. I've been so caught up in retracing Jane's past through James and Edgeworth that I forgot my original plan, which was to go to the fair. And now there's no time for resorting to subterfuge; I'll have to come right out and ask Mary to take me. That, I believe, would suit both of us.

But when I come to the breakfast table, my speech all prepared, Mary is sniffling and wiping her nose with a handkerchief.

"Are you all right?"

Before she can answer, a sneeze shakes her body, and she blows her nose.

"You poor girl." I put my hand on her forehead, which is only slightly warm. "I don't think you have a fever, or at least not much of one, but you should go back to bed immediately. Why don't I have Mrs. Jenkins bring a tray to your room?"

Mary sniffs. "But what about our plan to find some new ribbon for your bonnet?" Her voice is raspier than ever. "I would hate to spoil the day over a silly little cold."

"What would be sillier is if you went out like this. As for my bonnet, I doubt that one more day, or even twenty types of ribbon, would make much difference."

Aided by Mrs. Smith, who is as set against Mary's going out as I am, I persuade her to go to bed, and I extract a promise that she'll stay there the rest of the day. I know that her strict sense of honor will not allow her to go back on her word, even after Mrs. Smith leaves the room and I break the news to Mary of my intended outing. I would rather keep it a secret, now that it's clear she can't possibly go with me, but quite frankly I need her carriage. The fair is outside of Bath, and I'm hardly prepared to start figuring out how to hire myself some transportation.

It takes some persuading to convince Mary that I have no intention of releasing her from her promise to stay in bed, as well as that I have no intention of wavering in my plans to go to the fair, with or without her.

"Very well. I shall send Mrs. Smith with you," she says.

"You know as well as I that she'll insist on staying here to take care of you."

"Hortense, then. She is a good sort of girl, and I do trust her discretion."

"I refuse to have Hortense glued to my side, especially if I have my fortune told."

"Do be reasonable, Jane. This is not merely a question of propriety; it is dangerous for a lady to go to such a place alone."

"But there will be people everywhere."

"Exactly. I shall send Hortense, and that is the end of it."

Mary launches into a fit of coughing, and I surrender to the inevitable. After I fuss around her a bit, plumping her pillows and tucking her in, she begins to look like she might even take a nap.

"You will be careful, Jane?"

I kiss her softly on the forehead. "I promise."

Her face relaxes and she snuggles into her pillows, and I leave her room shaking my head at the absurdity of having to bring an entourage with me. It's like being unable to go to the movies without a limo driver and personal assistant in tow.

As the carriage rattles its way to the fair, I wonder how I'm going to ditch Hortense when we arrive. What I want is the freedom to wander around, look for the fortune-teller, and drink in the atmosphere as Jane might have experienced it, and I don't want company.

Not an easy wish to fulfill. Turns out that not only has Mary saddled me with a limo driver and personal assistant, but a bodyguard as well. This one is in the form of a liveried footman who, at a nod from the coachman, follows us from the coach.

Hortense is so childlike in her enthusiasm for the noisy groups of pleasure seekers and colorful booths, the jugglers and vendors and squawking of chickens, not to mention a couple of young men, one of whom winks at her as soon as he catches her eye, that I figure I could easily persuade her to enjoy herself on her own. However, the footman appears to be impervious to anything but his assigned task.

Unless . . . I turn around and look at him. "Would you be so kind as to see if I dropped a letter on the ground? Back there?" I point in the opposite direction of where we were walking. "It was in my pocket just a minute ago."

The footman glances behind him, then back at me uncertainly.

I smile in an attempt to reassure him. "I'll wait for you right here."

He cuts his eyes at Hortense, then bows to me. "Very well, miss. I shall be back directly."

Watching his retreating figure disappear into the thickening crowd, I pull coins from my purse and put them in Hortense's hand. "Why don't you buy us all some gingerbread from that nice old woman over there?"

Hortense looks toward the vendor, who is only about five yards away.

I point to another booth that's about halfway between where I'm standing and the gingerbread lady. "I'll be right there, looking at ribbon."

"But what about . . . ?" She gestures in the direction the servant went to hunt for my nonexistent letter.

"You're right. I'll wait here."

"Yes, miss." Hortense drops a curtsey and scurries off to buy gingerbread, and as soon as my view of her is blocked by the crowd I take off.

Oh, the comfort of being sometimes alone! I know how Jane Fairfax must have felt after ditching her companions and throwing off the oppression of social niceties, if only for an hour. I wander around the fair, trying to blend in with the crowd while keeping a watchful eye out for my entourage. It's a mixed crowd of people, many of them from the working classes, but also a fair number of middle-class folks and some high-collared, carefully coiffed, spit-shine-booted young men who weave and stumble in the unmistakable manner of those who've had too much to drink.

Are the looks I'm getting from some of the men—the more refined-looking ones as well as the ones who look like farmers—more leering than they were when I had Hortense and the footman by my side? Or is that my imagination? No matter. It's still nothing compared to what I became used to in my student days in New York, when I developed what I called my jungle stare-down. That look usually scared a couple of my friends much more than it did my targets, but I never got mugged or unduly hassled.

I pause for a moment to look at a puppet show, or rather to wonder how so many adults could possibly be as amused as they apparently are by the crude theatrics on the tiny stage. In the midst of the rough laughter and continual talking of the rowdy audience, I feel someone standing just behind my left shoulder. The tiny hairs on the back of my neck stand up, and I turn to see a man, his face hidden by shadows, bow deeply to me and say, "If you please, miss, my mistress is expecting you."

His voice is barely a whisper, but I have no

trouble hearing him. Before I can say anything in reply, he gently indicates the direction in which he wishes me to go, and I follow one step behind him, arguing with myself that I should be on my guard, that he could be some kind of lunatic or cutthroat, but unable to convince myself of being in any kind of danger.

He stops at a small tent and turns to me. "My mistress will be with you directly." Then he bows again and disappears into the crowd.

The man must have recognized me. Could I possibly be so blessed as to meet up with the same fortune-teller that Jane saw? But nothing outside the tent indicates who or what is inside. No sign or decoration, just plain, mud-brown cloth that is patched in a couple of places.

As I wait outside the dingy tent, a red-faced, grimy-looking man of indeterminate age emerges, reeking of alcohol. All gap-toothed smiles, he waves at another man, evidently a friend, who's waiting for him a few feet from the tent. The red-faced one triumphantly holds up a little drawstring bag and shows it to his companion, loudly proclaiming how he "got the goods" and "just wait till ol' Martin gets a bit o' this lot in 'is porter. That'll teach 'im."

Oh great. I've gone to all this trouble to see a quack who pushes love potions for the lonely or laxatives for the vengeful. Maybe I should just turn around and get the hell out of here. Suddenly I feel heavy and tired. Despite my skepticism, I didn't realize till now how much hope I'd been hanging on this event.

A whiff of something in the air distracts me. Delicious, sweet. Could it be freesia? I move without thinking toward the fragrance, which appears to be coming from the tent. As I move closer, the flaps part gently, and I find myself walking inside.

Softly lit by candles, the inside of the tent glows invitingly. Though it's made of thin fabric, the sounds and bustle of the fair outside are obliterated. The welcoming, citrus-sweetness of freesia makes me want to linger there forever. A thought lazily flits through my mind that I'm being enchanted somehow by its proprietress, but I don't care. That's when I notice her, though she could hardly have escaped my notice when I entered.

She's old, with a kind, grandmotherly bearing. She smiles at me with perfect teeth, unusual for an old person here. Her dress is black and simply cut. Her shawl is richly embroidered silk, but not overdone. There's no jewelry, bangles, big earrings, nothing fortune-teller–like about her appearance.

"You were expecting someone different?" she asks, and before I can protest she's suddenly middle-aged, black-haired, gaudily dressed, and jeweled from head to toe.

I gasp, and she switches back to her grandmotherly self. "Either way suits me. You choose." Her voice is silky smooth.

"How did you do that?"

"For the people who come to me, I am whoever they need me to be. Smells lovely in here, doesn't it?"

"I love freesia. But I don't see any flowers in here."

She looks at me impishly and shrugs her shoulders as if to say, *And your point would be . . .*

I laugh.

She sits up straighter and indicates the chair opposite her for me to sit. "Now, what can I do for you today?"

"I just want you to know that I don't want to put any spells or whatever on anyone else, like that man who was in here before."

"Oh, him." She rolls her eyes. "I gave the poor creature exactly what he wanted. A powder that will do no harm to the man he wishes to harm. So he can keep on blaming someone other than himself for how miserable he is. Those who want the truth, get truth. Those who want lies, get lies no matter what I say."

She looks me over for a moment, and I feel the flesh rise on my arms. "Though you are getting bits of the other one's memories, I do not see that your last visit to me is one of them. So I shall tell you what I told her."

Liquid light floods my veins. To be talking to

someone who knows! Who understands without my having to say a word. I start laughing with the pure joy of it, tears running down my cheeks.

She takes my hands in hers. "Jane was someone who did not want truth, though she needed it most urgently. She longed to have a different life; she found her own suffocating. I told her that wherever and whatever she placed her attention would manifest in her life. And that she had a destiny to fulfill. It's no use fighting our destiny, you know."

"I don't understand."

"I know, dear. But I have faith you will."

"But how could I just fall out of my life and end up here, in Jane's? And in a different time? Can I leave here and return to my old life in the future? Will Jane come back to hers if I do?"

"What could I say that would make sense to you? You who believe time is as rigid as a straight line."

She raises her cup of wine, lets a few drops fall out of the glass, swirls the liquid around inside for me to see. "Time is as fluid as the wine in this cup. You can be here, and you can be wherever you came from. What is real right now is where your attention lies. You have chosen to focus on where you believe you are right now."

"Wait just a minute. I haven't *chosen* anything. I went to sleep and woke up here. And haven't been able to get back home since."

"Choosing happens in many different ways. Our

heart chooses for us, or a tiny whisper inside that is too faint for us to hear."

"Whatever. I still want to know how this happened."

"There are many possibilities. The night your attention left your home was a time of a rare planetary configuration, the likes of which had not been seen in hundreds of years. Such a formation takes the fluid quality of time and makes it like quicksilver, with little clusters forming, breaking apart, and reforming. Then it becomes like the air, floating, escaping through the tiniest openings, before it becomes its usual liquid state. Anything is possible during such events. It is when the doors that are already there open wider than ever before, and time defies its usual boundaries, if boundaries they could ever be called."

"But why me? Why Jane?"

"You are linked, as we all are. The idea that I am actually separate from you is just an idea, not the whole truth. Surely your desires and fantasies about this time, as you call it, are evidence of your connection to Jane. Both she and you must have done something that ripped apart the barriers of what we refer to as time and space."

"Like what?"

"A dream, a wish made, an illness, a mishap . . ."

"Wait. Jane did have a bad fall before I came here and took her place."

"Ah, yes. I warned her of it."

"But what about me? I didn't have an accident."

"Are you sure?"

"Don't you think I would know such a thing?"

"Of course, my dear."

"Then what could it be?"

"Does it matter?"

"Jane isn't taking over my old life, is she?"

She smiles, her eyes full of compassion. "There is no old life or new life. There is only life. And I can tell you only what you can hear."

"But can she return here? And can I go back to who I was?"

"Only a fool would wish to go back to who he was."

"You can't mean that."

"Do not take what I say so literally. Of course you can return to your old life, as you put it. As Jane can return to hers."

I jump out of my chair. "I could kiss you! How do I get back?"

"Ah, yes. That is the question. How."

I don't like the sound of this.

"Sit, sit," she says, and I do.

She reaches for my hands and holds them firmly but gently. "You, like everyone else, have a destiny to fulfill. You must stop resisting your destiny. Be where you are right now. Live your life. You are only hurting your chances by struggling so, just as Jane struggled."

"But this isn't *my* life!"

Her black eyes bore into me.

I can only croak out a whisper. "Is it?"

"Did you think this was just some accident?"

The flesh rises on my arms. "I don't know what to think."

"Perhaps then it is best you do not think at all. It is something you do entirely too much of, my dear."

She reaches for a teapot and pours two cups of tea, then gently smiles at me and hands me one. I take a sip. Delicious. I wonder how she heats tea when there's no fire or stove, but I don't want to ask.

"What's been going on in my old life while I've been here? I mean, I can't very well be in two places at once . . ."

"My dear, all these questions will give you the headache, to be sure. You shall discover all when you are ready."

Come to think of it, my head is beginning to ache. I rub my temples and look at her. Is this her doing?

She hands me another cup filled with warm liquid. "Here. This will ease the pain."

I sip it and instantly the throbbing stops, replaced by a calming balm throughout my entire body. Nineteenth-century Vicodin? Somehow I don't mind being drugged by her. Or is that the drug talking?

My mind drifts to Edgeworth. "May I ask you another question?"

The woman raises her eyebrows and gives me an impish grin. "Ah, love. That is what they all wish to know. Let me see . . ."

She produces a smoky crystal ball, makes some theatrical wavings over it, and says in an equally dramatic voice, "You will marry a tall, handsome stranger."

"Come on. Be serious."

"Oh, but I am serious, my dear."

My heart pounds. "Edgeworth?"

"What do I look like? A fortune-teller?" At that she becomes the hoop-earringed gypsy again. She laughs so hard that she begins to cough, and at my not-so-amused reaction she collects herself and gently takes my hand again.

"You take yourself far too seriously, my dear. Besides, he is not your problem. Nor is the other one; Frank is his name? Or your friend Wes, for that matter. Your problem is your mind, which, as I said before, does entirely too much thinking. You know, it is a little known fact that thinking is entirely overrated. The world would be a much better place if we all did a lot less of it."

She pats my hand. "There, there. It will all work out. Now, let us conclude our business. How shall you wish to pay for my services today?"

Flustered, I stammer, "I, uh, hadn't thought of it. What would you like?"

"I would like to have your lovely pearl necklace. Yes, that would suit me."

"But I don't have it with me."

"Do you not?"

I touch my bare neck and reach for my purse. I open it to show her. "See, all I have is some money and a handkerchief."

"Look again."

I follow her eyes to the inside of my purse. And there it is, the strand of pearls I wore to the ball the other night.

I look at her, then back at the pearls. "But how—"

"If you could be here, coming from so far away and in such another time, why would it be so difficult for your pearls to make a mere trifle of a journey?"

She smiles and holds out her hand, and I put the strand of pearls in it.

I start at the sound of a deep, male voice behind me. "Forgive me, madam, you must away."

I turn to see the man who led me here standing in the now open tent flaps, his features obscured by the brightness of the sunlight behind him. I turn back to the fortune-teller, whose eyes register only a flicker of alarm.

"There is talk of arrest," he says to her. "You must make haste."

"On what charge?"

"Murder." He holds up a dusty drawstring bag, like the one the red-faced man carried out of the tent. "This here was found with the corpse."

"Preposterous. What is in there wouldn't harm a baby."

"Still, you must away. And fast. There's talk of witchcraft."

He turns toward me with a slight bow. "Begging your pardon, miss, but if I was you I'd make haste."

I can hear the faint pounding of horses' hooves and men's voices shouting. The fortune-teller, once again a plainly dressed old woman, snatches up a large linen bag, stuffs a few items in it. "Go," she says to me. "Now."

"But I still don't—"

"Stop struggling to be somewhere else." She's already starting to crawl under the tent on the opposite side of the flaps, the man moving quickly to assist her. "Fulfill your destiny."

The frenzied sounds of the approaching crowd and the neighing of horses are getting closer.

"I don't understand." My heart pounds with the rhythm of the horses' hooves.

Her body is halfway through the underside of the tent, surprisingly agile for such an old woman. "Just be where you are. That is the only way to get where you're supposed to go."

She disappears behind the tent, and I can feel the man's hands pulling me toward the floor, helping me crawl through the same small opening. I scrape my knee as my dress hikes up, then scramble to my feet and feel his hands pushing me toward a crowd of pleasure-seekers who are still enjoying the fair and merely curious about the approaching horses. I look around to thank him, but he's gone. Hands shaking, I make a weak attempt to straighten my dress and dust myself off while walking briskly and trying to act composed, the result being that I stumble into a high-collared, foppishly dressed young man with a sweaty red face.

He puts an arm around my waist. "I say," he whispers into my face, his sour, beery breath nearly making me gag. "Where are you off to all by yourself?"

I try to extricate myself, but his grip is like iron.

"Get off me!"

"Leave the lady alone, Stiles." This one's in his twenties, impeccably dressed and sober. Stiles loosens his grip, and I pull away.

Stiles's friend makes me a sort of half bow and a shrug, grabs the sweaty one's arm, and hauls him away.

I shoulder my way through the crowd, pushing against a tide of thrill-seekers who are surging toward all the excitement. I hear the words "murder" and "arrest" several times. I shudder, and hope to God my fortune-teller has managed to get away.

Twenty-six

At the edge of the fair, I spot Mary's coach and her coachman. With a great surge of relief, I run toward him. Grim-faced, he bows stiffly. I catch sight of Hortense, who is huddled against the back of the coach, wiping her tear-stained face with a corner of her shawl. She straightens up when she sees me, and bobs a curtsey with downcast eyes.

"Hortense, you're not upset because I—because we got separated?"

"No, miss," she mumbles, her eyes on the hard-packed dirt of the road.

As she and I settle into the coach, I see my erstwhile bodyguard walking toward it, looking apprehensively at the coachman. The coachman's back is to me, but whatever is on his face causes the footman to flinch.

When the coach rattles off down the little country road, I turn to Hortense, who is attempting to hide her tears by covering her face with her shawl.

"What is it then, Hortense?"

She uncovers her face, her eyes red and swollen.

"When I went looking for you, miss, there was all these men on horseback talking of murder and hanging. They were so angry that I swear if they weren't getting near to doing more murder. Two of the ones on foot began hitting each other, and two more joined in, and the magistrate had a time of it making them stop. I was near frightened out of my wits, but that wasn't the worst of it—"

"You mean they didn't find the murderer."

"They did not, miss, I am sorry to say."

"Good."

"Begging your pardon, miss?"

"Good that you told me, I meant. Anyway, you're safe now."

"Begging your pardon, miss, but I don't—" With that, she retreats under her shawl again, her shoulders shaking with sobs. After a couple of futile attempts to get her to talk, which only seem to upset her more, I give up.

When we arrive home, I check on Mary, who is asleep. Mrs. Smith is dozing in a chair by her side, a book on her lap. I tiptoe out, and realize how hungry I am. Might as well have a dinner tray sent up to my room.

A couple of hours later I am contemplating the pink and gold sky from my window and puzzling over the fortune-teller's words when Mary storms into my room.

"Is it true, Jane?" She has her hands on her hips, her brown eyes trained on me.

"Mary, what are you doing out of bed?"

"Hortense said she did not know whether I would be angrier if she told me herself what happened at the fair, or if I found out from my coachman."

"Is that what she's so upset about?"

Mary's eyes narrow. "So it is true. Do you know my coachman told her he would urge me to dismiss her? That he has already urged me to dismiss Matthew, not for any reason he chose to disclose to me, of course."

"Who's Matthew?"

Mary laughs, but without humor. I've never seen her like this. "Matthew is the footman I sent to watch over you at the fair. For someone who claims to care about the welfare of servants, your actions say something quite different."

"This is insane. They had no idea what I was going to do."

"How could you, Jane? How could you put yourself in such danger?"

"I just wanted to be by myself. I didn't think—"

"No, you most certainly did not. If you care nothing for your own safety, your own reputation, have you no thought for mine?"

"Mary, I'm begging you. Please don't send Hortense or Matthew away." I grab her hands, hot tears springing from my eyes.

Mary gives me a long look, then sinks into a chair. "Oh, Jane. What am I going to do with you?"

I squeeze her hands, and her face relaxes into tenderness. "Besides never speak to me again?" I ask.

"Do be serious."

"I won't cause you any more grief. I won't play any more tricks on the servants. I promise."

She pulls out a handkerchief and wipes away my tears.

"Are we still friends?"

"Have you no more faith in me than that?" she says with her sweet smile.

"What about Hortense and Matthew?"

Mary pats my hand. "They are safe. I cannot expect a footman, let alone a silly girl I had a notion to train up as a lady's maid, to be gaolers. I shall say it was all a mistake, that you saw your cousins in the crowd, went to greet them, and lost sight of Hortense and Matthew. That may satisfy John coachman as well."

Mary goes off to make peace with her servants and then early to bed, and I spend the rest of the night pondering what were—and what could have been—the consequences of my actions. Just as Elizabeth Bennet reflected on Darcy's social position and the responsibility it entailed, I reflect on my own. *As a brother, a landlord, a master, she considered how many people's happiness were in his guardianship!—How much of pleasure or pain it was in his power to bestow!—How much of good or evil must be done by him!* And I see how much power even a single woman who is dependent on her parents, who can't even go to a ball without a chaperone, has over the welfare of others. No matter how unwillingly I might have assumed guardianship of Jane's life, the power that comes with it is mine as well.

• • •

The next morning, Mary behaves as if we never had a disagreement. In fact, when I bring up the previous day's debacle she tells me not to distress either of us by mentioning it again. Even Hortense gives me a timid smile with her curtsey. Mary doesn't even ask if I got to see the fortune-teller, and I'm happy not to have to tell her half-truths.

Before breakfast, she announces her intention to return to the hot baths. Her cold is nearly gone, and the hot baths will be the crowning cure. I try my best to talk her out of it, but she's determined. I can only hope that her absolute faith in the powers of those putrid waters will provide not only a placebo effect against any cold that might still be lingering, but also guard her against picking up something new.

After Mary leaves with Mrs. Smith for the baths, I spend the first part of my time alone pacing my room and thinking about what the fortune-teller said. Obsessing is more like it; it's too irresistible not to do so. I try to take my mind off it by answering a letter I received from Mrs. M yesterday. I hate to do it, but after all, she does hold the purse strings.

Happily, I discover that I can play dutiful daughter while indulging my taste for passive-aggressive behavior. To wit: I pointedly ignore her questions as to whether I've heard any news of Edgeworth from his sister. I gleefully imagine

Mrs. M worrying over whether Mrs. Talbot's matrimonial plans for her daughter are progressing. With even more glee I deny her even the bare fact that I have seen him. No doubt she'll hear about it from Mrs. Randolph, but that will only increase her aggravation at not having heard it from me first. Excellent. I smile as I drip wax on the edges of the paper to seal the letter.

Now what? I try losing myself in my embroidery, but my hands are independent of my brain, which rehashes over and over what the fortune-teller said, what I said, what I should have asked her but didn't, what she might have meant but perhaps I misinterpreted, ad infinitum.

Then, somehow, without preamble, I go into that semi-meditative state that I have experienced several times while embroidering, and I am completely at peace. And every time the thought of how I'm going to leave here and what I should do comes up, I simply decide that I will not obsess. And I don't.

For me, this behavior is nothing short of miraculous. Of course, the old behavior keeps poking its nose into my peace every now and again. *You're in denial*, it says. *You're getting sucked into Jane's life*. And even worse, *You're possessed.*

And still, a new voice, a calmer and quieter voice, keeps coming back to echo the fortune-teller's words. *Be where you are now. Stop struggling to be somewhere else.*

New-age platitudes, the old voice sneers.

New age, my foot, I say. From my vantage point, looking out the window at horse-drawn carriages, bonneted women strolling arm in arm, and men rushing by in tall hats and morning coats, the world looks anything but new. At least by my old standards.

That shuts up the old voice. For now.

"Jane?"

I bolt up from a slumped position on one of the drawing room sofas, my neck stiff and sore.

"What time is it? I must have fallen asleep."

"It is time to get those ribbons for your bonnet. The bath did me a great deal of good, the sun is shining, and a walk to Milsom Street is just what I need. Mrs. Smith has engaged to spend the rest of the day with an old school friend, and I am in need of your company."

I shrug the kinks out of my neck and shoulders. Actually, Mary does look better. Her skin has a healthy glow, and the pale yellow dress she has on is perfect with her coloring.

"Give me a minute to get my things."

About ten minutes later we have just reached Pulteney Bridge when Mary, who has been walking beside me, stops abruptly, grabs my arm and turns completely around, blocking my path, her face about three inches away from mine. She opens her mouth to speak, but nothing comes out.

Then her body sags, and I grab both of her arms to steady her.

"What is it? Are you ill?" If she collapses on the street I don't know how I'm going to get her home.

"It is he—right there—do not look—dear Lord, do not let me faint in his presence." Her face is white and her lips are trembling.

"What? Who?"

Still grasping my arm with one of her hands, Mary fumbles in her bag with the other and extracts a handkerchief. She dabs at her brow, her voice a raspy whisper. "Please. Say nothing. And no matter what, do not release my arm."

She turns back around, while I hold her arm, bracing myself, for what I have no idea. And then I see a thirtyish man and a tall, striking-looking woman of about the same age walking deliberately toward us.

"Miss Edgeworth. What a delightful surprise." The man's voice is deep and smooth. He bows and then regards her appraisingly, with a familiarity I don't like. "It *is* still Miss Edgeworth?"

Mary nods. "Indeed it is." Her voice is strong again, but I can feel her trembling.

"I cannot say I am sorry to hear it," he says, raising an eyebrow. His eyes are large, almost black, with the illusion of being outlined and the kind of long, thick lashes that women are never lucky enough to be born with. His full lips curve into a smile, revealing large white teeth. The better to eat you with, little girl.

I squeeze her arm. She turns her head toward me, her eyes a mute appeal. And then: "Allow me to introduce Mr. Templeton to you."

Templeton? Will Templeton? No wonder she's trembling. This is the man she was—probably still is—in love with. Not only is she running into him for the first time in years, but he is with another woman, probably his wife. I get hold of myself and we exchange courtesies. Is anyone going to say anything about the elephant in the room, i.e., the woman on Templeton's arm? No demure virginal type, this one, with cleavage up to her neck and a dress that somehow manages to cling to every curve, despite the empire waist. She's observing us from behind heavy lids, a look of detached amusement on her face.

I hold onto Mary's arm with one hand and stroke her arm reassuringly with the other.

Mary clears her throat. "Would you do me the honor of introducing me to your wife?"

Templeton exchanges an amused glance with the woman. "Miss Edgeworth, Miss Mansfield, this is Mrs. Lawrence, an old family friend."

Mrs. Lawrence entwines her arm even closer within Templeton's, as if to demonstrate just how close a friend she is.

"I beg your pardon," Mary says, curtseying to Mrs. Lawrence.

Mrs. Lawrence arches an eyebrow and looks like she's struggling to hold in her laughter.

"What brings you to Bath?" Mary says to Templeton, her face now bright red.

"Oh that." His black eyes twinkle with amusement as he exchanges a conspiratorial smirk with Mrs. Lawrence. "I have come in search of my wife."

And then he looks at both of us confidentially and lowers his voice, as if we're a couple of guys throwing back a few beers after work. "Like many women born into wealth, she does not understand the business of men, nor should she. I have the unhappy task of explaining that to her and bringing her back home, which is where she belongs.

"With all due respect to the ladies here present," and he makes a sort of flourish with his hand, like a courtier's bow, "there is divine wisdom behind the principles that put a woman's property into the hands of her husband, and make his word her law."

I do my best to skewer him with my eyes. "I have news for you, sir. Those days are numbered." I can feel Mary almost sinking against me, and I put my arm around her. "And you," I say to Mrs. Lawrence, who is stifling a yawn, "should be ashamed." Her only reply is a bored shrug.

"Come on, Mary," I say, steering her back toward the house. "This conversation is over."

Templeton calls after us, "I hope to repeat the

pleasure of seeing you again, Miss Edgeworth. With or without your lively friend."

He laughs, and I feel Mary stiffen against me. "Keep walking," I say, stealing a glance at her face, which is death on a stick. "We're almost there. Don't look back," I tell her. "Never look back."

Twenty-seven

About half an hour later, Mary timidly peeks in at the doorway to my room, and I jump up, motioning for her to come in. I've been waiting for her, figuring that once she's cried herself out she might want to talk.

Her face is blotchy, and her eyes are rimmed in red. I move toward her, wanting to give her a hug, but she holds me off, her palms up.

"No, Jane. I do not deserve your pity. I, who have turned you against my brother. Charles spoke the truth about Will, but I refused to see it."

"You're too hard on yourself."

Mary starts pacing the room, becoming more agitated with every step. "How could I not see how odd it was that Will never renewed our friendship, even after I came of age? How could I see only cruelty in Charles, rather than the natural feelings of a brother?"

She pauses in her pacing and flushes to the roots of her hair.

"And now I can hardly look you in the eye, dearest friend. For did I not accuse Charles of fathering my servant's child, and did I not try to convince you of his guilt as well?"

"What does that have to do with Will?"

"Can you not see that nothing is what it seems?"

All I can see is the recurring image of Edgeworth

brushing bits of straw from his coat, the pretty auburn-haired woman emerging from the stables, and the way she touches his arm. True, Edgeworth didn't mistreat Mary or her boyfriend, as it turns out. But as for that incident at the stables, I'm afraid the evidence is more than circumstantial.

And then it hits me. What would Edgeworth have thought if he saw me sneaking around the house to kiss James, if he saw me using another man—and a man under my power; isn't that the term Mary used?—to get over him, or maybe even get back at him? Would he have tried, convicted, and sentenced me on that evidence? Is there anything remotely innocent about what I have done? Am I any better than what I think Edgeworth is?

I, I, I. Is there really any separation left between Jane and me? Am I losing my mind?

I jump when I realize that Mary is staring at me, waiting for my reply.

"What about what you witnessed with your own eyes?" I finally say.

Mary resumes pacing, twisting her handkerchief in her hands with frantic energy. "Yes, of course that was wrong. But that does not mean that he, that they—If I could be so wrong in my estimation of Will's character, how can I trust my conclusions about Charles?"

That I can certainly relate to. When have I ever been a good judge of a man's character, especially a man I found attractive? All the more reason to stay on my guard, despite my wish to second guess what I saw, and despite anything Mary thinks. I cannot allow myself to trust Edgeworth, not after all I've been through. I trusted Frank—and Wes; of course I trusted Wes—and look where it got me. Every time I let down my defenses, that image of Edgeworth at the stables intrudes. It has to mean something, despite any guilt I might feel over what I did with James.

I attempt a smile. "Don't worry about having influenced me, Mary. I can assure you that I'm incapable of making a fair assessment of a man's character, with or without assistance."

Mary looks even more distressed.

"That was a joke, Mary."

"I see," she says woodenly, sinking into the sofa and massaging her temples.

"Headache? Shall I get you something for it?" Though what's on offer I can hardly imagine. Leeches? Eye of newt?

"I am well, I assure you." She smiles weakly, as if to convince me. "But if only I could rub these thoughts out of my head, I would feel much better."

"Let's see. What do I do when I want to stop obsessing?" And lord, do I need to stop obsessing right now. I mentally flip through the usuals, if I were home, that is: a chilled bottle of the finest vodka and a jar of green olives; one of the Xanaxes I stole from my boss's desk drawer, but only for dire emergencies; Googling old boyfriends; calling Paula to offer a sympathetic ear for her latest man woes, which she spews out in a nonstop stream-of-consciousness rant, thus obliterating any thoughts of my own; going to the shops on Vermont . . .

"That's it: shopping!"

Eyes wide with fright, Mary shrinks into herself and hugs her shawl to her shoulders, as if I've just suggested she dance naked in Sydney Gardens.

"Sorry, no, of course not." I slap my hand against my forehead. Stupid, stupid. That would involve leaving the house, and risk our running into the angel of death again.

"I know!" I jump up and rummage through my armoire, retrieving the first precious volumes of each of Jane Austen's first two novels and triumphantly holding them aloft. How could I have forgotten the best and most foolproof cure there is? "Let's read *Sense and Sensibility*! Or better still," I say, thinking that perhaps Willoughby's villainy might be too reminiscent of Will Templeton's, "*Pride and Prejudice*. Nothing beats the blues better than *P & P*."

"Thank you, but I have already read them both."

I try to hide the shock and disappointment that must be apparent on my face by busying myself with replacing the books in my armoire. Poor Mary. I cannot imagine a world in which one can read Jane Austen only once. Perhaps I can persuade her of the unnecessary poverty of such an existence . . . and then, I notice something at the very back of the wardrobe, a glint of gold and lace. I reach in and—

"I've got it!" This time I am holding up what appears to be an eighteenth-century coat, encrusted with pearls and gold embroidery. "Let's play dress-up!"

Mary's expression is less than enthusiastic, but this time I'm not letting her get away with it.

"Let's see," I say, holding up the jacket against her. "Perfect."

"But it is a man's coat."

"So what? We're not leaving the house in it, we're going to play right here. Didn't you ever go through your mother's clothes and jewelry when you were a little girl, and parade around in her things?"

"Well, I—"

Instead of giving her time to answer, I grab the coat and Mary's hand and pull her down the hall till we reach the bedroom of Mary's aunt. Apartment, more like it, is what I think when I open the double doors and enter the carpeted expanse and head straight for the first of three wardrobes.

"No, Jane! I cannot go through my aunt's things." Mary quickly closes the doors behind her and flattens herself against it, lest any of the servants see us engaged in such a scandalous activity.

"Well, I can. And I trust that with everything

you've told me about your aunt's kindheartedness and generosity and devotion to you, she would not object to a little harmless game of dress-up and—"

Wait. What's that on the top shelf? It's a group of jars and brushes that look suspiciously like cosmetics.

"—and makeover!" I open one of the jars to reveal something that could indeed double as blush and lip color. Yes!

"Especially," I say, steering Mary to a cushioned seat before a mirrored vanity table and pushing her gently down into it, "when its purpose is to divert the thoughts of the brokenhearted."

"But Jane—"

"Hush. You're in my hands now. I am going to transform you. And you, my dear, are going to have fun."

And with that, I get up and lock the bedroom door.

Two hours later, with the help of a couple of glasses of sherry or whatever alcoholic reddish stuff is in the Venetian glass decanter in the aunt's bedroom, I have transformed a now giggling Mary into a goddess, some kind of throwback to early Prince music videos. Maybe not a throwback, come to think of it, since Prince is in the future. But anyway, she is wearing a sort of half-male, half-female, and definitely all femme fatale costume: hair back in a low ponytail, knee breeches and fancy stockings with a floral design at the ankle, the embroidered, golden coat with lace cuffs and pearls everywhere, the latter open over her stays, which I insisted on once I got her to take off her dress and saw that she actually has a gorgeous, voluptuous hourglass figure that her empire waists completely obliterate. And the best part is that I've made up her face. I've reddened her lips and cheeks and even improvised heavy eyeliner with a brush and some coal dust. Talk about smoky eyes. She looks staggeringly sexy, and I tell her as much, which makes the rest of her face red before she collapses in giggles on the sofa.

I am also sort of half dressed in one of her aunt's gowns, which was my means of persuading her to cooperate in the grand make-over/dress-up party. I told her that if I was already in her aunt's clothes, there wasn't much more harm in her wearing them as well. Besides, I said, most of what I wanted her to put on must have belonged to her uncle, who is long dead and surely wouldn't mind.

I look absolutely ridiculous in the aunt's dress, which is so enormous on me that it keeps falling off my shoulders. Its only saving grace is that it has a waistline. Unfortunately, the circumference of said waistline is probably twice that of mine.

I realize that one of my necklaces would be the perfect finishing touch to Mary's outfit, and I am about to run down the hall and grab it, then change into my own dress, per Mary's request, so that I can order tea from Mrs. Jenkins; God forbid she should see either Mary or me in Mary's aunt's clothes. I close the aunt's bedroom door behind me and sigh. Mary still has some loosening up to do. But I've certainly made progress.

I think I hear a bustle downstairs in the foyer, but am almost instantly distracted by the sound of the aunt's door opening.

"Jane," Mary says, now in the hallway, "do ask Mrs. Jenkins for some sandwiches, too. And—"

At that moment we both hear the front door closing, and down in the foyer we see that Mrs. Jenkins has just let in Edgeworth and his friend Stevens. They are both looking up at us in our full costumed glory.

Mary gasps. "Do excuse me!" she says and darts back into her aunt's bedroom, but not before grabbing my wrist and pulling me inside with her.

"Oh dear!" Mary says, her face flushed as she looks at herself in the mirror. "Embarrassing enough if it were only Charles. But Mr. Stevens, too."

Mrs. Jenkins is instantly at the door, an anxious expression on her broad face. "I beg your pardon, miss. I had no idea you were—" She trails off and looks down at her shoes, clearly at a loss to describe just what it is we've been doing.

"You are not to blame," says Mary. "For I did tell you to admit Mr. Edgeworth no matter what. How were you to know that we were engaged in, in"—she clears her throat—"private theatricals."

Mary turns to me, her wide brown eyes asking for my confirmation.

"Exactly so, Mrs. Jenkins," I say. "We are rehearsing the new play by"—I cast around in my mind for the name of a playwright, but I'm ignorant in this department—"Sir David Mamet."

Mary gives me a quizzical look and then, "Do show my brother and his friend into the drawing room, Mrs. Jenkins. Bring tea and sandwiches, and tell them that I will be with them in a few minutes. And have Hortense come up at once."

As soon as Mrs. Jenkins is out of the room, Mary says, "You will come downstairs with me? And do me the honor of witnessing my efforts to make amends to my brother?"

My stomach goes into freefall at the thought. "I think you two need some privacy."

"That is hardly likely with Mr. Stevens here. Besides," she says, her gold-and-brown eyes imploring, "I will keep you only for a few minutes. Then you may make any excuse you wish."

One of the maids buttons and laces me into my dress with lightning speed while I try to slow my breathing. Casual, just be casual. He has no power over you, I tell my reflection as I give it a once-over in the mirror. What's with the blue-and-white checks on this fabric? Why am I wearing a tablecloth instead of a dress? I should have put on my yellow dress. And washed my hair.

What am I thinking? I can't go down there.

As soon as the maid leaves me alone, I give myself the respectable version of Regency-era makeup, which consists of biting my lips and pinching my cheeks. It figures that I was just about to make up my own face when we were so rudely interrupted. So close, yet so far. Did I just say "my own face"? It scares me how quickly I'm getting used to thinking of it as such.

I search for a shawl to camouflage the hideous fabric, then throw it down on the sofa. Who cares how I look (or how Jane looks, for that matter), let alone whether we look good enough for a man that neither one of us should want to see anymore.

Maybe I'll slip into the yellow dress after all. Not a good idea. Mary might notice the change in clothing and read too much sub-text (or even worse, exactly the right amount) into it. Besides, the idea of "slipping into" one of these dresses is a laughable impossibility. Tablecloth it is.

I begin to make my way toward the drawing room, gripping the banister and steadying myself inwardly with the thought that wearing table linen more than makes up for any hint of color I might now have summoned to my lips and cheeks, and therefore I have little chance of appearing alluring or looking like I wish to appear alluring.

I take a deep breath, willing my hands to stop trembling, and open the door to the drawing room.

Twenty-eight

Edgeworth smiles at me, cheek dimpling, and bows his greetings. Stevens stands up and mumbles something.

Mary, whose face is scrubbed of all traces of my ministrations, is just unlocking the tea caddy. I still haven't figured this one out. What do they think is in there anyway, controlled substances?

Mary looks up from her high-security operations and smiles at me. "Jane, I was just telling my brother how sorry I am to have been out when he was kind enough to call on us. And how glad I am that he was persistent in his efforts."

Edgeworth arches an eyebrow. Can't say I blame him for being skeptical.

But what he says is, "I hope to have the opportunity to repeat the pleasure many times," and then looks at me as if for a clue to his sister's apparent personality transplant.

"Shall I see you both at the ball this week?" he says.

Mary darts her eyes at me before answering her brother. "I cannot say. You see, I—that is, I find that Bath does not agree with me, and I am thinking of asking Miss Mansfield," and now her voice breaks a little, "if she would mind cutting short our visit here."

Stevens, who has been staring at Mary with

undisguised admiration, gasps and looks as if someone just punched him in the gut. Then he starts coughing.

"Are you well, Mr. Stevens?" Mary asks.

"Perfectly," he croaks, pointing at his sandwich plate. "It seems to have made a wrong turn."

Edgeworth pats him on the back. Mary pours him some more tea.

"I am ready to leave Bath whenever you are," I tell Mary.

Her eyes fill. "You will not be disappointed?"

"Not a bit."

Edgeworth looks from me to Mary and back at me again. "That is a pity. Stevens and I were just saying that the cooler weather has made Bath a much pleasanter place to be, were we not, Stevens?" He looks at his friend encouragingly.

Stevens blanches, apparently realizing we all expect him to speak, then promptly flushes to the roots of his hair. "Y—es."

Edgeworth glances at his friend, then fills in the ensuing pause. "I have spent entire summers wondering why the geniuses of fashion were not as kind to men as they are to women."

"You can't be serious," I say, conscious of what feels like a stiff piece of wood inside the front of my stays. "Besides, I don't think you would look well in a gown."

Edgeworth smiles at me mischievously. "I shall take that as a compliment, Miss Mansfield. But I speak of fabrics, not of forms." He fingers the material of his green coat to underscore his point, then looks at his friend. "What say you, Mr. Stevens?"

"I—that is . . . indeed. A coat is abominably hot in summer. I would not wish its encumbrances on anyone who—" At this Stevens turns bright red again and looks at Mary, and then at me, his eyes imploring. "Forgive me. I did not mean—"

Poor Mary's own cheeks are flaming as she busies herself with the sandwich tray, no doubt imagining the picture she must have presented in her costume. "Not at all, Mr. Stevens," she says, her tone barely audible. "Miss Edgeworth and I were merely engaged in private theatricals when you arrived."

"I would not for the world have intruded on your privacy," says Stevens, looking down at his shoes.

"What a pleasure it was to see you both at the ball," says Edgeworth, apparently eager to turn the conversation from embarrassing topics. "I do believe I never enjoyed a dance as much as I did that night." And this with a significant smile at me. "What say you about the number of people, Mary?"

And just like that, the tension dissipates. Edgeworth takes over the bulk of the polite discourse, clearly eager to put both Mary and Stevens at ease. Mary visibly relaxes, and Edgeworth even coaxes a few words out of his friend.

As for me, every time Edgeworth looks in my direction with those hazel eyes, all I can think of is how much I want to put my arms around him.

It's exactly how I felt after Frank got his stuff from my apartment. Instead of making sure I wasn't at home, I had watched him pile clothes and books and CDs—including my Bjork *Debut* CD and my copy of *Mrs. Dalloway*, among other ancient treasures—into ratty cardboard boxes from Von's, probably because he was too cheap to buy new boxes from a packing store. But instead of exploding with indignation over his thievery (surely salt in the wound of infidelity) I kept gazing at the taut curves of his ass in faded jeans as he bent over to abscond with more of my belongings, wishing he would turn around and smile his crooked smile to tell me it had all been a mistake. But of course he didn't. All he did was mumble "I'm sorry," shrug sheepishly, and walk out the door. And all I wanted to do was talk to Wes when he rang me for the tenth time that day, instead of letting the machine pick up again. "I have to talk to you, Courtney. Please." I wanted to cry into his shirt, feel his arms around me, hear him murmuring soothing words into my hair, like he did after my work Christmas party, most of which I had spent watching Frank flirt with other women. I didn't even have to tell Wes what had happened, and he was good enough not to ask.

No. If I barely had the strength to resist Wes, who had unquestionably betrayed me, then I certainly do not have the strength to resist a man whose injuries to me might not even be real.

At that moment Edgeworth hands me a cup of tea that Mary has just poured, and his fingers brush against mine, sending a thrill through my body. I mumble something about a letter I have to answer, and dash out of the room.

About an hour later, which seems like three hours because I've spent most of it pacing the room and reliving the touch of his fingers on mine and replaying every sound he uttered and searching for meaning in every word and gesture, I hear a soft knock at my door. Mary comes in, her face swollen and tear-streaked, but smiling nonetheless.

"I could do with some tea," she says, pulling the bell for Mrs. Jenkins and settling into a chair. "I did not even remember to drink mine."

"You told him."

She nods. "Mr. Stevens left the house shortly after you went upstairs. What an embarrassment. I do not wonder at his wishing to escape after seeing me in such unladylike attire. That look on his face I shall never forget. Charles was not in the least discomposed, of course, but then again . . ." She blushes and looks confused, perhaps thinking about all the preconceived notions she had of her brother. "In fact, he was quite sorry to have unwittingly turned the conversation to what I would not have alluded for the world."

Mary looks down at her hands. "I would have kept Charles here longer, as there is still so much I wish to say to him, but he had an engagement he could not break."

"And?"

"He said very little, but what he did say was more than kind. And no doubt more than I deserve."

She reaches into a pocket for a damp handkerchief and wipes her eyes. I move to comfort her, but she waves me away.

"No, Jane. It is right that I feel the weight of my own foolishness. How else am I to have any hope of amendment?"

The tea arrives, and Mrs. Jenkins has made up a tray with some thick slices of dark bread, plus a sharp white cheese and cold beef. For a few minutes we eat and drink in silence.

Mary takes a bite of her sandwich, and a big blob of mustard falls out on her chest. She looks down at the offending stain on her white dress, then at me, mortified.

"Yellow suits you," I say, dunking my napkin in water and blotting the spot. We both laugh.

"And so does strength," I add. "You're handling this whole thing beautifully."

Mary starts crying again. "How very blessed I am. My brother, to whom I have been barely civil for years, instantly forgives all, and my dearest friend, whose heart my brother might have won had it not been for my vicious tongue, sees nothing but goodness in me. How do I deserve this?"

"Mary, you are not responsible for how I feel about your brother."

"But it was I who told you—"

"True, but you haven't considered the possibility that I might have made my own observations."

"What do you mean?"

I cast my eyes into the dark dregs of my cup.

"Jane?"

"Let's not talk about this now."

"Dearest friend—"

"Listen to me. You are not responsible."

I am not about to tell Mary what I think I saw or remembered. I don't even know if it's real, and even if it is, what good would it do Mary? She's just begun to repair her relationship with her brother, and why should the quality of their relationship be dependent on the quality of mine? Couldn't he be a perfect brother to her and a perfect liar to me? Wasn't Frank always doing favors for his sister and bailing her out of trouble? Did that make him a better boyfriend to me?

"Jane, do you really not mind leaving Bath? I did not plan on broaching the subject to you with Charles in the room; it just came out unbidden."

"Do you think I could enjoy myself in this town, knowing you were constantly worried about running into Will?"

"If we stay, it is inevitable that I shall. In time I will be stronger, and it will not signify."

She smiles sheepishly. "Do you know that of the thousand things that were going through my head today when I saw Will, the one that clamored loudest for my attention was the thought that I looked a perfect fright?"

"You did not, but I know what you mean. Which is why we need to keep you out of harm's way."

Which is exactly what I tried my best to do after Frank depleted my CD tower and bookshelves along with my self-esteem. I did everything in my power, short of leaving town—the slight inconvenience of my job preventing that from being an option—to avoid seeing him. Or Wes. Any restaurant, bar, or store we ever went to together, any place I thought I might have the chance of running into either of them, I avoided. And except for the one time I saw Wes on Vermont, and the one time I bumped into Frank at the farmer's market two weeks after we broke up, I'd been successful. Like Mary, all I could think of when I came face to face with Frank was how I looked, my unwashed hair held up in a clip and no mascara, my body, eight pounds slimmer from the heartbreak diet, completely and unjustly hidden in a pair of shapeless overall shorts. What I should have been thinking was how he deserved to die a slow death at my hands, and that I would not wish to ruin a good outfit while doing it.

Yes, leaving town is the best thing I could do for myself as well as Mary. Except suddenly it hits me that leaving town means going back to Mrs. Mansfield. The thought of being stuck in a room with her and enduring endless questions about Edgeworth and Bath (for surely she would have found out by now that Edgeworth was in Bath) is unbearable; there's no way I can handle that.

I feel Mary's eyes on me. "What is wrong, Jane?"

Everyone's always told me that I wear my feelings on my face, and I suppose having a different face hasn't changed that about me.

"I was just thinking how much fun it would be if we could extend our trip to another destination."

"What a splendid idea. I would offer my brother's house in London as our next destination, were it not in the midst of improvements. At present it is not fit to be seen. I do, however, have a cousin in town who has been urging me to be her guest. We could go there at once and delay our return home."

"Are you sure she wouldn't mind my coming along?"

Mary laughs. "Mind? Louisa loves nothing more than to surround herself with as many people as she can. My dear cousin's biggest fear is being alone with her husband, so I must warn you that if it is peace you seek, you will not find it in London. And certainly not at Louisa's. Would a few days there suit you? I fear you may not be able to tolerate much more than that."

I hug her. “It sounds perfect.”

“Such gratitude does not come from one who savors the thought of returning home.”

“Believe me, Mary—”

“No, do not say it. You are making a sacrifice by leaving here, and I am sensible of it. So, I will do everything in my power, both in London and at home, to make it up to you.”

But Mary won’t have to make up anything to me. I’m so excited about not having to face Mrs. Mansfield and the boredom of her house I could scream. Plus I’ll get to see London, not the London I saw briefly as a twenty-first-century tourist—a three-day blur of jet lag, somnolent sightseeing from atop a double-decker bus (I have a vague, bleary-eyed memory of barreling past the Houses of Parliament and Big Ben while battling the leaden weight of my eyelids), and a Dramamine-less, barf-bag-less nightmare of a Thames boat excursion.

No. I am going to the pre-Starbucks, pre–Madame Tussaud’s London. I am going to see the London of two hundred years ago, the London of Jane Austen. Not the London of Edgeworth, or Wes, or anyone else who pees standing up. What are men to shops and theaters, Gray’s of Sackville Street, or even the wild beasts at Exeter Exchange?

Mary kisses me on the cheek. “And now, dearest friend, I must write a note to Louisa. And change my clothes yet again.” She smirks, indicating the splotch of mustard on her dress.

Twenty-nine

Not ten minutes later Mary bursts into my room, dressed in a clean gown, her face flushed with excitement.

"Dearest friend, do you know we could actually leave Bath as early as tomorrow?" she says. "Even Mrs. Smith seems positively cheerful about it, though I feared she had not given the waters their due."

"Shouldn't we wait to hear back from your cousin? What if she is out of town? Or has already filled her house with guests?"

"Impossible. Just two days ago Louisa was lamenting the lack of company and the various obligations that prevented her leaving town. I need only send her word of our imminent arrival. That is, if you are agreeable to such a plan."

I assure her of my eagerness to go, though I keep the reasons to myself, and she runs off to her room to pen the note to her cousin.

I start going through drawers and organizing clothes and books in neat little piles on the bed. Not that I need to do any of that, with all the servants at my disposal, but the busy work is what I need right now to stop thinking about Edgeworth's eyes and the way he looked at me when we were dancing and whether Mary is actually more right about him now than she was when she was trying to warn me about him. I can't let myself think about any of that, because putting some distance between him and me is the smartest thing I can do, and leaving Bath is the best thing for Mary, and besides, isn't there the tiniest chance that being in the same city I'd visited in my real life might somehow bring me back home?

Stacking hatboxes on the bed and debating whether I could find a proper container in which I might borrow some of the rouge in Mary's aunt's room, and whether she'd miss any of it, it occurs to me that there's another advantage to leaving immediately: There's no chance I'll get a letter from Mrs. M urging a postponement of our departure. She can't possibly object to the propriety of the London trip, since we are to stay with Mary's cousin, but she will most certainly object to its geographical distance from Edgeworth, should she know by now that he is in Bath. The thought of her frustration makes me smile.

Mary and I spend the rest of the evening packing our trunks (or more precisely, supervising Hortense, who is supervised by Mrs. Jenkins; we are absolutely superfluous) and planning quick take-leave visits to the three people for whom Mary insists we must do more than leave a card: Mrs. Randolph, Susan Randolph, and Edgeworth.

Our first stop the next morning is the Randolphs'. I cross my fingers that her daughter will still be in bed, as the hour is early for visiting.

No such luck. The only fortunate thing is that Mary and I can keep our visit short without Mrs. Randolph's urging us to stay, because the first thing we tell her is that we're leaving that very morning.

Susan is oddly silent at first; she appears to be focused on some sewing in her lap, and an occasional nod or murmur of assent is the only proof that she's paying any sort of attention. The only time she puts her needlework down and trains her dark blue eyes on us is when Mary mentions that our next stop is to say good-bye to her brother. Susan lifts her brows in surprise or skepticism when Mary says how sorry she is not to have a chance to spend more time with him in Bath. I find it sweet that Mary is so anxious to make amends to her brother that she makes it a point to advertise her newfound affection for him to the first people she sees.

Susan catches my eye, instantly turns her attention back to her needlework, and says softly, "And I suppose you too have had little time to spend with Mr. Edgeworth, cousin, what with all the time you devote to taking exercise in Sydney Gardens."

She looks at me again and holds my gaze, this time with the detached yet focused look of a cat that has cornered a mouse.

I clear my throat. "I am not sure I understand you."

Susan resumes her needlework and makes a

slight shrug. "Perhaps I am mistaken then. Perhaps I saw you there only the once. I believe you were much engaged in conversation that day and did not see me, and then you seemed in a great hurry to leave, which is why you did not see me when you passed me by. I remember thinking you looked exceedingly well, and how the exercise must agree with you, for the flush in your complexion told me that you must have spent a great deal of time walking that morning. A most courageous undertaking, I thought, considering it was such a dirty day."

And then, with a falling sensation in the pit of my stomach, I remember the woman with the bloodred ribbons on her bonnet, the woman I ran past when I left James, the woman who seemed vaguely familiar to me, but whose face was a blur in my panic to get out of there.

What is she up to? I feel my pulse quicken and my face grow hot. I open my mouth to confront her, but I feel Mary's eyes boring into me, and so all I do is mumble that perhaps she is mistaken, but if indeed I was the person she saw in the Gardens, then I was sorry I did not see her as well.

"It does not signify," Susan says, "for whether it was your mistake or mine, it was most assuredly an innocent one."

"Would it be anything but?"

A clatter of teacup on saucer—Mrs. Randolph's—turns my attention from Susan. Mrs.

Randolph opens her mouth as if to speak, but Mary stands up abruptly and gently insists that we must say our good-byes if we are to leave in good time. I kiss Mrs. Randolph warmly; as for Susan, I barely touch her cold fish of a hand and look her in the eyes with what I hope is an intimidating glare. She is the first to look down, which gives me a little tingle of triumph.

As soon as we leave the Randolphs' house, Mary starts saying over and over again, "Oh dear. Oh dear. What shall we do?"

"I know exactly what I want to do, which is what I would have done had I not felt you begging me not to with those puppy dog eyes of yours."

"Thank heaven you did not admit you were actually there. It is her word against yours, and it is entirely possible that she was mistaken. That is what you shall say."

Mary is so worked up that she's practically racing down the street, and I can hardly keep up with her.

"Could we slow down just a bit? I couldn't care less what Susan saw. Or how it may have looked."

At this, Mary stops walking and looks at me, her eyes wide with alarm. "Oh God. What exactly did she see?"

"How would I know?"

Mary's eyes dart around, no doubt assessing the proximity of a plump matron and the five teenage girls she has in tow. We are in the middle of the circular, cobbled expanse of the Circus, an echoey place to have a discreet conversation. Mary moves close to me and waits until the women are a good nine yards away. She hisses into my ear nevertheless. "Could it be worse than seeing you meet, unchaperoned, a young man whom she may have recognized as a servant in your parents' house? Do you realize how serious this situation may be?"

I flinch at Mary's vehemence, but I will myself to slow the pounding in my chest. Why am I getting so rattled?

"I held his hand," I say loudly into the otherwise empty Circus. "And touched it to my cheek."

"Are you mad?" Mary hisses. "For heaven's sake, lower your voice."

She grabs my arm and drags me out of the Circus, not slowing her pace or saying a word until we are halfway down Brock Street.

"Tell me it isn't true," she says.

"I was merely asking his forgiveness, not that it's any of your concern."

Mary starts walking rapidly again, repeating over and over to herself, "Oh dear. Oh dear."

"Calm down," I say, shuffling to catch up with her. "If Susan has nothing better to do than spread rumors, why should we care? We're leaving tomorrow anyway. Besides, if she were going to gossip, why wait almost a week to do it?"

At this, Mary stops again and turns around with a fierce look in her eyes.

"Now you listen to me, Jane. If she decides to gossip about this, and you do not flatly deny it, then it will matter little where we are and why Susan decided to speak now rather than then. If your reputation is tainted, then I will suffer as well, as you are my traveling companion and my guest. If my relations will not receive you, then where does that leave us? We will each of us be confined to our own homes."

"Are you suggesting your brother would refuse to let you see me?"

"Charles would never believe such gossip."

"Even so, would he want his sister to associate with a woman the rest of the world saw as a whore?"

"Jane!" Mary gasps. "You will deny this, and that is all there is to say on the matter."

We continue our breakneck pace in silence. How could I have romanticized this world? A world where a woman's place, substandard as it is, hangs by a thread. Where a man, even a man like Edgeworth, would be just as turned off by the thought of my rendezvous with James as the rest of these hypocrites would be. If I had known I was forfeiting my good name by meeting with James, at least I could have had the satisfaction of all-out sex instead of a measly touch of his hand on my cheek.

The shattering of any remaining illusions I have about Edgeworth is actually a blessing. It'll make forgetting about him that much easier. I suppose he'll expect the next woman he marries to come to the marriage bed without having so much as kissed another man. God forbid the wife should have prior knowledge of sex, let alone enjoy it. What sort of meaning would a husband read into that? No, I imagine he must think that the only women who enjoy sex are those of the lower classes, who maybe aren't expected to be so pure when they finally get married. Or maybe they are, but the ones who hire them as servants just indulge in sexual harassment whenever the mood strikes, and always with impunity.

After all, here is a place where the pregnant employee leaves her job in disgrace, and where not all bosses are kind enough to send them off with a reference, as Mary had done for her servant. I am in a thoroughly disgusting, absolutely hypocritical society, a prison for women of all classes, and the sooner I get out of here, the better off I'll be. All I have to do, as the fortune-teller said, is be where I am. Ha! That's about as clear as the germ-infested waters of Bath.

"Jane, are you listening to me?"

Mary has stopped walking and is staring at me.

I realize I am standing in the middle of the huge lawn in front of the Royal Crescent. I've been so immersed in my thoughts that I don't even know how I got here. "What?"

"Will you promise to deny Susan's accusations,

should she decide, heaven forbid, to spread them?"

"Yes, yes. Can we please stop talking about this?"

"Thank you."

We reach the door of Stevens's house in the Crescent, where Edgeworth is staying. Mary is composed, at least outwardly, as she raps on the door, and I feel an empowering sort of indifference.

We are shown into the thickly carpeted drawing room, where Edgeworth and Stevens join us. Stevens glows as he greets Mary and stammers his apologies for not being able to present his mother and sisters to us. Edgeworth says what a sad loss to Bath our going will be and how he hopes to join his sister in the country soon. Mary is effusive in her encouragements, insisting we will be in London for only a brief stay. I watch them all play-acting, and say nothing. Can we get this over with and get on our way already?

Yet, as I sit there in silence on the pale green sofa while we wait for our tea, while I listen to Mary and Stevens and Edgeworth engage in the usual polite nothings of what passes for conversation in this world, my detachment grows. I see nothing of depth in anything Edgeworth has to say; I see only that he is the perfect man of his class and his era, bred to think highly of himself and much less of women, regardless of the outward trappings of gallantry and deference. It is all an elaborately structured ploy to lure women into marriage, rob them of financial independence, turn them into breeders, and keep them in a luxuriously padded cell while they raise the heirs to the family fortune.

For the first time I am immune to Edgeworth; his face and form are beautiful to look at, but there's nothing behind the mask that interests me. Suddenly I have my appetite back, and I eye the silver bowl of summer fruits that Stevens's servant brought out. A plum is what I want. I'll eat and drink and murmur like everyone else, and I'll look Edgeworth in the eye without the slightest bit of discomfort.

I can tell he is off-balance by my unselfconscious silence, especially when his sister is being so openly approving of him. He tries to draw me out but gives up after a few minutes. Mary lets me be; I imagine she is grateful I'm not talking about unchaperoned meetings with single males of the lower classes and shouting out words like "whore." Perhaps she hopes my silence is a thoughtful one in which I can meditate on the error of my ways. And she's right. Never has there been a woman so cognizant of her errors as I am at this moment.

There is one pleasant aspect to the visit, and that is my continuing observation of Stevens's huge crush on Mary. He stammers and blushes whenever he speaks to her. Mary appears to be entirely oblivious to it.

When we finish our tea, I remind Mary that we still have a lot to do before we leave Bath, and she takes the hint. As we say our good-byes, Edgeworth shakes my hand and clasps it firmly, then covers it with his other hand for a brief moment. His face is grave as he catches my eyes with his; we are both still until finally I look away, my stomach fluttering. Damn him.

Thirty

After clattering around in Mary's coach for who knows how many hours, my bones have become castanets. Sleep is not an option, but I attempt it anyway. I open my eyes when I feel the coach slowing, and I welcome the sight of a roadside inn, its smoking chimney and candlelit windows inviting. I emerge from the carriage stiff and sore and hobble toward the door, anticipating a comfortable break from the rigors of the road.

How wrong I am. At the doorway to the inn's dining room, in which a few bedraggled patrons listlessly spoon greasy chunks of a mystery stew into their faces, I am riveted by the sight of a ragged, spindly creature walking toward their table with a steaming plate of food in one hand and the other hand feverishly scratching his stringy mop of hair. I know if I stand there another moment I'll have the stench of congealed grease in my nostrils for a month, but I cannot stop staring.

This can't be where we're staying. I can only imagine the conditions of the bedding in this place. Even in my own more hygienic world I hate to touch the bedspreads on hotel beds, which I know are not washed on a daily basis. The first thing I always do in a hotel room is throw off the bedspread and ball it up in a corner, then apply liberal amounts of antibacterial wash to my hands from the little purse-sized bottle I always carry with me (if only I had it now). The few who have witnessed this ritual dismiss me as a contamination-phobe, but I have seen too many of those "hidden universe"–type shows on the Discovery channel, the ones that reveal the colonies of microscopic beasts that live on our skins and in our houses, to be otherwise.

"Jane? Is something the matter?"

Mary's smoky-sweet voice jolts me from my downward spiral.

"Mary, this place is filthy. Do you think we could just rest for a half hour and get back on the road?"

Mary pats my hand reassuringly. "Do not worry. It is an inconvenience, to be sure, but we shall make the best of it. Hortense has bespoken a private parlor for our meal and will secure the cleanest and best rooms. She and I will keep you safe and snug. And to ensure our comfort further, I have brought my very own bed linens. I never travel without them, being a fastidious sort of person myself."

I am about to plead my case further, when Mary lets out a tiny sneeze. I know that if I press the matter she'll give in, but I don't want to risk her cold getting worse, not when it's almost gone. So I resign myself to a night in germ paradise.

Granted, the private parlor is tidier and less rancid-smelling than the dining room, and instead of Rumplestiltskin's brother serving us our meal, we have a moderately clean-looking maidservant who doesn't scratch herself once. The roasted chicken she places on the table smells tantalizing and looks harmless, but I cannot get myself to take a bite, despite the grumblings of my stomach, Mary's urgings, and the odd look from Mrs. Smith, who eats heartily herself. Finally, I settle on a chunk of bread and a boiled potato, both of which I examine minutely before saying a silent prayer and washing them down with a large glass of wine for its disinfectant as well as its tranquilizing effects.

Mary and I share a bed that night, which Hortense has covered with Mary's bed linens. Despite that precaution, I spend a disastrous night, waking, it seems, every ten minutes, torn between fears that relaxing my vigilance will invite worse horrors than insects and germs into my bed (my fantasies by this time have settled on mice and rats, the staring eyes of the creature in the trap back in Mansfield House taking a starring role), and the soft but nonetheless irritating snores of Hortense, who is sleeping on the floor, wrapped in blankets, at the foot of the bed.

Mary, of course, sleeps like a baby; Mary, who could eat salmonella chicken and bathe in *eau de typhus* and get nothing worse than a cold. I suppose that one possible advantage of being born and bred in this time period is developing a stalwart immune system, and I suddenly realize that the body I am inhabiting is used to such customary insults to hygiene, unlike the daily-showered and antibiotic-treated one I am used to in my own era. But then I remember what I read of the life expectancy and infant mortality rates of previous centuries, and toss my way through another interval of insomnia.

When I awake from my last ten-minute nap, Mary is already dressed and downstairs, and Hortense invites me to wash myself in the "fresh" water she has just placed in the washbasin. The room looks even worse in daylight, the wear and tear of thousands of weary travelers no longer camouflaged by candlelight. Even worse, the washbasin has a ring of dirt in it, which apparently neither Hortense nor Mary noticed, since it is impossible for Mary's white neck to have left that kind of color behind. I don't have the heart to make Hortense lug the basin downstairs again and have it scrubbed (or scrub it herself), so I just splash a bit of water on my face, clean, as it were, my teeth with the scouring powder that passes for tooth-paste, and let Hortense maneuver my weary limbs into clothes as I steel myself for the sights and smells awaiting me below.

I am wise enough to avert my eyes as I walk past the main dining area toward our private parlor, but my nose is assaulted by the ill-smelling fare being served up. The fact that I am now thinking as well as saying things like "ill-smelling fare" is disturbing enough. What's worse is that I practically brush shoulders with the skeevy waiter from the night before. His stench is unbearably pungent, and though Mary does her best to talk me into having some breakfast, I can't get the thought out of my mind that he might have touched some of the food laid out for us. By this time I'm starving, but decide I will have nothing more than tea. It takes all my powers of persuasion to convince Mary that my fast does not indicate illness.

We resume our journey, and for the greater part of the day the bouncing around in the carriage is nothing compared to the itchiness I now endure. Once I start scratching I find it almost impossible to stop, despite the fact that it has to be psychological, since neither Mary nor Hortense, nor Mrs. Smith, for that matter, are similarly afflicted. Though Mary gently expresses her concern for my comfort, it's clear she has no fears of catching whatever I have. Mrs. Smith simply raises her thin eyebrows and stays characteristically silent, focusing her attention on the book in her lap. Hortense, however, looks as if she is fighting the desire to fling herself from the moving coach every time I shift anywhere near her.

Mercifully, the lack of sleep and food finally catches up with me, and I sleep for who knows how many hours, waking only when we arrive at our destination. I stumble out of the carriage, bleary-eyed and dry-mouthed, and look up at the tall townhouse that is to be our home for a few days. I hardly notice or care what the house or the London of Jane Austen looks like, since I can only think of a comfortable bed and a hot bath and dread being introduced to a stranger when I feel so beaten up and dirty, not to mention barely able to form a sentence. I am even too tired to itch.

In the entrance hall, an attractive, fiftyish woman, done up in an elaborate hairstyle and headdress, rushes toward us in a cloud of gardenia perfume. The first thing that strikes me about her is that she is wearing makeup, almost the first woman I've seen here wearing powder and blush and what has to be color on her lips, and certainly the first person wearing makeup that I've been introduced to.

She and Mary embrace, and Louisa oohs and aahs, exclaiming at how Mary is "a preserver of life itself," and how her last few guests had "cruelly absconded to the country and left her bereft of company."

Whatever. Just get me to my bed.

Mary introduces her cousin as Lady Ashwell, but before I can say anything Louisa says, "You poor bedraggled darling. Do not even attempt to dissemble. Name what you wish this moment, and it shall be yours."

"A bath," I say, "and a bed."

"Done," she says, and goes to ring the bell. "You are quite pretty, you know. Even in your travel-weary state I can see that. I have a notion," and she turns to Mary, "that it is my destiny to find your friend a husband. What say you to that, Miss Mansfield?"

"You needn't put yourself out. I'm perfectly capable of making a mess of things on my own."

Louisa laughs. "Cousin," she says, "I am pleased to see that your friend is no simpering country girl. I like her already."

"Likewise," I say, which sets Louisa off into even more laughter. Easy audience. Then a maid comes and whisks me off to my room, where I get my glorious bath and then sink into the softest, most inviting bed I've ever slept in.

"Jane?"

I open my eyes to what I dub from that moment the "bridal room," everything covered with white frothy fabric, from curtains to bed hangings, and there is Mary, sitting on the edge of my bed, her pale pink gown the only spot of color in the room.

"From that smile on your face may I surmise that you slept as well as you look?"

I stretch out my arms and yawn, nodding. The feel of the clean bedding on my clean skin is delicious. And Mary smells of lavender.

"We did not have the heart to wake you for supper last night, but you must be hungry."

Come to think of it, I'm ravenous.

"Shall I send Hortense in to dress you, and then see you downstairs in the breakfast room?"

I nod gratefully.

I inhale my breakfast, while Louisa watches (she will not allow me to call her Lady Ashwell, because she says it makes her sound far too old, and I'm grateful, because I know I'd end up calling her "Laura Ashley" by mistake).

In the harsh light of day I can see that "makeup" is an inadequate term to describe what Louisa has done to her face. Raggedy Ann–like blotches of red are exclamation points on her Kabuki-white cheeks.

"I adore your cousin's natural, unspoilt beauty," she declares to Mary. "And such a prodigious appetite, so unlike most women who eat like baby sparrows in company." And this from someone who has been poking at a lone piece of toast on her plate without taking a single bite.

When I put my fork down for a moment and take a breath, Mary and Louisa ask me if I approve of the plans they've made for a day of shopping followed by a musical party at the house of someone named Lady Charlton.

Louisa adds, "I am sorry there is nothing more exciting in the way of entertainment to offer you, but London is rather thin this time of year."

I pat my full stomach. "Thin or not, Louisa, I am ready for London."

Louisa laughs. "You know, Mary," she says, continuing her pattern of talking about me as if I were not in the room, "I do believe your friend means what she says. Delightful girl!"

I don't know why Louisa is getting on my nerves, but she is. Perhaps it's because she's pegged me as a mistress of witty dialogue when I've hardly even spoken a word to her. On the other hand, what's wrong with being encouraged to speak my mind and thought of as entertaining? Perhaps I'm just being judgmental because she's allowed to wear makeup and I'm not, especially when she has no idea how to put it on in an attractive manner and I do. Or perhaps I'm even shallower than that. Truth be told, the white mask isn't the only thing that makes Louisa hard to look at. Her teeth are brownish, a fact she attempts to hide with her fan as best she can, and I can see that the heavy hand with which she applies the face powder is a futile attempt to camouflage acne scars. Still, had she the benefit of modern dentistry and cosmetics, not to mention a chemical peel, she might have been a pretty woman.

So again I have to ask my judgmental self, why am I so bothered by her? The only conclusion I can draw is that I resent her de facto pronouncement that I am an amusing curiosity. And I resent it being a truth universally acknowledged, no matter what era I find myself in, that a single woman of thirty must be in want of a husband.

I particularly resent Louisa's holy-grail view of

marriage when she can barely be civil to her own husband, a rotund man in his sixties who pops his head into the breakfast room to say a warm good morning to me and welcome me to his house, and I resent the fact that she rolls her eyes the moment he leaves.

I also resent that I find myself wondering what Edgeworth is doing. And whether he's thinking of me. But this too shall pass.

Shortly after breakfast we go out, and I have plenty of diversions; in particular, the most fascinating dose of people watching I've yet experienced, and my very first look at a horse-drawn traffic jam. London is a landscape of sensory opposites: the hint of a blue sky peeping from behind the gray cover of a million coal-burning fires (and I thought the smog back home was bad), the shouting of the street vendors and the rhythmic clip-clop of hooves on the cobbled pavement, the perfumed air of the shops and the stench of horse droppings in the streets, barefooted children with grime-streaked faces begging for pennies from gloved ladies in immaculate gowns.

We spend a lot of time in the shops; Louisa is on a mission to spend as much of her husband's money as she can (her words, not mine), and Mary and I are dragged in her wake. After a few hours of conspicuous consumption, however, the novelty of my surroundings wears thin. I enjoy shopping as much as the next person, but in small doses. Here there are not enough clothes to look at and too much fabric, and how many bonnets could I examine, especially when I hate them all? I'd much rather watch the people going in and out of the shops than look at the wares. Even Mary's determined cheerfulness is getting to me, and as I stand in yet another shop fingering merchandise I care nothing about, I decide it's time to call it a day. I'm just about to venture a hint that perhaps it's best for Mary's health that we think about going home, when I hear something that stops me in my tracks.

It is a shop clerk saying, "Miss Austen? Here it is, wrapped as you specified. Thank you, miss. Good day to you."

I wheel around to see the clerk smiling at the back of a woman, who is walking out of the shop. Could she possibly be *the* Miss Austen?

"Mary," I say, "I'll be back."

"Are you all right?" she says as I rush toward the door.

And out the door I fly in pursuit of the rapidly retreating figure, certain of nothing but that I must have a real-life look at her.

Thirty-one

My whole body surges with adrenaline. If this is who I think it is—she looks, from behind, to be the right age, and I thought I caught a glimpse of brown hair as she left the shop—then there's a good chance I'm going to faint before I reach her. This isn't just any celebrity sighting, and living in L.A. I've had my share of those. She isn't even a person in the normal sense of the word, and no matter how much celebrities are adored, it's hard to forget they are also real people who can be caught with their tops off on a beach or trashing a hotel room after checking out of rehab. But *she* isn't a person in that sense of the word. She is a legend, an icon, an object of speculation by people who have made her life their life's work, or her work their life's focus.

She's also been dead for almost two hundred years.

This can't be happening. More than the can't-be-happening aspect of everything that is happening to me, this definitely cannot be happening.

I've just about caught up to her. Please let it be her.

"Excuse me, are you Miss Austen? Miss Jane Austen?"

She stops and turns around, a quietly pretty woman in her thirties, with large brown eyes; very dark, elegantly arched brows; and her face tanned to a golden brown, which strikes me as unusual. A few dark curls tumble out of one of those unflattering, matronly caps that she looks too young to be wearing, and over that is a cream-colored bonnet tied under her chin with a light green ribbon. She's not gorgeous, but she's far prettier than the pop-eyed portrait of her in the back of one of my books.

She shifts her parcels to the other arm, her large brown eyes unguarded. "I am she. Are we acquainted?" Her voice is clear and sweet.

Oh. My. God. It really is Jane Austen. My knees turn to jelly, and it's all I can do to keep the tremor out of my voice. "No, but may I introduce myself? I am Jane; I mean, Miss Mansfield, and I could not help but hear the shopkeeper address you, and—"

I can feel her guard go up slightly as she sizes me up. I can see in the glinting sunlight that her large, widely set eyes are more gold than brown. She is waiting for me to speak, offering nothing to ease the awkwardness.

My stomach flutters. "I know this will sound insane, because I know that no one is supposed to know, but I am a huge fan of your books."

She lifts her eyebrows momentarily, then composes her face and gazes at me steadily. "I do not know what you mean by 'fan,' and I am afraid you have mistaken me for someone else. Good day." And with that, she begins to stride briskly away.

"Please," I say, running after her.

She doesn't even slow her pace, so I just continue scuttling alongside her.

"You have mistaken me for someone else," she says firmly, without looking at me or breaking her stride.

"But I know your work. *Sense and Sensibility. Pride and Prejudice. Mansfield Park*—"

At that she stops and faces me, naked astonishment in her eyes. Her face downshifts through a succession of emotions: fear, then incredulity, then a hard-eyed challenge.

"What do you know of *Mansfield Park*?"

"I've read it."

"Impossible."

"Every word."

"It has not been published."

"It will be."

Her face changes again, as if going through mental calculations. Her eyes narrow. "You are a friend of Henry's, are you not?"

"No. I just wanted you to know how honored I am to meet you, what a privilege it is, and how much your books have meant to me, will always mean to me."

Her features soften minutely at this, and she bows her head slightly. "I wish I could thank you for the compliment, but I am sure it is meant for someone else."

"What would you say if I told you you're

wasting your time trying to be anonymous? That two hundred years from now millions of people will have read your books, and your name will be known by many more as the author of those books? Think of it: Millions of women will dream of living the lives of your heroines and meeting heroes as handsome as Edward Ferrars."

Here she starts to laugh, a deep, resonant laugh. "Edward Ferrars? Handsome? Are you certain you have read the books you claim I have written?"

"And seen the movies."

"Movies."

"Perhaps not all your heroes are that handsome in your books, but they certainly are in the movies. How else would they sell tickets?"

She is no longer smiling. Her eyes are sizing me up again. "Of what are you talking, Miss . . . Mansfield, is it? Or is that a joke, too?"

"I'm sorry. That was silly of me."

She shifts her packages to her hip. "If I am to have a conversation on a public street, the least I can expect is to know the name of the person to whom I am talking."

"That's not what I meant. I mean, Jane Mansfield isn't my real name, but that's not why I said it was. I mean, it *is* my name, at least that's what everyone insists my name is; everyone here, that is. But that's neither here nor there. What I wanted to say is, and I know this will sound strange, but one day, people will be able to go to a theater, and instead of seeing actors on a stage, they will see actors on a screen, moving around and talking as if they were there in person, but of course they are not actually there. What they will see on the screen is merely a flat but very realistic picture of those actors."

By now she has a distressed look on her face.

"It's a harmless form of entertainment. You would like it," I add desperately.

I didn't mean to, but I sort of have her backed up against a wall and her eyes are darting around, probably in search of an escape.

"Anyway, what I really want to say is that the people who made movies of your books decided the heroes should be handsome. And that there should be a love scene at the end, you know, with kissing and an actual proposal, even though you left that sort of thing to the imagination. But see, that's the thing about movies. Nothing is left to the imagination. You read a book, and you see a picture of the characters and the scenes in your mind. You don't have that with a movie. It's all either up there on the screen laid out for you, or it isn't there at all. And you can't blame people for wanting kissing and romance and handsome heroes, because without them they would feel a bit deprived. And don't get me wrong, I adore your books, but sometimes even I feel a little deprived by those proposal scenes."

She looks at me for a minute, as if hooking onto

a bit of lucidity in the middle of my nonsense. And now I can see that she clearly doesn't like that piece of lucidity. She suddenly looks much taller than before, and there's steel in her eyes.

"You will excuse me," she says, "but I must go."

I move aside—I don't dare prevent her from going—but as I watch her take her first few brisk steps I know I can't just let her go off feeling insulted. If she would even stoop to be insulted by me, that is. Who am I to insult the greatest novelist who ever lived?

I quickly catch up alongside her. She gives out an exasperated sigh but keeps her eyes straight ahead as she strides on. I can't believe I've become a stalker. Of Jane Austen.

"Forgive me, Miss Austen. I had no right to say anything that might be construed as remotely critical of your work. Not that it matters to you what I think. You probably think I'm insane, as well as rude and annoying. But I'm not. Insane, that is."

I hear what sounds like a stifled laugh, but her face is still averted and hidden by her bonnet.

"Anyway, I just want you to know that one day you will be famous beyond your wildest imagination. And revered. Scholars will write books devoted to your work. Biographers will catalogue every detail of your life. Every word that has ever issued from your pen will be devoured by your adoring public. And still they will crave more."

She stops walking for a moment and turns to me

with the kind of smile you give to children; that is, if you are someone who doesn't like children.

"Miss Mansfield, or whatever it is your name might be. I fear you have been reading too many novels. Consider adding a measure of less fanciful prose to your daily studies." And with that she sails off.

I stand there watching her until she disappears around a corner. I don't dare follow her.

I hardly know how I got back to the shop where I left Mary and Louisa. I had wandered so far down the street and was so confused as to where I'd left them that had they not had the sense to wait outside the shop, I don't know where I would have ended up. It occurs to me, in fact, that I don't even know Louisa's address. But there they are, and I do my best to convince them there's no cause for alarm. I don't even know what I manage to say other than that I needed some air and got distracted by all the shops, which Louisa takes as further proof of my worthiness, queen of shopping that she is. Mary doesn't look as convinced.

We have a couple of hours to get ready for dinner and our night out, and I take the opportunity to spend some quiet time in the white vastness of the bridal suite. I've actually met my favorite dead author, and alive no less. And left her, no doubt, with the desire for a nineteenth-century version of a restraining order. Why couldn't I keep my mouth shut? Come to think of it, why didn't I see this meeting as a chance to find a way out of this time warp or whatever it is—why didn't I see that she could be the key to my getting back to my real life? After all, isn't she the surest link I have between both places? I feed my Austen addiction at home to such a point that I end up not only in what could be the setting for one of her novels, but I meet the woman herself. This can't be mere chance; it has to be the key to the mystery. But no, I waste this precious chance. I start holding forth on the pros and cons of adapting great literature to the big screen, and not just to the author of that great literature, but to the author who never gave her consent to a future world that butchers her great literature, and to the author who cannot possibly think any more of that conversation than that she had the misfortune to be cornered by a madwoman who claims to know the future.

By the time she got home she probably rationalized it all away. Or maybe I really gave her a class-A freak-out. I didn't mean to scare her, but who knows; perhaps she'll open her mind to the possibility that what I said was true. Maybe time is as fluid as the fortune-teller said it was, which means the future is up for grabs. Who knows; perhaps the rantings of this insane woman will influence my favorite author to make different choices. Maybe she'll start taking credit for her books, or mix more in literary circles, and who knows how that might affect her future? Maybe she'll meet some really interesting guy who appreciates her talents as a writer and sees her as an equal instead of breeding stock, and then she gets married, and then who knows how many other novels she writes? Maybe I won't be limited to her six books when I get back to my own time. And so maybe my meeting with Jane Austen could accomplish something after all, even if it doesn't give me the key to getting back my real life.

Then again, I can't imagine that marriage could prevent the illness that ultimately kills her, but who knows what the power of love might do? On the other hand, what if she becomes so enamored of married life (or so worn out raising kids) that she doesn't complete the rest of her books and I end up back in a future where the yet-to-be-published books never got published? Am I willing to sacrifice my own literary pleasures for the thought that my favorite author found true love?

It's all a perverse sort of wishful thinking anyway. The anonymous lady novelist will remain the anonymous lady novelist, and the memory of the crazed prophetess she encountered on the street will fade. *Stop resisting your destiny*, was what the fortune-teller said. *You, like everyone else, have a destiny to fulfill.* Jane Austen, with those penetrating eyes, steely will, and honey-sweet voice that could rip me to shreds if she so desired, sure looked like someone determined to fulfill her destiny, and nothing, certainly not me, would take her off her course.

Is the future so depressingly set in stone? Don't we have free will as well as destiny? Can't Jane Austen exercise her free will and still fulfill her destiny? Can't I go back to my own time and live in a world where she has still written all six novels or even more *and* died in her beloved husband's arms? Can't I use my own free will here to fulfill my destiny, and still get back to the place I'm supposed to be? Does that mean I'll alter my future in my own time? Will I go back to a reality where my entire life and personal history has changed? Will I even know it happened? My mind is becoming a contortionist again, and the chimes of the big clock down in the entrance hall remind me I have to stop ruminating on destiny and the future and get myself ready for a night out with my hosts.

It's a good thing Mary sends Hortense in to help me dress for the evening, because if she had not I might have come down to dinner with half my dress unbuttoned or no dress at all. That's how preoccupied I am, and day-to-day concerns like getting dressed just seem like a big waste of time. I manage to get through dinner without saying much, though I do drink a lot more than usual, thanks to Louisa's husband, Sir William, who joins us for dinner and makes sure my glass is refilled constantly. I still can't figure out what Louisa finds so repugnant about her husband; he's plump and shiny-faced but has kind eyes and good teeth, a quality not to be underestimated here. Most important, he seems attentive and polite to her, but who can say what goes on between them when they don't have houseguests.

By the time we leave for Lady Charlton's house, I am pretty tipsy. Which is nice, because I feel little of my usual trepidation at entering a strange home in which I'm expected to make small talk when all I usually want to do, even in the familiarity of such gatherings in my own world, is camouflage myself in a corner of a room. Tonight, however, all I can think of is the juxtaposition of destiny and free will, and whether it makes no difference what I do, or all the difference in the world.

Thirty-two

"So happy you could come to my little soirée, Miss Mansfield," says Lady Charlton, a stout, heavily jeweled woman swathed in aubergine silk.

Little, indeed. The two hundred or so guests are swallowed up by the palatial proportions of her house, or more precisely, her mansion, and through tall French doors I can see vast, torch-lit gardens and scattered groups of more guests strolling about. If this is what Louisa thinks London is like when it's "thin," then I can't imagine her life during the busy time of year.

Louisa stations us near one of the fireplaces and introduces me to so many people that faces blend into one another and I give up trying to remember a single name.

One thing does stand out, though, and that's the tone of this party: It's much less stiff and mannered than other social experiences I've had here so far; there are more smiles and meaningful looks passing between men and women, more out-and-out flirtation and less restraint than I've witnessed before. And besides, I see several women who are definitely wearing color on their lips and cheeks as well as face powder, and some of them actually know how to put it on. There aren't quite enough of them to approximate my worst nightmare, but still enough to make me more conscious than ever of my own naked face.

Between the unrestrained atmosphere and the wine in my system (which circulating servants take care to replenish almost as soon as we walk in), I am much more inclined to enjoy myself and much less obsessed with the question of destiny and free will than I would have imagined. Louisa further helps matters by demanding my opinion—the more frank and insulting, the better—of almost everyone who stops by to chat with us. What do I think of Lady Atwater's turban? Or of Sir Edward's flirtatious manner? When I suggest that the former's headdress is big enough to house a family of six, but too small for the latter's sense of self-importance, Louisa's squeals of delight only encourage me to continue playing the role of visiting wit.

I realize there is silence, rather than laughter, from my other female companion of the evening, and when I look over at her, she quickly looks down at her lap.

"Mary?"

After making sure Louisa is safely distracted by one of her friends, Mary says in a lowered voice, "Jane, I must confess I am not quite at ease with these new friends of my cousin's. I observe much here that I am not used to seeing in a party of respectable people."

As if to punctuate her words, a tall, imposing man who is standing near us and has been talking to a shorter man and a petite woman (the latter a couple, I would presume from their body language) takes the opportunity of running his index finger along the back of the woman's neck the moment her escort's back is turned. I can only imagine how something like that appears to Mary's virgin eyes.

Mary whispers into my ear. "I wonder if my cousin knows in what danger she may be placing her reputation."

"I'm sure you have nothing to worry about."

She doesn't look convinced. "Thank heaven Mrs. Smith did not accompany us." When Louisa demands my attention again, Mary goes back to examining her gloved hands in her lap.

"Miss Mansfield," Louisa says, "here is someone to give us fresh sources of amusement."

But this time, instead of a boxy matron decked out in too many diamonds or a candidate for midlife crisis in pants that are so tight he might as well be wearing a sausage casing, I am introduced to a fine specimen of manhood with dark brown hair, dark blue, almost violet, eyes, and a sensual, toothy smile. He is standing with a slender, delicate-featured woman who is far more demurely dressed than most of the other female guests, many of whom must have discovered some Regency version of the push-up bra, if I am to judge by their standing-room-only décolletage. His wife, I suppose. Too bad.

Louisa introduces him as Mr. Andrew Emery and his female companion as his cousin, Mrs. Haverstock.

Much better.

What am I thinking?

A little diversion never hurt anyone, did it?

"Shall I tell you what the charming Miss Mansfield had to say about a few of our acquaintance?" Louisa says, and begins whispering into Mr. Emery's ear. He looks at me with raised eyebrows, then bursts into laughter, and I find myself wanting to slap Louisa for making me into a spectacle.

"She is very naughty, is she not, Emery?" Louisa says.

"Very naughty indeed," he replies, caressing the words with his full lips and appraising me with those violet eyes.

"And so many amusing opinions, too," says Louisa. "Shall I tell Mr. Emery your views on marriage?"

She is clearly trying to amuse her friend by embarrassing me. "As you wish."

"Very well," says Louisa, and flicks her fan. "Did you know, Emery, that when I told Miss Mansfield she should waste no time securing a proper establishment for herself, she said she had not yet decided whether marriage was, in the words of one of her friends, 'an institution designed to subjugate women.' Have you ever heard anything like it? I declare my cousin's pretty young friend is the most amusing creature! I am most indebted to you, Mary, for bringing her to me."

Mary inclines her head politely, but I can see she's in agony.

"Miss Mansfield," says Mrs. Haverstock suddenly, "would you care to take a turn with me in the gardens? If your friends can spare you, that is."

"Go, go," Mary whispers, apparently as pleased as I am at this means of my escape from her cousin and her cousin's friend, and I allow myself to be chaperoned out of the room by the respectable-looking, cleavage-less Mrs. Haverstock.

As we walk into the gardens, which are much emptier than they were when I first arrived, we seem to be the only pair walking away from the house rather than toward it. I look over my shoulder to see liveried footmen in white wigs opening the French doors for the last few sets of garden-going guests, and in answer to my unspoken question, Mrs. Haverstock says, "The musical program is starting, I believe. Do you mind terribly? I do so enjoy the sweetness of these gardens, which are all the sweeter without the crowds."

"Not at all."

We stroll in silence for some time, the only sounds the crunching of gravel under our slippered feet and the faint strains of music and laughter coming from the house. While the gardens are fragrant and the air fresh, my mind is occupied with the scene I left inside. My instinctual dislike of Louisa wasn't unjust after all. Here she is, using me, a person she barely knows, to insult people she's probably known for years. Why should I think she would pass up an opportunity to make me look foolish in front of her attractive male friend, despite all that crap about finding me a husband? More important, why should I care if my words (well, Frank's words, to be precise) sound foolish to someone as insignificant to me as Andrew Emery?

Why then was I so thankful to leave that room? Maybe it was Louisa's coldness. It was the same coldness that I saw in how she treated her husband. I was only shocked at seeing it directed at me because I had allowed myself to mistake her momentary fascination with me for genuine admiration.

I shiver, and wrap my shawl around me more tightly.

"Dear me," says Mrs. Haverstock. "It is chilly indeed. Shall we explore this charming little summerhouse and warm ourselves inside for a moment?"

We are, at that moment, walking past the first of a row of small enclosed structures, each separated from the other by ornamental hedges and shrubs. This one, like all the others, is windowed but completely curtained, so it is impossible to see inside.

Why not, I think, and put my hand on the latch of the door, half expecting it to be locked. But it opens easily, and in the softly candlelit interior I can see piles of plush cushions arranged on the floor and lightweight white fabric draping the ceiling and walls, giving an Arabian-nights effect to the small space.

"Here," says Mrs. Haverstock, picking up a dark red velvet throw and putting it over my shoulders. And fastening it. It's not a throw, it's a cape. "Wrap yourself in this. And why not sit for a minute until you warm yourself."

"What about you?" I say, my words trailing off as the door opens and Andrew Emery slips in.

"What a pleasant surprise," he says, bowing. Then, he turns toward Mrs. Haverstock, and whether he gives her a look or some sort of signal I can't tell, but she curtseys to me and disappears into the darkness outside the door.

"What's going on here?"

He puts his finger to his lips and glides noiselessly to the pile of pillows I'm sitting on.

"Why did she leave?"

Again he doesn't answer. Instead he sits down with me and reaches for my gloved hand.

"Do you mind?" he says, swiftly pulling off my glove and bringing my hand to his lips.

I sputter with laughter to cover up my shock—his stripping my hand of its glove somehow feels exciting and forbidden and wrong all at the same time—and pull my hand away. "Is this Louisa's idea of a joke?"

He raises an eyebrow. "Your friend, if I may rightly call her that, knows nothing of our meeting. I would never compromise your honor."

"Oh, no. Of course not. You only show up, uninvited, to what you refer to as a meeting, dismiss your cousin so you could be alone with me. And—kiss my hand." (I can't even bring myself to say remove my glove.) "None of which, I have it on good authority, is considered appropriate behavior. What will Lady Charlton's guests think if Mrs. Haverstock returns to the house alone? Or if I return alone? Or if I'm found in here with you?"

I realize I'm not even half kidding. I, who have spent many a night alone with many a man in much less clothing than I am wrapped in at present. Yet part of me is outraged at this man's audacity.

"You may ease your mind on all those points. Mrs. Haverstock will certainly not return to the house alone. She will wait for us and accompany you back to the party. As for anyone discovering us . . ." He goes to the door and bolts it, then makes a little bow.

"And as for my kissing your hand, I hope you will forgive me. I was overcome by my good fortune in meeting a woman who does not surrender to the tyranny of social convention. I supposed you were as weary as I of what passes for conversation in a room full of strangers. And thus I seized my chance when I saw you and my cousin enter this room."

Emery produces a slim flask from an inside pocket of his coat and a couple of small metal cups from another pocket. "Shall we drink to the honest discourse of friends?"

"Why not." He does have a point, and he looks harmless enough. After all, he only removed my glove.

Emery sits beside me again, and I take one of the small cups from his hand. We raise our glasses to each other, and I drink. Or attempt to. Whatever is in my cup is so strong I almost choke. I was expecting wine or maybe the watered-down version of wine I've become used to drinking, and instead I'm tasting something more like whiskey, and not very smooth whiskey at that.

"I apologize," he says. "May I offer you something else?"

I laugh. "I don't suppose you have a full bar hidden in those pockets?"

"I do have a small bottle of good wine, which I stole from the house."

He reaches for my cup. "May I?" He downs its contents, then uncorks the wine bottle and pours me some.

The wine is red and delicious, with a faint taste of blueberries, and as I sip it I take as good a look at his face as I can in the soft candlelight and decide he's not going to try and pull anything funny, especially not with his cousin waiting outside. Though there is something a little off about her role in all this.

"May I speak plainly, Miss Mansfield?"

"No, lie away."

He smiles. "I do understand. You are not sure I am to be trusted. After all, it was Lady Ashwell who disclosed your confidences to me in such a public manner. If a friend could have such little regard for your feelings, how could you credit a man of her acquaintance with more?"

I hold out my cup for more wine. "Good point." Though he did laugh at said disclosures.

"I can only hope you will allow me to prove myself worthy of your company. I have only the highest respect for you."

"If you say so."

He refills my cup and his own, and for a few minutes we drink silently, listening to the faraway sounds of stringed instruments, a piano, and what sounds like a tenor coming from the house.

The wine is spreading a pleasant warmth through my veins, and I lean back into the pillows. Then I remember Mrs. Haverstock.

"Don't you think your cousin must be cold waiting outside?"

"I can assure you," Emery says, softly caressing my hair, his voice fading to a whisper and his breath warm on my cheek, "that she is neither cold nor waiting outside. She is as safe," he continues, punctuating his words with soft kisses on my forehead and eyelids, "and as warm, as we are."

He softly touches my lips with his own, and, what the hell, I let him kiss me, open-mouthed, tongues exploring. I fall into that familiar, heightened sensation of desire and wanting and mindless heat accompanied by an overly mindful analysis. It is that excitement that is all about newness and unknowns, the newness of this man, of this situation, the triumph of knowing I'm desired, of hearing him breathe and feeling him grow hard as he pushes himself against me, and that anticipatory wondering of how far I will venture into the as-yet unknowns. Will I let him take off clothes and which ones, will I let him into my bed, will he be a good lover, will *I* be a good lover . . .

Wait a minute. I don't even know this man. Not that such considerations necessarily stopped me before, given the right mixture of loneliness and alcohol.

He moves his lips to my neck and runs his fingers down my one bare arm, sending a tingling sensation all the way down to my toes. Yes, I am tired of what passes for conversation in a room full of strangers. I am tired of surrendering to the tyranny of social convention. I want to be drunk and have sex and forget everything I'm supposed to do or be or say.

Emery is now maneuvering one of his legs

between mine, a preparatory move that sets off alarms, those of the birth-control-sexually-transmissible-disease kind. But there is no bathroom to retreat to in order to insert diaphragm, nor a drawer from which to retrieve condoms. Nor is there any hope whatsoever that my inadvertent partner of the night has a supply in his pants pocket or wallet, or in this case, in one of the inside pockets of his long coat with tails.

Am I really about to risk unprotected sex in a world without antibiotics, a woman's right to choose, or adequate personal hygiene? And with a total stranger, no less?

Are you kidding me?

"Uh, Andrew," I say, attempting to gently maneuver myself out from under him.

"Say my name again." His knee is now engaged in raising my skirt.

Gentle maneuvers are out. "Andrew, stop."

"I beg your pardon?"

"Stop." I have my hands up against his chest now, pushing him away.

He rolls off me, but keeps one leg resting against mine.

"What is it, my love?"

"There are potential consequences to our actions, which I am not prepared to deal with."

"You shall have my protection, and every comfort you desire. A house in town. The finest jewels. Just name your wish."

Apparently, some things haven't changed in two hundred years. Is there anything a man won't say to get laid? I've heard them all, from "I can't wait for you to meet my mother" to "You're the first person I've ever told that to," after which I'm lucky if I get so much as a perfunctory, post-coital I-had-a-great-time-with-you email, let alone an actual relationship.

And now I'm expected to believe that Andrew Emery, an acquaintance of under one hour, despite his attempts to mark me with his scent, is planning to make me his kept woman? In an era when I imagine there would have to be serious cash up front—or the deed to an estate—in order for a woman to make such a no-turning-back sort of choice? And even if he is sincere, who would want such a thing? It's bad enough to be a baby-making machine with no epidural in sight in exchange for the state-sanctioned title of "Mrs." before one's name. But to be a "Miss" with an ever-increasing brood of children, just waiting for her man to grow weary of stretch marks and spit-up? No thank you.

And then it hits me. Regardless of what era I'm in right now, or how I'm supposed to fulfill my so-called destiny, I refuse to make my destiny a lifetime of nights in the arms of yet another man I don't care about but want to care about because the alternative is being alone, or even worse, a man I care about even though I know he can never give me what I really want. I'm tired of settling for two strange bodies fumbling with buttons and zippers and each other to reach the momentary high of sexual release only to have that replaced by the inevitable abyss I fall into afterward. I will not settle for that kind of destiny. Not here. Not anywhere.

And suddenly, I truly understand free will.

And in that moment, I realize that Andrew has grabbed my hand and is moving it toward his now-opened pants, which reveal the largest penis I have ever seen in my life. *Guinness Book of World Records* material. If I weren't as struck as I am by the absurdity of the situation, I might run out of the room screaming. Which is when I begin to laugh. And laugh. The human sexual act can be seen in a comic light under the best of circumstances. But in this case it is downright hilarious. No doubt the wine plays some part in my amusement, but I can hardly straighten my clothes I am so doubled over with laughter.

My laughter, to put it delicately, softens Andrew's resolve, and with a face so red I can see the color in the candlelight, he quickly buttons his now-sleeping beast into its former hiding place.

"I'm so sorry," I say, in between snorts of laughter. "It's not you."

He looks so humiliated that I manage to regain control by biting my lip. "It's nerves. Fear, really. I have laughing fits when I'm frightened. Please forgive me."

His eyes are ice. "I shall distress you no more, Miss Mansfield." He bows curtly, puts his hand on the door latch, and turns to go.

"And your cousin? Will she be waiting to escort me back to the house?"

He looks at me coldly. "You appear to be perfectly capable of taking care of yourself."

"Appearances can deceive. Which is why you might want to find her and ask her to walk me back. After all, I wouldn't want to worry about returning alone and be carried off by a fit of nervous laughter. People might start asking me all sorts of questions, and what would I say then?"

"I am at your service," he says tightly, and leaves the room.

Within five minutes, Mrs. Haverstock knocks softly on the door and silently walks me back to the party. I decide there's no reason to worry about Andrew's spreading gossip, since the farce in which our tryst concluded likely trumps any triumph he might have felt, or wished to disclose, in nearly compromising my virtue.

Compromising my virtue? Are these thoughts really mine? Or have I already lost my mind?

As I enter the house and part from Mrs. Haverstock without a word, I shudder. I catch sight of Mary at the back of the music room; her smile is innocent, trusting. She has no idea what I just did—or what I almost did. As I make my way toward her, I feel a rush of gratitude for her friendship. Thank God I came to my senses before things got out of control. At that moment I spot Andrew Emery across the room; we both avoid making eye contact.

I settle into a chair next to Mary and try to turn my attention to the music. Within less than half an hour, I see Emery and his cousin, if that's really who she is, leave.

Thirty-three

When there is a break in the music, Louisa asks me if I know where Emery is. I just shrug with as much wide-eyed innocence as I can manage, and finally I overhear one of her friends telling her that he and his cousin left quite some time before. Louisa gives me a penetrating look from over her fan, but I ignore her and turn to Mary.

Louisa then attempts to return me to my role of court jester. What do I think of so-and-so's hat, or gown, or wife? I refuse to take the bait this time, and answer her with bland neutrality and perfect, ladylike propriety.

Louisa's eyes narrow, and her fan increases in velocity.

Mary, however, pats my hand and whispers, "Well done."

Louisa soon disappears into the crowd, presumably to seek out more amusing companions. I figure she's successful, because by the time she takes us home in her carriage, she seems to be in a cheerful mood again.

The next morning I wake up feeling like I've smoked a pack of cigarettes, and Mary, I hear from the maid who comes in to help me dress, is in bed with a cold, Hortense reluctant to leave her side to deliver the news herself.

A gap in my room's white curtains reveals a sky

that is sooty gray. I don't even want to think about how polluted the air must be. Nor, as I watch the coal in my fireplace burn and glow, will I ever think of a barbecue in quite the same way.

I head down the hall and check on Mary, who is under the covers, a few damp strands of hair stuck to her forehead. She gives me a weak smile as I feel her forehead and cheeks with the back of my hand. Not particularly warm, just clammy.

"I don't think you have a fever." I blot her forehead with a cloth.

"I think the worst of it passed during the night."

"Didn't sleep well?"

She shakes her head.

"Poor girl."

"A bit more rest is all I need."

"Shall I send up some breakfast?"

She shakes her head. "Must sleep."

At the breakfast table, when I tell Louisa why Mary isn't coming down, she drops her butter knife on her plate with a clatter and springs up to ring for her cook, housekeeper, and maid, dispensing orders that they should do everything to make Mary comfortable, including summoning Louisa's physician immediately.

I suppress a groan. "You are not going to have her bled, are you? She is weak enough as it is."

Louisa glares. "I imagine that is for Adams to decide."

"Did I happen to mention last night that I heard

Lady Holloway and Mrs. Davis saying how only the backwards country doctors still bleed their patients, and that in town such practices are considered *très outré*?"

Louisa snatches up her fan and creates a small wind tunnel. "I can assure you that Adams is highly regarded amongst many of my acquaintance."

I only nod, keeping my eyes steadily fixed on hers until she looks down and clears her throat. She rings the bell again for her maid, who comes breathlessly into the room seconds later.

"Send Mr. Adams in to see me before he attends Miss Edgeworth."

"Outré!" says Louisa, the second the maid closes the door behind her. "As if Eleanor Holloway and that vulgar Fanny Davis do anything but embody the word."

She gazes out the window, the weak sunlight highlighting the pockmarks on her cheeks. As if reading my mind, she raises the fan to her face again, then peers at me from behind its protection.

"What else did that pair of harridans have to say?"

"I am afraid that is all I heard." Of course, I heard nothing at all.

"A pity. They can be so amusing, you know."

After breakfast I check on Mary, who appears to be sleeping peacefully, Mrs. Smith having resumed her maternal post in a chair next to the bed.

"She will be all right, won't she?"

Mrs. Smith regards me with a kinder expression than she's ever bestowed on me before. "Miss Edgeworth has been prone to sniffles and sneezing ever since she was a little girl. But she is always well again."

"Would you allow me to watch over her till she wakes up? She seems to be sleeping peacefully, and it would give you a chance to have some breakfast."

Mrs. Smith assents, but unfortunately Mary's rest is short-lived, thanks to Louisa's making a brief, noisy appearance in the room to coo over her cousin, plump up her pillows, and apologize for her "absolute uselessness in a sickroom," while congratulating Mary for having in me "a most faithful and competent nurse."

I think I'm going to be sick myself.

As soon as Louisa sails out, leaving a cloud of gardenia in her wake, I soothe Mary back to sleep, which, luckily, isn't difficult.

After a couple of days of hovering over Mary—which is about all Mrs. Smith and Hortense allow me to do—and avoiding Louisa as much as is possible while staying in her house, I can see that Mary is a hundred percent stronger. The doctor agrees and orders her to the country as soon as possible for a change of air. I suspect he's just as anxious to have us gone as Louisa, to whom we can no longer provide amusement. He has grumbled several times about not being able to give his patient the best treatment and how much faster she would have recovered with a little blood-letting.

Within twenty-four hours, we are packed and ready to carry out the doctor's orders. Louisa dabs her dry eyes with a delicate handkerchief and kisses me on both cheeks, but if she's fooling anyone it's certainly not me. As the carriage door closes behind me and I settle in for a bone-jangling journey back to Jane's village, I am happy to leave behind the smog and pretense and duplicity of Jane's London. And I hope my favorite author soon has the chance to do so, too.

A couple of skin-crawling nights in the best of England's coaching inns and a few bruised bones later, I'm back home, such as it is. If being in a city I've visited in two different time periods and meeting Jane Austen herself haven't given me the magic key to getting back to my real life, I don't know what will. I no longer feel desperate about it, though. I realize this with quiet certainty rather than resignation. It doesn't mean I've given up. I'm just tired of struggling, that's all.

In the meantime, Mary's heartfelt good-byes and entreaties that I call on her soon, and Mr. M's warm hug as I step out of Mary's carriage almost make me feel like I have come home.

Until, that is, Mrs. M greets me in the entranceway with a double air kiss, and the temperature in the room drops about thirty degrees.

Thirty-four

"Come into my dressing room after you have removed the dust of your journey," Mrs. M says. "And be quick about it, dear," she murmurs into my ear, withdrawing with a smile that in no way reaches her pale blue eyes. "I have missed you."

Mr. M slinks off, mumbling something about his atelier, and I shiver as I head toward the stairs and my room.

A grin splits Barnes's broad face as she greets me with a curtsey, then swipes at her eyes with a corner of her apron, asking me to pardon her silliness. Instead, I give her a hug. "Oh, miss," she says, turning away and dabbing at her face until she is composed enough to face me again. "Let's get you out of those clothes."

Within a few minutes I am sponged, perfumed, wearing a clean gown, and padding down the hall to Mrs. M's dressing room.

I tap on the door, and even before her imperious "Enter," my stomach does its habitual two-step.

She is settled regally on a sofa beside a window, the fading daylight and candles in sconces giving her pale skin a golden glow as she reads a letter. Should I really be intimidated by someone in a frilly cap and ruffles around her neck?

She looks up from the letter. "You can be at no

loss, Jane, to know why I have summoned you here."

I am unable to repress a snort of laughter. "Sorry. You sounded just like Lady Catherine De Bourgh when she showed up at Longbourn to frighten Lizzy Bennet away from marrying Darcy."

She taps the letter with her forefinger, her eyes boring into me. "Do not flatter yourself. If this report is true, you are less likely to marry than Miss Bennet's sister was before Darcy bribed her seducer into marrying her."

Suddenly I'm not so amused. "Report?"

She sits back against the cushions, eyeing me like a cat who is wondering whether to kill the mouse or torture it.

Can she possibly have heard about Emery? No; that's impossible . . . isn't it? My knees start to tremble, so I move toward one of the chairs opposite her.

She holds out a hand, as if to bar my way. "I did not invite you to sit."

Very well. I'll just stand here and see who blinks first.

She smiles. "Were the shops in Bath to your liking?"

"I—yes, of course." What is she up to?

She eyes my figure appraisingly. "I was simply noticing your new gown. That buff color suits you. Must look well with the buff ribbons on your new bonnet and brown shawl."

I am about to open my mouth and tell her I don't have a new bonnet or a new brown shawl, but something tells me not to—wait a minute. Brown shawl? Buff-colored ribbons? That's exactly what Mary lent me for my rendezvous with James.

That's exactly what Susan saw me wearing. She must have written the letter Mrs. M is holding.

I will myself to betray nothing with my voice or facial expressions. "It is a pity you were not there to advise me on my purchases, Mama. For I bought no such shawl or bonnet, though you are right; they would look well with this gown."

Mrs. M narrows her eyes. "Do you know to whom you are talking?"

I keep my eyes on her, commanding myself not to flinch.

She rises off the sofa and shakes the letter at me. "My dear niece Susan informs me that you, clad in that very same bonnet and shawl—and God help you when I find them in your wardrobe—come, we shall settle this now." She grabs my hand and pulls me out of the room, down the hall, and into my bedroom.

"As I was saying"—she flings open the doors of my armoire, pulling out gowns and bandboxes, rifling through every article of clothing and dumping them on the floor, on my bed—"You were seen in, shall we say, intimate discourse with a man in Sydney Gardens."

Mrs. M continues to go through clothes and

drawers and boxes, while I try to smooth away the terror that must be on my face. Did Susan recognize James as a former footman in this house? If so, I'm finished.

"And this man with whom you were conversing so intimately, according to my niece, was neither your brother, nor any man of her acquaintance. This man, who has not even the air of a gentleman, in her words, who is perhaps a common tradesman" —and here she stops ransacking my room to watch my face—"is seen in public, with *my* daughter, touching her cheek, as if they were lovers."

I try not to sigh my relief audibly. Thank God Susan didn't recognize James.

"Do you deny it? Consider carefully before you answer."

I stand as tall as I can, meet her eyes, and summon some quiet outrage into my voice. "There is nothing to consider. Of course I deny it. The only possible explanation is that Susan saw someone else and mistook that person for me. As you can see, I own no such shawl or bonnet. And I was in Sydney Gardens only with Miss Edgeworth and Mrs. Smith, not with any man. Ever."

"I do not suppose Miss Edgeworth has such a shawl or bonnet?"

My eyes never waver from her face. "Surely you do not think my friend is the person Susan saw."

"You are a cool one." She circles around me, her look detached and predatory. "Should I discover anything to disprove your claim, you shall find yourself confined to this house, without so much as a shilling at your command, until such time as I find a proper situation for you. One that will make a sojourn in Newgate sound like an agreeable alternative."

She gestures toward the mess on the floor and glares at me accusingly. "Now look at all this time I have wasted, when I still need to prepare for my own journey tomorrow."

She's going away? I feel the corners of my mouth twitching as I will myself not to smile, and I cough to cover it up.

She pulls out a lace-trimmed hankie and holds it up to her mouth. "I hope you have not caught a cold. I do not wish to be ill for my journey."

"Where are you going?"

"To see Clara, as I told you at least three times in my letters, if you would ever pay attention. With a slight detour to see my niece in Bath first." She bares her teeth in a chilling smile. "I do not know what you are about, dear daughter. I do not even want to know. However, I shall make certain Susan sees that the sword of false witness can cut both ways. Depend on it."

She gives me a sort of can't-be-bothered little wave with her handkerchief. "I shan't see you in the morning." She flourishes the hankie toward the piles of clothes, hats, and bandboxes. "Do put that in order."

And that's it, it's over. She's gone.

That was close, too close. I sit down in a chair, taking deep breaths, trying to slow the beating of my heart. It's all right. She doesn't know anything. And as soon as I can get word to Mary, I'm going to ask her to burn both bonnet and shawl. I owe my freedom to the fact that they are in her closet, not mine.

In the meantime, I'm going to turn this room back into an orderly place. Just looking at the piles of gowns and shawls and bonnets makes my stomach knot. I start picking up clothes and fold everything into neat piles. I want to get it all put away. In the closet. Just like my meeting with James. Just like my tryst with Andrew Emery.

Oh, God. How stupid have I been? If Mrs. M was this incensed over an alleged touch of my face by a strange man in a public place, what would she do to me if I'd succumbed to self-destruction and actually bedded Emery? What would she do if I was pregnant? If he abandoned me? Would I ever be able to get back to my old life with a baby inside me? Would I want to?

And then it hits me. Even if reclaiming my old life is still an option, what sort of life would I have left behind for Jane? If she was able to reclaim her own life, she would have every reason to regret having done so. I would have doomed her to a life of social ostracism, of, at best, expulsion to a remote farmhouse somewhere, like Maria Bertram of *Mansfield Park.* Or at worst, a descent into prostitution, tuberculosis, and a poorhouse, like Eliza Brandon of *Sense and Sensibility.*

Some guardian of this life I've been. Like Willoughby, *the whole of* my *behaviour, from the beginning to the end of the affair, has been grounded on selfishness.* When I ditched Mary's servants, I never gave a thought to how it might affect them. Or Mary. When I was indiscreet with James, and when I nearly slept with Emery, I gave no thought whatsoever to the consequences for Jane. I gave no thought to what it might mean for a woman whose entire well-being hinges on obeying the inflexible laws of propriety, or at least giving the appearance of doing so.

Like Darcy, *I have been a selfish being all my life.* Or at least in Jane's life.

I'm sorry, Jane, I whisper into the darkness as I lie in bed, sleepless despite my fatigue. I'll do better. For both of us.

Thirty-five

Without Mrs. M's tyrannical presence, the entire routine of the house is different, as is Mr. Mansfield. At breakfast he shovels his food with even more gusto than before, and without his wife's sarcasm and general disapproval in the air, he is even talkative. He wants to know every detail of my trip, and after satisfying him with a highly edited version, I persuade him at dinner to tell me about his day in the atelier. It doesn't take much to open the floodgates, and with a little more encouragement, he is soon pouring me a glass of wine in his sanctum sanctorum.

I sip my wine and walk around the room, inhaling the heavy scent of oil paints and trying to make out what's on some of the canvases stacked along the walls and behind almost every piece of furniture. There are a couple of easels draped with paint-splotched cloths, and I pause before one of them. "Is this the one you worked on today?"

"How did you know?"

I move my hand toward the cloth. "May I?"

He clears his throat. "It is not nearly finished, and I fear the subject may not be suitable, though I have made some improvements lately."

He shrugs, then uncovers the canvas and reveals a semi-repesentational painting of two lovers entwined.

He takes a long drink of wine. "The figures were, how shall I say, undraped before. But I feared that if I kept them in such a state they might shock those with delicate sensibilities."

The pale skin of the two figures is set off by bold swirls and splotches of color behind them, and I wonder whether the lovers might not make a more powerful contrast without the purple swaths of cloth that strategically cover their bodies.

"I like it," I say, "but I can't help but wonder why you would alter your work just to placate a bunch of prudes."

Mr. Mansfield lets out a short sputtering laugh. "That is just what Mr. Edgeworth said when he made his take-leave visit here, though in far more polite terms than my daughter." He attempts a disapproving frown, but the corners of his mouth are twitching.

I ask to see more of his work, and one by one he lifts up each canvas and props it up on his desk. Most are completely non-representational, wild streaks, swaths, and dashes of color, some angry and dark, others bursting with golden and pastel lights. Again I am struck with how ahead of his time his canvases are, a universe away from the formal portraits and sedate landscapes that comprise the typical paintings I have seen elsewhere. I imagine his passion must be a lonely one, and he glows with pride when I praise his work.

As I am about to leave, I notice a small framed

picture on his desk. It is covered by a cloth except for a corner that's sticking out. "May I look?" I ask, and he hesitates before nodding his assent. I lift the cover and see a portrait of a young man, quite handsome, sitting in a garden, his face suffused with sunlight. It is a small painting, but the details are so fine that I can read the expression on the subject's face. He looks happy, content.

"Who is this man?"

He clears his throat. "It is a likeness taken of me when I was but one-and-twenty."

"Who painted it?"

He stammers his reply. "Her name was Miss Allcott, now Mrs. Lyle."

"You were very handsome."

"Ah, well." He fusses with the cover as he replaces it on the picture, and puts it into a desk drawer.

"Tell me about her."

"Who?"

"Miss Allcott."

He averts his eyes, his face crimson, and busies himself by rearranging a few of the stacked canvases. "You mean Mrs. Lyle. I heard she married into a family of—"

"No, I mean Miss Allcott."

"Jane—"

"You were in love with her, weren't you."

He almost drops the canvas he's holding. "You forget yourself, Jane."

"But I'm right, aren't I?"

"Jane, your mother—"

"This is not about her. I want to know about you—Papa." Saying that gives me a warm feeling inside that has nothing to do with the wine.

Mr. Mansfield sighs and puts down the canvas, then sinks into a chair and takes a sip of his wine. "It is getting late."

"Tell me about her. Please?"

"It was a long time ago. I was very young, she had no fortune, and my father forbade the match. Her parents sent her away, and of course, I met your mother."

"And Miss Allcott?"

"I never saw her again."

I don't know why, but I tear up, and I can tell he sees it happen. He swallows hard and springs up, busying himself again by covering up the canvas of the lovers.

"Thank you for showing me the picture," I say. "The lovers are an inspiration. With or without clothes."

He smiles. "Good night, my dear."

"Good night . . . Father." I hug him hard, which generates an embarrassed chuckle.

"Well, well, Janey girl. It's heaven to have you back."

When I go up to my room, I wonder how different my life might have been if I'd had a father like Mr. M instead of the sorry excuse for a dad whose face I can hardly remember. Or how different Mr. M's life would have been had he married this Miss Allcott, someone who loved him as only a woman in love could make the spindly Mr. M look like a hero from a novel.

But life doesn't usually have happily ever afters. Mr. M is stuck with Mrs. M, just like my mother is stuck with the boyfriend she'll never leave for fear of dying alone, and just like I was almost stuck with Frank for fear of never getting married.

But I'm not stuck with Frank now, so why should I even think of myself in such terms? Besides, not getting married couldn't possibly be a worse fate than having Frank for a husband. In fact, in some circumstances not getting married might not be so bad at all. For example, if Mr. M were a widower, sharing his house might not be so bad for an unmarried daughter.

Still, things change. Say his unmarried daughter got married after all. And he got lonely. What if Miss Allcott's husband were dead?

I laugh when I realize I am fantasizing about the deaths of two people, which seems to be the only option in this world for getting out of a lousy marriage. Better to stay single than to venture into that territory.

I wonder what kind of marriage Edgeworth had. I suppose it couldn't have been too bad; why else would he be willing to do it again? Then again, his wife could have been a humorless priss. That would be a sorry fate indeed for someone with Edgeworth's sense of the ridiculous. I smile, thinking of his having made a similar comment about the lovers painting.

No, he doesn't suffer fools gladly. But that doesn't change the fact that he's not to be trusted.

But are you not tempted to hear the accused testify before pronouncing your final sentence?

Of course I am.

No. I am not. I will not be tempted by him, or by Wes. One thing I must say on Frank's behalf. He never even tried to explain himself. After all, there's no denying one's nature.

Thirty-six

At breakfast the next morning, I am sipping my hot chocolate while Mr. Mansfield demolishes a stack of toast. Suddenly he looks like he's just bitten into a rock and puts down a half-eaten slice.

"I almost forgot. Your mother decided to return in three weeks instead of the six she had planned."

"Ah." And thus ends my career as an old maid living in happy contentment with her single father.

Mr. M puts down his napkin and leaves the table, mumbling something about going into his atelier.

As for me, I intend not to waste a single hour of freedom from Mrs. M. Today I'll start by rereading a few chapters of her first edition of *Sense and Sensibility* and maybe taking a stroll.

When I pull all three volumes from their shelf in the library (where I only just returned them after their travels with me to Bath and London), I notice the third volume has a bookmark in it; for some reason I hadn't noticed that before, probably placed my own slip of ribbon right over it when I got to that page. Randomly placed? Or did Mrs. M stop reading at a certain point?

I open the book to see, and get sucked right in. It's the part where Willoughby, having heard that Marianne is dying, shows up to seek forgiveness.

I remember the first time I read that chapter; I actually felt a little sorry for Willoughby. But the second time I read it was right after a breakup, and I changed my tune. Thereafter I would always get a bit irritated that Elinor was such a pushover for Willoughby's sufferings, despite her attempts to remain unmoved. Is his pain supposed to eclipse the fact that he abandoned Marianne's predecessor after knocking her up, then dumped Marianne for an ice princess with a fat checkbook?

Is Wes's pain supposed to eclipse the fact that his alibi made it possible for Frank to cheat on me? Would I be as seduced by his sufferings—if I ever returned his phone calls—as Elinor is by Willoughby's? Of course I would. Which is why I had to shut him out—why I'll still have to shut him out; that is, if I ever get a chance to do so.

Maybe I should start the book from the beginning and skip that scene when I get up to it. Who am I kidding? As if I'd ever skip any scene that Jane Austen wrote.

I pick up the first volume and take it up to my room, ready to settle in for a couple of hours of reading. But first, I'll get that knitted blanket from the bottom of my armoire and prop up my feet. That'll be nice and cozy.

I go to pull out the blanket, but it appears to be caught on something in the back of the armoire. I tug a little harder, and out comes the blanket, as well as the bottom panel of my armoire, which reveals the top of a rectangular compartment I've never seen before. But why would I; there's no apparent handle or groove for one's finger. In fact, I suppose if it weren't for Mrs. M tearing everything out of my armoire, which must have jarred the lid of the compartment enough to catch the knitted fabric of the blanket when I put everything back, I never would have discovered it myself.

Could this be where—I peer into the compartment, and sure enough, there are packets of letters tied with ribbon, several journals, and a book whose leather covers with gold-tooled edges give me a jolt of recognition. The book is impossibly familiar, but how could it be? Yet I know I have held it in my hands before. Many times. The title page reads, *Poems by William Cowper* and the date, 1806.

The book is place-marked with several strips of paper and lengths of ribbon. I open to one of the places marked with paper. There are a few lines underlined in a poem called "Mutual Forbearance, Necessary to the Happiness of the Married State":

The kindest and the happiest pair
Will find occasion to forbear;
And something, every day they live,
To pity, and perhaps forgive.

This is what Edgeworth said to me at the ball. I turn over the strip of paper, and penned in tiny letters are the words *Whatever I have done, I beg you take pity and forgive—C.E.*

I open to another page marked with a ribbon. Underlined is a passage from "The Progress of Error":

Remorse, the fatal egg by pleasure laid
In every bosom where her nest is made,
Hatched by the beams of truth, denies him rest,
And proves a raging scorpion in his breast.

Is this in response to the first passage I read? Did I even read them in the proper order?

And all at once I know that this is a conversation in passages, the book passed back and forth between Edgeworth and Jane, each underlining passages for the other, hers marked with ribbon, his with paper.

There are more than just strips of paper marking Edgeworth's underlined passages; there are larger folded sheets tucked in here and there. I pull out one at random, and in Edgeworth's spidery handwriting is a passage he attributes to Scott's "Lay of the Last Minstrel":

True love's the gift which God has given
To man alone beneath the heaven.
It is not Fantasy's hot fire,
Whose wishes, soon as granted, fly;
It liveth not in fierce desire,
With dead desire it doth not die;
It is the secret sympathy,

The silver cord, the silken tie,
Which heart to heart, and mind to mind,
In body and in soul can bind.

I reread the same three passages over and over, and each time I see myself in the one marked by ribbon. Each time it is less as if someone else had marked it. And I know that remorse—the beams of truth that deny me rest—is a confession, not an accusation.

There is a quick rap at the door. I shove the book into the recess in the armoire, and Mr. M pops his head in to tell me he will be out for a couple of hours. I stand up and stretch—I need some air before I can examine whatever else is in that book. And then there are the journals, the packets of letters. I have days of reading ahead of me. Now that I've finally discovered Jane's writings, it is almost too much to face. I need to walk first.

Closing everything up securely in the compartment, I go down to the library and open the French doors to the garden, and the mild warmth and blue skies are irresistible.

I literally have one foot out the door when Barnes appears at the entrance to the library and announces Edgeworth.

My stomach goes into freefall. I'm not ready for this. I could tell Barnes to say I'm not here, but before I complete the thought I hear myself say, "Send him in."

I have half a second to prepare myself before he appears at the library door, his face flushed and the ends of his hair slightly damp, as if he's been running, or swimming. His eyes are questioning, and my knees turn to water.

"Would you like to sit?" I say, wobbling into the nearest chair myself.

Edgeworth perches on the edge of a sofa and fidgets. He opens his mouth to speak, which is the exact second that I do the same.

"I—"

"Please."

"No, you first," we say in unison.

A pause, and then we both stammer out a syllable at the same moment. We both stop cold, and at the exact moment start laughing.

"One thing you could say in favor of such a conversation," Edgeworth says, "we will never have occasion for conflict."

I sober. "You don't need language to have conflict."

He's not smiling anymore.

I clear my throat. "I was just about to take a walk."

"Shall I leave or—may I join you?"

I nod, and we leave the library through the French doors. I am hyperaware of his proximity to me, vigilant about not brushing against his shoulder, even though he is at least four inches to my right.

We enter a grove of trees, and he breaks the silence. "I have a lot to say to you."

A chill rushes up my back. That's exactly what Wes said to me when I ran into him on that last day of my old life.

All of a sudden I'm trembling. Edgeworth doesn't seem to notice. He does stop walking, however, which is good. I cannot possibly walk this rigidly and hold a conversation at the same time. I lean against a tree trunk.

He points toward a bench. Not, thankfully, the same one where he proposed to me. "Shall we sit?"

This is an even better way to camouflage the shaking of my knees. What's wrong with me?

He keeps a comfortable distance from me on the other end of the bench, looking down at his hands before he finally raises his soft hazel eyes and says, "I know what Mary told you about me."

My stomach drops.

His eyes bore into me. "I want you to know what happened."

"All right, then." And I look him in the eye right back, affecting a bravado that I don't feel.

But he doesn't speak right away; he drops his gaze and moves off the bench, breaking off a twig from the tree above us and stripping its leaves. "Mary did see me kissing a lady who was in my service. It was wrong, but it happened only once. A kiss, nothing more."

He drops the naked twig on the ground and looks at me. I keep my face as expressionless as I can.

He clears his throat and flushes a deep red. "Not that I was not tempted, willing as the lady was, and unattached as I was then. You see, I had not yet met you."

He thrusts his hands into his pockets and looks down at his boots. "Mary would not speak to me of what she saw. When next she mentioned the lady's name, it was to accuse me of fathering her child. Which I most certainly did not do."

He sits on the edge of the bench again and looks me in the eye. "Now you know everything."

I stand, drawing myself up to my full height, which is pretty tall in this body. "You know what's most astonishing? You actually look like you believe what you're saying."

"I do not understand," he says, springing to his feet.

"Why don't I spell it out for you then. Jane—I mean I—saw you coming out of the stables followed by a woman with auburn hair. And that was *after* you had met her; I mean, me."

His face pales, and he swallows hard. "Dear God." He buries his face in his hands.

"My thoughts exactly."

"Stupid, stupid. How could I be so stupid?" He thumps his forehead with the heel of his hand.

"Spare me the *mea culpas*." I stalk off toward the house.

Within seconds I hear the crunch of his rapid stride on the gravel path close behind me. "Jane."

He catches up alongside me. I keep my eyes trained straight ahead. In a couple of minutes I'll reach the house.

He grabs my hand and pulls me to a stop, stands in front of me to block my path. "Jane, nothing happened. I swear to you. She wanted my advice, and I agreed to meet with her. I could not do so in the house, for I did not wish to . . . I had no idea if others in my household had the same mistaken notion of my role in the young lady's situation as my sister did."

If this is a lie, he's a fast thinker.

"She said she trusted me because I did not take what she had so freely offered. I urged her to tell me who the father was, but she would not. And so I added to the sum already promised her by my sister. What more could I have done?"

His eyes are imploring. He looks sincere. No, I'm not going to fall for it. "You sure looked like you did a lot more than that," I say, remembering the straw in his hair and the way the woman reached for him. But my words sound hollow even to my own ears.

What is stopping me from believing him? What am I holding on to? Fear? Guilt? Shame creeps over me as I remember how I ran into James's arms the second I doubted Edgeworth. And how I almost lost my virginity to Emery, a calculating, and by all appearances, experienced seducer.

I ran into James's arms? *My* virginity? I'm starting to get dizzy.

Edgeworth's voice brings me back. "I won't deny the lady, shall I say, attempted to express her gratitude in a manner I did not encourage."

He puts his hand on my arm, but I shrug out of his grasp. Why did I do that?

"Jane." His voice is breaking.

I look up into his face, which is almost as pale as his shirt. A tear is running down his cheek.

"Not only would it be dishonorable to accept remuneration of any kind for my charity toward this lady, but I had also already met, and fallen in love, with you."

"But I thought—"

Edgeworth flings out his arms. "You're not listening to me."

He grabs my shoulders. "Don't you understand? There is no one else."

He pulls me close, wrapping his arms around me. And my whole body relaxes its grip on all the anger, all the bitterness, all the fear I've been holding onto for so long. I'm so light I could float. I don't even think I'm resting my weight on my own feet. And then his lips graze my neck, leaving a trail of tiny featherlight kisses as he works his way up to my mouth, and I hold his face between my hands and kiss him back, drinking in the taste of him, the warm-linen-and-soap scent of his skin that is so inexplicably familiar, yet so new and unexplored.

He kisses me harder, and for a second his glasses knock into my cheek. I want to laugh, but instead I put my arms around his waist and feel the muscles of his back through the thin material of his T-shirt. I marvel at the newness of him, the way the ridges of his spine feel against my fingertips and the softness of his lips against mine. How can I be kissing Wes, my friend Wes, my ex-friend Wes, the best friend of my ex-lover? How can it be that I want him more than I've ever wanted anyone?

But this isn't Wes. I open my eyes, and Edgeworth is stroking my cheek with his hand, his hazel eyes glowing. I want to ask him what is happening to me but he finds my mouth again with his and I close my eyes, and I feel little kisses on my eyelids, and I touch his coat and it's Edgeworth's coat.

And in my ear is a whisper, and it's Wes's voice. "I love you, Courtney. I've always loved you."

I hold him tighter and Edgeworth says, "I love you, Jane. I've always loved you."

I pull away, the flesh rising on my arms.

The look on Edgeworth's face is so tender, so like Wes's face, that I can hardly breathe.

"I want to marry you," he says.

"On your terms, Jane. With all the freedom you want."

He kisses me again, and my whole body aches for him. His scent, the touch of his lips, the feel of his chest as he crushes me against him. So exciting, yet so familiar. Those words roll through my mind, over and over like a mantra. So exciting, yet so familiar.

I look up into his face. I shiver. He pulls off his coat and puts it around my shoulders, rubbing my back. I put my arms around his neck and hold him close, find his lips with my own and we kiss again, long and deeply. I am so light that I'm part of the air, the boundaries of my body so gossamer-thin that they dissolve into his; there is no separation between him and me. No separation between me and Jane. No Jane. No Courtney. Only complete and absolute surrender. And in one kaleidoscopic moment all the bits and pieces and memories and identities and self-images and projections and pasted-on images of who I am and who I think I am and who she is and who I think she is peel off me and fly away in a whirlwind of thousands and millions of sheafs and sheets of flat, vivid, two-dimensional images. And in that explosion of color I am everything they are and were and will be. There is no thought, no struggle, no doubt. Only surrender and an eternal laugh of unfettered joy.

And in that moment I am home.

From the Diary of Mrs. Charles Edgeworth, 7 July, 1814

My happiness is so great, this moment so complete that I must find a way to preserve it, if only with ink on paper. I know I will return to these pages when I am old and my memory begins to fail, and I will be glad that I once took the time from my day to enshrine this miracle of happiness so that an old woman might savor it and remember better days.

If any one had suggested not one year ago that I would now sign my name as Mrs. Charles Edgeworth; any one but my mother, that is, I would have laughed in pity for that poor creature's understanding. Yet here we are, recently returned from my dear Mary's wedding to her most excellent Mr. Stevens, and I glow with the thought of him, the sight of him, the thrill of writing his name and calling it my own. How could I have been so blind to his perfections?

This change of heart is not the only change, which is why I must soon put aside my pen till tomorrow.

For this, too, I wish to remember when I am old: I am become my Charles's Scheherazade. Every night he entreats me to tell him more of the tale of the woman who is not who she seems to be, the woman who lives in a faraway city in another land, hundreds of years hence, and finds herself living the life of an Englishwoman not unlike myself.

When he first made this strange request, I could not understand what he wanted. He insisted, however, that I had told him such stories before, and I decided to humor him by saying the first thing that came into my head. But nothing came out at first, and then all at once I remembered, or thought I remembered, something. I saw myself with him one night on our wedding journey, saying the words, "I must tell you something, Charles. I must tell you something very strange." I remembered having said those words to him, and I remembered the urgency and fear with which I first began to tell him the story of the woman. It was almost as if at first I believed the story to be real. It was like a secret I had been carrying with me, and I needed to unburden my soul to my husband. I wanted no more secrets between us, no more misunderstandings. We had had enough of those, and I wanted our marriage to be founded on honesty and trust.

But as I began telling the story, it lost its urgency within me, and I no longer felt it was a burden, or that it had happened to me, and I knew it was only a story, or at most, a dream I was just remembering at that moment. As I told it, a sense of lightness came over me. I felt free, of what I know not, but the telling of it gives me as much pleasure as it does my dear Charles.

I have not stopped telling this story since, though I have no idea whence it comes. It is like one of those memories in dreams, when you remember a whole history that has nothing to do with your waking life but which makes perfect sense in the context of the dream, a connection you discover that makes the illogical logic of the dream click into some sort of order that you couldn't possibly articulate when awake. And you wake up and know that this dream has more meaning, more depth than the usual dreams. It stays with you as a feeling, an impression, but then it fades, and try as you might to recapture it, to remember that history, it slips away and nags at the back of your mind, wanting to be remembered but elusive nevertheless. It is like a butterfly whose wings are too fragile to be touched. When you try to put words to that feeling, they sound like nonsense, but in the dream it somehow made all the sense in the world.

I never knew I had the gift of the storyteller before, but it makes my Charles so happy that I hope this gift will be with me always. And, I must allow, it pleases me as well. I feel as if I know the heroine of my stories. I feel her whispering to me at odd times and telling me her tales. I hear her voice softly speaking as I drift off to sleep. I feel her presence when I walk in the garden.

I cannot clearly state how any of this came to be,

not the stories of the woman, not the love I have for my husband. Perhaps, as my favorite heroine in my favorite novel said, *It has been coming on so gradually, that I hardly know when it began.* I certainly owe no thanks for my present happiness to my mother, whose mercenary intentions nearly worked against my seeing Charles's true worth, at least at first. But who knows? Perhaps if I were to be absolutely honest with myself, I would say, *I believe I must date it from my first seeing his beautiful grounds at Pemberley.* How I laugh every time I read those words.

I only know that once I surrendered to his love, I could hardly remember ever having disliked him. Of course, it is not that I claim to have forgotten the past. It is, however, as if I stand outside myself while I peruse those recollections. It is as if I am watching someone else, but not myself.

As my favorite heroine put it, *Perhaps I did not always love him so well as I do now. But in such cases as these, a good memory is unpardonable.*

Acknowledgments

I humbly thank my beloved teacher and dearest friend, Aurelia Haslboeck, who saw me through every step of the way, critiquing draft after draft, sharing her priceless knowledge of storytelling and character, even meeting me in England and turning my research trip into a magical experience. Aurelia, I am blessed by your generosity, patience, and love. You instilled your faith in me and made me believe it was possible. Without you, this book would not exist.

I am filled with love and gratitude for my husband, Thomas Rigler, my very own Mr. Darcy, who gave me that most elusive gift: time. Thank you for your unfailing faith in me, your vision, your patience, your insightful story notes, and for even learning how to do English country dance so that you could take me to a Regency ball.

I am tremendously grateful to Marly Rusoff, a dream of an agent whose kindness, grace, and vast knowledge of all things publishing imbue everything she does with a vision that is irresistible. I owe many thanks to Marly's fellow agent Michael (Mihai) Radulescu, an infinitely patient man who is responsible for making the foreign-language versions of this book a reality. I am also grateful to their reader Julie Mosow, who, along with Marly, put me on the road to perfecting the book.

Just when I thought I couldn't be more fortunate, I landed in the hands of Trena Keating, editor in chief at Dutton. Thank you, Trena, for your collaborative spirit, wise story notes, and generous nurturing of this book through every step of the process. I am also grateful to Susan Peterson Kennedy, Kathryn Court, Brian Tart, Lisa Johnson, Rachel Ekstrom, Amanda Tobier, and Lily Kosner.

I owe many thanks to a host of others. High on that list are the members of JASNA, the Jane Austen Society of North America, for giving me a warm and welcoming community of fellow Austen addicts with whom I can celebrate all things Jane. I am particularly grateful to Margery Rich, who vetted the historical details of this book and told me a thing or two about dangling modifiers. Many thanks to my fellow board members of JASNA-Southwest: Claire Bellanti, Mimi Dudley, Carla Washburn, Alice Marie White, Pat Cross, Diana Birchall, Carol Krause, Diane Erickson, Nancy Gallagher, and Jaye Scholl Bohlen for their support; and to the Pasadena Area Jane Austen Reading Group. Thanks to Keiko Parker and Pam Ottridge, co-coordinators of the Vancouver AGM; Barb Millett and Jan Fahey for their support; and Susan Forgue for sharing her database of facts about the period.

Many thanks to my early readers: Melitta Fitzer, Laura Graham, Randolf Hillebrand, Susan Lesser, Sara Levine, Cary Puma, Gabrielle Raumberger,

Uta Rigler, and Deb Zeitman, whose enjoyment of the book was a boost. Included in that group is Roxanne Rogers, who taught me a valuable lesson about my very first chapter; and Felice Levine, whose belief in me is so matter-of-fact that I started to see myself in the same way. I am also grateful to Anita Artukovich, who gave me a much-needed kick in the pants; Roman Jakobi, who took my photos; Bruno Rigler, who gave Mr. Mansfield his talent for painting; Steve Solodoff, who gave me a joke; the delightful Paula Breen; and the inimitable Bill Haxworth of the Mayor's Corps of Honourary Guides, whose walking tour of Georgian Bath I will never forget.

Center Point Publishing
600 Brooks Road • PO Box 1
Thorndike ME 04986-0001 USA

(207) 568-3717

US & Canada:
1 800 929-9108
www.centerpointlargeprint.com